"Vete   f
  m

"Leav
Ms.
read

"Bel

"Lo
Ca

CATHERINE PALMER

THE HEART'S TREASURE

Refreshed version of *LAND OF ENCHANTMENT*
newly revised by author.

Steeple
Hill®

Published by Steeple Hill Books™

STEEPLE HILL BOOKS

Steeple
Hill®

ISBN-13: 978-0-373-78581-0
ISBN-10:   0-373-78581-X

THE HEART'S TREASURE

This is the revised text of a work first published as
LAND OF ENCHANTMENT by Harlequin Enterprises in 1990

Copyright © 1990 as LAND OF ENCHANTMENT by Catherine Palmer

Copyright © 2007 as THE HEART'S TREASURE by Catherine Palmer

www.SteepleHill.com

Printed in U.S.A.

For Sylvia Johnson, a true friend who stood by me during the dark hours. May God bless you.

My thanks for research assistance to: Bobbie Ferguson, Terry Koenig, Dr. R. Lally, Dr. J. Moreno and Dr. G. Agogino.

Chapter One

❧

Kitt Tucker brushed away the powdery brown dust and stared down at the skull. Two gold front teeth, still in place, glittered in the brilliant New Mexico sunshine. She rocked back on her heels and stared at the earthen sides of the unmarked grave. Two gold front teeth…a memory long hidden slipped from the recesses of her mind and struggled forward. She flipped her long brown braid behind her shoulder and leaned over the skull again.

"Dr. Tucker." The voice startled Kitt from her concentration, and she shaded her eyes as she looked up from the six-foot-deep pit to find the portly Dr. Dean standing over her. "Dr. Tucker, he's back."

Frowning, Kitt rose and placed one foot in the step she had carved in the side of the pit, which let her stand high enough to survey the old cemetery site. The summer archaeology students were hard at work in the afternoon light, excavating graves and taking out remains that soon would be reinterred in another cemetery—one safely distant from the dam that would flood this area.

"I had to run him out of my tent. He was fiddling with the skeletal material. He's over by number fifteen now." Dr. Dean, self-appointed watchdog for the crew, nodded in the direction of the numbered grave of a small child.

"I'll ask him to leave," Kitt murmured.

The grizzled old man standing in the cemetery had proven to be harmless—though somewhat of an annoyance—since his first appearance at the project site nearly three weeks before. Kitt climbed out of the grave, walked over to him and gently touched his arm.

"Eh?" The intruder glanced at her, his watery blue eyes distant. "What's the matter, young 'un?"

"Sir, I'm afraid you'll have to leave the site. I've told you before, we cannot allow unauthorized people on the project."

"Why not?"

Kitt shook her head. How many times had she gone over this? A young intern listened as he worked quietly in the grave beside them. Somehow, she had to make the elderly fellow understand.

"This is sensitive work…even dangerous. Diseases may be living in the soil. We're all vaccinated." Kitt paused. "Some viruses can survive hundreds of years in skeletal remains."

The old man gave her a long look.

"Even more important," she went on, "the cemetery dates back only to the late 1800s. People in this county have relatives buried here. We're trying to conduct our work in a respectful manner."

"Respect for the dead."

"That's right, sir. We're not allowing the press or anyone else on-site until the project is complete."

The man took off his brown felt hat and looked away. The

afternoon sun had sent a rivulet of perspiration down his cheek. Kitt watched it meander into a crease and then slip beneath his worn, yellowed collar.

"Twilight is coming," he said at last. His gnarled fingers twisted the brim of his hat. "Twilight is coming, and I'll be here to see it."

She opened her mouth to object, then she noticed that a tear had escaped the old man's eye. He brushed it away with the side of his finger and put his hat on his head. Kitt cleared her throat.

"It's not long until dusk." She shifted from one foot to the other, unsure whether the man had been talking about the time of day. "I'm sorry, but you do have to leave. The rules are set by the Bureau of Reclamation, and I—"

"I'll stay." He looked at her so matter-of-factly that she realized it was useless to argue. He'd always gone away before, but he seemed too harmless to be a threat to the project.

"Listen, sir—what's your name?"

"They call me Hod." The old man grinned, knowing he had won. "I'll sit under that cottonwood. You'll never know I'm here."

Kitt nodded in resignation. "You can stay today, Hod. But I can't permit you to come back again. If you do, I'll have to—"

"Oh, I'll be back. I'm here to watch the twilight."

Kitt glanced at the student, who had continued working, silent but curious. He winked and tapped his temple. "Guess he's coming back."

Without responding, Kitt turned on her heel and headed back to the grave where she had been working. She could see Dr. Dean watching, and she knew she should come up with a good reason for letting the outsider remain. She had directed a number of similar projects for the Bureau—and she always felt it important to present a professional operation to visiting professors and government officials. After all, she had worked her way into the bureau's top archaeologist position with her no-nonsense attitude and levelheaded dedication.

"Looks like he's here to stay," the anthropologist said with a smile as Kitt approached. "There's always someone loitering around an excavation. Curious children, nosy neighbors, pesky reporters."

She sighed in relief. Dr. Dean had been at the site from the start, but unlike many of his stuffy predecessors, he had proven to be a warm and enjoyable addition to her crew. "His name is Hod, and he rambles a little. He's awfully old."

"Maybe he's got a friend buried here."

"A friend? He couldn't be *that* old."

The professor chuckled. "Nineties, I'd say. Maybe a hundred. Remember—I'm the physical anthropologist. I'm trained to analyze things like that."

"I suppose we could ask him." Kitt knelt at the lip of the grave pit again. She could see a few rib bones protruding from the dirt. The skull stared vacantly at her. Two gold front teeth. How odd, she thought. Most of the people buried in the cemetery had been impoverished pioneers. The dig had uncovered nothing of value—a few unmatched buttons, a scrap of denim, a wedding band.

"By the way, I took a phone message for you."

She looked up in surprise. In her growing curiosity about the skeleton, she had forgotten the professor's presence. "A message?"

"In my tent."

Sighing, Kitt stood and brushed off the knees of her jeans. What now? she wondered as she followed Dr. Dean. If it weren't some old codger who wouldn't leave, it had to be a broken camera lens or a hailstorm or a new government form to fill out.

Under the large, yellow nylon awning, the professor examined the skeletal remains in order to determine age, cause of death, sex and various other information. Kitt walked into the shaded area and swept the folded message from a card table. Flipping open the note she scanned it as he opened a crate containing yellowed bones.

"Great." Kitt stuffed the note into her back pocket.

"Problems?" Dr. Dean looked up. He held a skull in one hand and a set of calipers in the other.

"I forgot about a meeting." Kitt brushed a wisp of brown hair from her cheek. "A guy named Burton—an Affiliated Press reporter from Albuquerque—is passing through and wants an interview. I agreed, as long as he stays off-site. He's waiting at my motel."

"So take off. These skeletons aren't going anywhere, you know. At least we hope not."

Kitt grinned in spite of her annoyance. She wouldn't have time to change clothes or prepare what she wanted to say. More frustrating, she would have to leave the grave she had begun investigating. The strange skull flashed through her mind again and she lifted her chin.

"I'm afraid Mr. Burton is just going to have to wait a few minutes for his interview," she announced. "I have a more important date—and he's been waiting nearly a hundred years for me."

Dr. Dean chuckled as she set off again into the relentless sunshine. Glancing at her watch, she gave herself twenty minutes to complete a cursory examination. She would have to leave the detail work for a student. Project rules prohibited leaving graves open overnight.

Climbing into the pit again, she picked up her small brush and dusted the skeleton. Soon she had finished cleaning the skull and started on the shoulders. She brushed a filmy layer of dust from the skeleton's scapula and noticed a small protrusion. Taking an old toothbrush and a chopstick—her favorite tools—from her back pocket, Kitt cleaned debris until she could clearly see a knife tip. From the look of the bone, which had calcified around the metal, the man had lived for several years with the blade embedded in his shoulder.

Her curiosity mounting, Kitt carefully worked her way down the remainder of the skeleton. Nothing else unusual turned up, and she was about to climb out of the grave when her eye fell on a folded corner of newspaper. It was always strange to discover what time had chosen to preserve. The buried man's pants had rotted long ago, but in the spot where the pocket would have been, a scrap of newspaper lay in the dust.

Perhaps this held a clue to his identity. Shivering slightly at the prospect, she lifted the paper, climbed out of the grave and hurried to the yellow tent.

"What do you have there?" Dr. Dean glanced up from a microscope. "Looks interesting."

"Newspaper," Kitt said as she perched on a high wooden stool beside the table. With tweezers, she pried open the section of yellowed newsprint. The side folded in revealed a list of books and maps for sale—an atlas of the United States, a geography of the Mississippi River valley and a map of the New Mexico Territory. In one corner, the owner had scribbled what looked like an address. Probably the source for the maps.

She flipped the paper, hoping for something more revealing.

"Cattle market results," Dr. Dean observed, leaning over her shoulder. "Your fellow must have had a few head of cattle. Did you finish his grave?"

She shook her head. "No time. I'll have to let one of the students do the sifting." At the camera table, she photographed both sides of the newspaper clipping. Then she refolded it and set it in the box she would use to store the skeleton.

"It's strange," she murmured, half to herself. "The skull has two gold front teeth."

"Didn't I read about a fellow…Native American who ran with the old scalp hunter, James Kirker? What was his name? A real terror, as I recall. Black Dove—that's it." Dr.

Dean said the name that had been playing at the edge of Kitt's mind. "The Native American was buried someplace in Mexico, wasn't he?"

"Guadalupe Y Calvo. It's a town in southern Chihuahua." Kitt brushed her forehead with the back of her hand. "While Dr. Oldham and I were working together at Northern New Mexico University, he found the records of Black Dove's burial."

"I read the paper you wrote on Kirker's exploits. Fine work. In my opinion, Frank Oldham is the leading authority on the Indians of the Southwest. You must have learned a lot working with him."

"I wish he were still teaching. Students loved him." Kitt smiled in memory. "I've considered expanding the paper into a book for the NNMU press. Should get some attention—white scalp hunters have been getting a lot of play since our account came out."

"You're the person to do the book, if anyone."

"Thanks." Kitt hung her head for a moment, feeling unworthy of the compliment. She had worked hard to earn her educational degrees and her professional reputation, yet something inside whispered that she was still inferior. Things would go wrong, she would fail and people would find out the truth about her. Kitt knew she was hard, tough, intelligent and competent. But sometimes she felt like a brittle shell with nothing inside.

Pushing down the lump of self-doubt, she faced Dr. Dean. "I guess I'll head into town—I've kept that reporter waiting long enough. If I'm lucky he'll have gone home. Shut things down for me, will you? And let me know what you find out about our mystery man."

"Yup." He nodded, again absorbed in his examination.

Kitt slung her leather bag over her shoulder and picked up her worn jacket. Striding toward the Bureau's pickup, she glanced across the site. Students moved around in the waning sunlight. She paused and studied them as they labored in the cemetery, digging, photographing, conferring in low tones. The scene warmed her heart, let her know she belonged, gave her purpose and helped fill the hollow feeling inside.

Starting the engine, she glanced down at herself—a woman in faded jeans, dusty boots, a khaki work shirt. This was who she was…Kitt Tucker, head anthropologist-archaeologist for the Bureau of Reclamation in New Mexico, Oklahoma and West Texas. Thirty-two years old. Single.

Throwing the truck into gear, Kitt noted a lone figure beneath a stately cottonwood tree in the distance. Old Hod tipped his hat to her as she drove out of the cemetery.

Kitt scanned the dry landscape as her pickup sped along the two-lane road toward town. The clay soil and arid climate had worked unusually well to preserve remains at the cemetery. Too bad she hadn't had more time to examine that skeleton. By tomorrow the skull with the two gold teeth would be sealed in a new coffin, and soon it would be set in the ground again to rest in silence forever.

Black Dove. Legendary Shawnee war chief.

Retracing time, Kitt thought back to the two years she had spent working with Frank Oldham. Her primary focus in the academic paper Dr. Dean had mentioned had been white scalp hunters of the early 1800s—men who had killed Apaches for the Mexican and United States governments in exchange for up to two hundred dollars a scalp.

Details of Black Dove's life slowly sifted back into place. He had been one of James Kirker's right-hand men for many years, ruthlessly slaughtering men, women and children for bounty. He had been tall, powerfully built and handsome. He'd had two gold front teeth.

And he was buried in Guadalupe Y Calvo, Mexico.

A tumbleweed rolled across the highway, and Kitt swerved

to miss it. Those had been good years at the university. She had entered as hardly more than a child, aching to fill the void in her heart left by the sudden end of her brief, tempestuous marriage. She had worked hard to put away her past, to grow beyond it. And nine years later she had completed her doctorate as a mature woman, capable and skilled.

Kitt rounded a bend in the road, and the small oil town of Catclaw Draw came into sight, pink-glazed by the setting sun. The thought of her marriage opened a floodgate of emotion, just as it always did. How intensely she had worked to dissipate the effects of that year of reckless passion and tragedy…that year as the wife of Michael Culhane.

She hadn't spoken that name aloud in years. Not long after he had walked out the door, she had severed his name from her own, just as she had tried to sever all her memories of that time…holding each other close in their little trailer, enjoying picnics and laughing down by the creek, parents arguing ceaselessly over the hasty wedding and the child… most of all their child.

Blinking back tears she never allowed herself to cry, Kitt sped through town and swung the pickup into the motel parking lot. No—she wouldn't cry now. She was too knowledgeable for sentiment. Statistics showed the marriage had been doomed before she and Michael ever said their vows. They had been too young. Too silly and irresponsible. Both sets of parents had fought the union from start to finish. Babies born to teenagers were often small, often premature. The odds had been stacked against them from the beginning.

There was no point in going over barren ground. She had closed off that part of herself.

Kitt climbed out of the pickup and stepped to the turquoise motel door. Fortified against her past, she inserted the key and slipped into the darkened room, shutting off emotion as she shut out the sun setting behind her. She lifted a hand to the light switch just as a hard pounding sounded on the door.

For a moment she stood in frozen silence, staring into the blackness. Then, with a melting wash of relief, she realized it must be the reporter. Dropping her leather bag onto a chair, she turned and pulled open the door.

"Hello, I'm—"

Her eyes fell on the man leaning against the door frame, and the words suddenly garbled on her tongue. In the faint breeze, his dark blond hair lifted from his forehead, and at first she wasn't sure. The shoulders were different somehow, and the jaw. And then she looked into his eyes. Gray-blue with a golden halo around the dark center.

"Michael."

"Kitt?" His voice was deeper than she remembered. He stood to his full height—and he was taller than she remembered. "What are you doing here?"

"This is my room. What are *you* doing here?"

He looked away for a moment, his expression rigid. Then he turned back. "I came to get a story on an archaeological site. I'm supposed to interview the project director in room 112."

"But Mr. Burton—"

"Burton's down with the flu in Las Cruces. I was heading back from an assignment at Carlsbad Caverns when I got the call to fill in for him."

"You're a reporter? You're supposed to be a farmer."

"And you're supposed to be a farmer's wife." Michael looked at Kitt again, as if uncertain whether the woman standing before him really could be that girl he once had known. "I've been with Affiliated Press for eight years. I went to college after we…uh, after things turned out…different. So do you work for the project director or something?"

"I *am* the project director." Kitt stared into the blue-gray eyes. "I went to college, too. I've been the anthropologist-archaeologist with the Bureau of Reclamation for six years. The cemetery relocation is my project."

"Kitt Culhane—"

"Kitt Tucker."

She watched him shove his hands into his pockets and bow his head. He had larger hands now, sunbaked to a golden brown. And his shoulders were broad and massive. But of course Michael was a man now. He was what…thirty-three? Impossible. He'd been just a boy when he had last leaned against her door frame and looked into her eyes. *I'll always love you*, he had whispered. *And if you ever need me, I'll be here for you.*

He had walked away then, gotten into his old car and driven out of her life. But she *had* needed him! She'd clung to his words, praying that somehow he would know to come for her. He hadn't come. He had never come back—until one day she knew she didn't need him anymore. She had made it on her own, and she didn't need anyone, least of all Michael Culhane.

"I need to do the interview and get back to Albuquerque." His voice startled her again. When had it lost that youthful lilt? "Give me the basics, and I'll get out of your way."

Just walk in and then right out again. Like he'd done before. "No," she said suddenly. "I agreed to an interview with Mr. Burton. I had a lot of work to do on-site this evening, and I—"

"Look, I've been waiting for you for three hours." Michael again rose to his full height. "Digging up a bunch of old graves isn't my idea of hot news anyway. So let's just—"

"Excuse me." Kitt turned into the room and shut the door firmly behind her. And it felt good. So good. Years ago, Michael had walked away from her, and she had always feared that if he came back she would weaken and open wide the doors to her heart. But he hadn't come until now. And she'd been able to shut him out. Victory.

Trembling, still aware of his physical presence imprinted on her consciousness, she flipped on the light and stepped to the closet. She would shower and change and then take herself out to dinner. A nice dinner…

The knocking began again. Harder this time.

"Kitt Culhane, open this door." Michael's voice was deeper, almost a growl.

She stared at the turquoise door shuddering on its hinges. Who was he, this stranger pounding outside? The Michael she knew would never have stayed and hammered his fist on her door. He would have gone away…quietly, gently…as he did everything. He had even left her tenderly, sadly, his voice filled with regret.

"Open the door," Michael called louder. "I'm talking to you, Kitt Culhane—"

"Kitt *Tucker!*" she yelled. "Tucker, Tucker, Tucker! Now go away. Leave me alone."

She ran into the bathroom and slammed the door. No, she wouldn't cry. She buried her face in a towel and pressed her eyes tightly closed. She hadn't cried over him yet, and she wouldn't start now. Just because he was out there, so close…just because they'd loved each other once. No, he was not the same man!

Kitt whirled and turned on the shower full force so she couldn't hear him. She peeled off her dusty boots, jeans and work shirt. Then she stepped into the stall and scrubbed the day's dust away with a thick white washcloth. Letting the water cascade over her sunburned face, she unbraided the long hair that fell across her shoulders and thoroughly shampooed it.

She expected her tension to melt as it always did under a good hot shower. But this time she couldn't pull her thoughts from Michael. They had been so close, so deeply in love during the early days when all was well. She could almost feel his arms around her, his hands strong on her back. She could almost smell that indefinable scent of his skin, so male and welcome. When she had begun to swell with their baby, he had run the tub full of bubbles. He had gently washed her back, and then they had marveled at the moving hills on her stomach as the child turned inside....

Whisking open the shower curtain, Kitt fumbled blindly for a towel. She dried herself, wrapped the towel around her hair and pulled on a pair of clean jeans and a T-shirt. She had business to think about. She needed to check in with her supervisor, Dave Logan. The Logans had been her good friends for years, and Kitt enjoyed having lunch with Dave's wife, Sue, now and then.

She stood listening for a moment with her hand on the doorknob. The shower dripped. Cars sped by outside the tiny steamed-up window. A truck honked. But there was no sound from the bedroom.

Pulling open the bathroom door, she padded barefoot onto the carpet and reached for her cell phone on the dresser. It was after office hours at the Bureau, so she dialed Dave's home number from memory. He wouldn't mind.

"Is Dave in?" she asked when Sue answered. Kitt stroked her fingers along the dresser's plastic wood-grain veneer as she studied the deserted parking lot through the single window. "Hi, Dave. Kitt. Just wanted to let you know we're almost through... Oh, five or six unmarked graves since we last talked. Nothing of any interest really... Looks like some syphilis and smallpox deaths. A lot of children... Babies."

Kitt swallowed as she listened to Dave. She nodded. "Poor folks, mostly. Tin and bone wedding bands. Hardly any boots. Oh, one fellow was a little strange—he had two gold teeth. Gold, yes!...Black Dove is the one you're thinking of. But he was buried in Mexico, remember? Guadalupe Y Calvo.... I'd say no more than four days should do it—I've ordered the markers. No problems, really. An old fellow hangs around the site, but I've told him—"

A gentle breeze tugged the corner of the towel wrapped

around Kitt's hair, and she realized suddenly that the window was open.

"You've changed in fifteen years." Michael's voice filled the room. He was sitting in an orange armchair, his boots propped on the bed.

"How did you get in here—" She caught her breath. "No, Dave. It's okay, it's just this reporter who… Yeah, I'll get rid of him. Call me when you have that final survey."

She dropped the phone into her jeans pocket, her eyes narrowing. "Did you climb through my window?"

"You forgot to lock it." Michael unfolded from the chair and stood. "Careless of you but good for me. If there's one thing I've learned as a reporter, it's never to let a story get away."

"I thought this was just some boring old cemetery relocation." She planted her hands on her hips. "Get out of my room, Michael."

"A cemetery relocation—and a skull with two gold teeth. But you say it couldn't be Black Dove. I just did a feature story on New Mexico's Apaches. Did you read it? Most of the papers picked it up—the *Journal,* the *Trib.* Old Black Dove was quite a character. Massacred Apaches left and right. So where were the gold teeth on that skull? In the front?"

"That was privileged information, and you had no right to eavesdrop. I'll release the results of the dig to the press when I decide it's appropriate."

"Appropriate? Black Dove will be back in the ground by then, along with his secrets."

"Black Dove is buried in *Mexico*. If you'd researched your article, you would know that. Go read some history books." She glared at him, wishing he would leave, and at the same time mystified that Michael had even heard of Black Dove. The only extensive mention of the Native American was from his years with Kirker. And what was this hulk of a man she hardly recognized doing in her motel room, anyway? "Michael, I'm telling you to get out of here, or I'm going to call the desk."

"Were the teeth in the front? The two top incisors?" He whipped a narrow spiral notebook and a ballpoint pen from his back pocket. "Black Dove disappeared in New Mexico, didn't he? Right after his stint with Kirker—"

"Black Dove is buried in *Mexico*. I helped Frank Oldham write the paper that documented it." This was absurd! She couldn't believe she was even in the same room as the man who once had been her husband. Was he totally unaware of her—all his senses trained on his story? And why did she even care where he chose to place his attentions?

"Our paper is in the NNMU library. It's all spelled out, Michael. There's no story *here* about Black Dove. The only information you need to know is that the Bureau is moving a historical cemetery because a dam is going to flood the area—"

"Were the teeth in the front? Just tell me that." Michael looked up from his pad, his eyes filled with an intense light Kitt had never seen there before.

"You're just a typical obnoxious reporter, aren't you?" She took a step toward him. Steam drifting from the bathroom had lent a misty moistness to the air. "Sticking your nose into places it doesn't belong. Trying to make something of nothing so readers will buy more newspapers. You'll insinuate that Black Dove is buried here, and then history buffs and treasure seekers will come pouring out of the woodwork—disturbing historical sites, moving grave markers, trespassing on government property."

"So the teeth were in front?"

"Get out—"

Michael's hand shot out and grabbed Kitt's wrist. "When did you get to be such a—"

"Professional? After you walked out of my life."

She stared into his eyes, willing herself to see only the hardness in them. Willing herself not to feel his fingers on her skin. He was close now, his presence filling the space around them. The muscle in his jaw flickered as she lifted her chin.

"I worked hard to get where I am today," she told him. "I'm not going to let you desecrate the things I believe in."

"What do you believe in, Kitt Culhane?" He dropped his voice. Glancing up, she saw the hardness had gone out of his face. His eyes had darkened to teal and his hair looked thick and clean. Touchable. Once, he had been all ears and crew cut and sunburned neck beneath his Cummins Diesel cap. His arms had been long, gangly with sinew. Now, white shirt sleeves rolled halfway to his elbows, he displayed the solid, rock-hard muscle and ropy veins of a man. Thick silver-gold hair matted his forearms. His hands were large and square, their blunt-tipped nails white against his deeply tanned fingers.

"Talk to me," he said. "Tell me about Kitt."

Despite her determination to stand strong against him, Kitt sensed herself slipping back into the girl who had once loved a boy so deeply. She'd been a woman-child then, soft, giving, a little scared of life. But a lot of hard work had erased that part of her, leaving a focused, competent woman. Or was she now no more than a shell, a lifeless vessel whose spirit and heart had been destroyed?

Michael's eyes studied her. Though years had passed between them, she knew what he was thinking. They'd had no choice but to separate. They had nearly destroyed each other's lives during their short, impossible marriage. If she hadn't been a teenager, their baby might have stood a better chance. The birth—it couldn't even be called that…the removal of that lifeless body inside Kitt's had nearly killed her, too. And afterward, the cold emptiness inside her had plagued him. They had been so young, so immature, so unprepared to suffer such a loss.

"Kitt, what do you believe in?"

Fighting tears, she summoned what little strength she could muster. "I believe that you should get out of my room, get in your car and go back to Albuquerque. I don't want you here, Michael. I don't want you in my life."

He dropped her wrist. "I'll take you to dinner. I'm hungry."

Kitt clenched her teeth as anger boiled. She dug in her pocket for her cell phone, but Michael's warm hand on her arm again stopped her. She lifted her head, her lips forming hot words that would unleash the years of pain, disappointment, loneliness. But he raised her hand and kissed it gently.

"Just come with me, Kitt," he said, his voice almost as young and loving as she remembered. "I'll take you out to eat for old times' sake. We won't talk about your project or Black Dove—"

"Black Dove is not in that grave, and—" Her mind reeling, she couldn't continue her train of thought. She wanted to shout at him, beat her fists against his chest for hurting her so much, prove to him that she didn't need him. But part of her longed to fall into his arms, lay her head against his shoulder, feel his fingers stroke her hair.

She pulled her hand from Michael's and went into the bathroom. Running a comb through her damp hair, she realized she should pull it up in a tight bun. He would hate that. Michael had always loved her hair hanging loose around her shoulders. Electing to leave it wet and clumpy, she leaned over the sink to brush mascara over the tips of her dark lashes. As she rubbed lotion on her sunburned cheeks, she paused and held her hand to her nose. A scent clung to her fingers—a smell so evocative that she closed her eyes and leaned against the wall. Michael's scent. Spicy, a hint of musk, but mostly the smell of *him*—his skin and his breath and...

Jerking upright, Kitt turned on the water and lathered her hands with the tiny bar of motel soap. Then she dried them, marched through the door to her suitcase and grabbed an old cotton sweater she had bought on a research trip to Mexico. The last she had heard, her mentor in the field of archaeology was living in retirement in Albuquerque. That could mean trouble. Michael might try to contact Dr. Oldham about the skull. But it was ridiculous to think Black Dove could have been buried in the old cemetery. She had gone through the professor's entire collection of research materials—interviews, photographs, tapes.

Straightening, she realized the room was empty and the door to the outside was closed. She stared at the imprint of Michael's boots on her bed. The coverlet was slightly rumpled, indented. So he had gone. Probably changed his mind about dinner. Good. She hurried to the bed and smoothed out the spread. Erase him, Kitt. Erase him again.

She slipped into her sandals and threw the sweater over her shoulders. For a moment, she stood silently. His scent was here, too. No one else would have known, but she had lived with it once. She studied the orange chair. He had sat in that chair. Walked on this carpet.

For one brief moment, he had come back…mistakenly, of course. Yet he'd entered her life, and now he was gone again. This time it wouldn't take long to crush the pain. She would know that in the intervening years he had grown hard and stubborn. He wasn't the man she once loved. It was over.

Picking up her purse, she flicked off the light and stepped out into the night. She took a deep breath of cool air, climbed into her pickup and rummaged for her keys. As she turned the ignition, the door on the other side of the pickup swung open and a tall, lean figure climbed onto the seat.

"Thought I'd better get my jacket," Michael said, pulling the door shut. "The nights are cooler than you'd think in the desert. So let's go."

As she numbly backed out of her parking space, he pulled out his notebook and pen. "I phoned my bureau chief and left him a message to get in touch with Dr. Oldham. So were the two gold teeth in the front of the skull?"

"Michael, you promised!"

"At dinner. Nothing about work at dinner." He flipped open his notebook and began scribbling. "Right now, I want to know about that skull. Remember, you owe Affiliated Press an interview, Mrs. Culhane."

"Tucker!"

Chapter Two

❧

Michael watched Kitt cut her enchiladas into neat rectangles. Then she halved the rectangles into squares. They had hardly spoken on the way to the restaurant. She refused to let out one tidbit of information about the unusual skull, and she would say nothing about her life since their marriage ended.

In the restaurant, she ordered and then sat picking at her food. Every effort to engage her resulted in anger or stony silence. She was no longer the skinny chatterbox who nestled in his arms and told him everything she was thinking and feeling. This woman had an exterior of ice.

"You planning to eat any of that?" he asked finally. As he reached to dip a tortilla chip into a bowl of salsa, his knee brushed Kitt's under the table. At the unexpected contact, he caught his breath. Across the table, she tensed, and her eyes darted to his for an instant.

This was ridiculous. He was thirty-three years old, but

he acted seventeen-skittish, his stomach twisted into knots, his heart hammering. He felt out of control, and he didn't like it.

The situation had to improve, but he couldn't figure out how to ease the strain between them. The woman had been the catalyst for everything bad that had happened to Michael. And everything good. In losing her, he had found God, or maybe God had finally found him. Michael's salvation experience meant everything to him, and he wondered where Kitt stood.

Both had been raised by churchgoing parents, but it wasn't until Michael's already reckless life careened out of control that he had given God the driver's seat. No matter where Kitt was in her feelings about Christianity, he knew he had to proceed with caution. She could easily interpret his claim to having a changed heart and becoming a new man as a cop-out from taking responsibility for the hurt he had caused her. On the other hand, life now was good, whole and complete thanks to his daily submission to Christ. And he wanted to show her that.

"Decent place to eat for a small town," he offered. He watched and waited for a response.

Kitt gave an indifferent shrug. "It's the best around, but the food can't compare to what they serve in northern New Mexico."

Michael couldn't disagree with that. He loved nothing better than a plate of blue corn enchiladas covered with hot, nutty red chile sauce in Santa Fe or Española. This restaurant's decor must have originated in some border town *mercado*—faded piñatas, ceramic parrots, sombreros. But maybe he was being too harsh. With Kitt sitting across from him, he could taste confusion and hurt more strongly than salsa.

"So where do you live these days?" he asked her.

"In Santa Fe."

"Alone?"

"Yes."

"Me, too. I never married again." When she didn't react, he went on. "Pretty expensive to live up there in the mountains with all those movie stars and artists, isn't it?"

Kitt gave another shrug. "I manage."

"That's all you have to say?"

"Look, Michael, you don't need to know anything about the life I've built for myself."

"Any children?"

"No, and stop talking about this. It's my life, okay? Private. Closed."

"What are you so afraid of? You think if you tell me anything about your life, I'll be a part of it again?"

"You might. In some small way. And I've worked too hard to let that happen."

They returned to their meals in silence. Michael fought the hardening in his heart. He didn't want to end up hating her. It wasn't right. They could at least be civil.

He tried again. "So how many more days until you finish the project?"

"You heard what I told Dave Logan on the phone. Don't play games with me, Michael."

Can't you see I don't want you? The message couldn't have been plainer if she had spoken the words. Michael watched her face for any break in the facade. But there was none. Maybe it wasn't a facade after all, this rigid exterior on display. Maybe Kitt was a block of stone right to the core. If so, it was his fault.

He swirled his tea and watched the ice cubes go around. His fault. The Lord knew Michael had to take part of the blame for killing her spirit. A big part. Long ago, he had asked God's forgiveness for his mistakes. But now, facing Kitt, he was convicted all over again and it settled heavily in his heart.

Was there any point in trying to bridge the hurt between them? Could God fix something that far gone? Michael studied Kitt as she poured honey into a *sopaipilla*. Her fingers, tanned by the sun, were still as long and beautiful as he had remembered them. Her hair—dry now, after her shower—draped across her shoulders in shades of deep brown that lightened to ribbons of gold. She was so beautiful it almost hurt him to look at her.

Maybe somewhere inside she was still soft and warm, the way she'd been when they loved each other so much. Maybe there was hope, though not a hope for rekindling that flame. He certainly didn't want that, and neither did she. But God had allowed them to find each other after all these years, and there ought to be room for kindness.

"I guess I should have expected you to do something in history or anthropology," he tried once again. She was poking at her frijoles. "Remember how we used to meet in the Southwest history section of the high school library at lunch? It was the quietest place—"

"Don't, Michael. I'm not interested in talking about the past."

"That old library," he continued. "I remember it well. The hard, brown wooden chairs. The off-white tile floor. The books smelled so musty. Remember the librarian, Mrs. What's-her-name? She wore bright pink lipstick and sat with her back to the room, eating her lunch of peanut butter sandwiches and bananas."

"Michael, stop this."

"You would read me books about famous New Mexicans—Geronimo, Cochise, Victorio. Billy the Kid and the Lincoln County War. Remember that?"

When she didn't answer, he drifted back in time to the chill room, his arm sliding around Kitt's shoulders, his fingers brushing against her neck, his stomach doing somersaults—

"So you don't want to talk about the past," he said, cutting off his train of thought. "And you won't tell me about the present. What about the future, Kitt? You going to stay with the Bureau?"

Michael watched her struggle to focus. She had been remembering, too. He could see the way her lips had softened and her face had gentled. She lifted her eyes to his.

"This is my job," she said. "The Bureau. My next assignment is to rehabilitate irrigation ditches that date back to the Spanish settlement."

He nodded, grateful for the crumb of civility she had tossed him. "These ditches…where are they?"

"Near Taos."

"Why does an anthropologist need to repair them?"

"In order to document their antiquity. I believe the ditches are unique and worth conserving, but the locals want to line them with white concrete."

He winced at the image. "What can you do about that?"

"The old ditches are as organic as the landscape around them. I need to come up with a creative way to keep them useable, but also to preserve their totality with the environment."

"I guess you run into a lot of conflict between progress and history."

"The past and the future always clash."

He pondered the statement, wondering if it were really true. He and Kitt shared a past. Did that mean they had to be at odds now?

To his surprise, Kitt picked up the line of their conversation and went on speaking. "It's my job to take problems with set parameters and solve them. In this situation, the locals won't give up the ditches, and I'm not willing to let them become glaring white scars on the terrain. I imagine we'll compromise. There might be a simple solution. Perhaps earth-toned concrete."

"Colored concrete." He had to smile. Maybe the softness and fun had gone out of Kitt—maybe she had become prickly and analytical—but this grown-up woman was also intelligent and resourceful and dedicated.

"It would work," she said.

"No question. When did you decide to go into archaeology and anthropology?"

She folded her napkin and set it beside her plate. "I took a course in college."

"Where did you go to school? NNMU?"

"Listen, Michael, I know you want to chat, but I need to be getting back to my room. I've got a lot of papers to review."

"I went to college after I got out of the service."

"Which branch?"

"Army. I enlisted right after we…right after I left Clovis. I worked at a Comcenter as a communications specialist. That was during the Gulf War. It gave me a taste of the field. When I got out I studied journalism at Texas University in El Paso. I was hooked. Paid my dues working for the local newspaper until finally Affiliated Press took me on."

"Have you been in their Albuquerque bureau all those years?"

"Digging into the past, are we, Mrs. Culhane? I thought that was forbidden territory."

"Digging into the past is my job."

"It's mine, too."

"You have an uncooperative subject tonight."

"I'm aware of that." He could see that she was trying to maintain her expressionless mask. But she wasn't succeeding. One corner of her mouth had turned up. "I stayed in El Paso for a couple more years. I really liked covering the border. Drugs, racial tension, illegal aliens. Good stuff. But they got shorthanded in Albuquerque and sent me up there."

"And what's in your future? Are you moving onward and upward?"

"I've applied to go overseas." He looked away, studying the print on the curtains. "The hotter the spot they plant me in, the better. Baghdad, Kabul, Jerusalem, Beirut—I'll go anywhere."

"Why, Michael?" she asked. The words slipped from her

lips, barely audible in the busy restaurant. "Why the army and why Baghdad? You were going to be a farmer."

He focused on her eyes. "Things change."

"But I don't understand. You used to take me out on your dad's big green tractor. We'd ride all over the farm, remember? You would show me the fields of milo and cotton. You had big plans for that place—trying new methods and improving the land. And you'd tell me the cost of seed and fertilizers and insecticide. It was so important to you. And you'd show me the owls up in the—"

"Yeah, I remember those barn owls." Michael chuckled at the memory. He had held on to those moments—they'd gotten him through some tough times. "We would walk into the barn to watch them. You'd be trying to look like you belonged on a farm. You wore a checkered shirt and overalls. Smallest pair of overalls I ever saw."

Kitt bit her lower lip. "They were designer overalls."

"You looked so cute. We'd be standing in the barn looking up at the owls, and I'd finally get brave enough to put my arm around your shoulder. And then kiss you."

"Michael." Kitt glanced at a waitress wheeling past with a cart loaded with salsa and chips.

"Remember climbing up the bales of hay to the top where we were almost level with the owls? They would watch us with their big yellow eyes."

Instinctively, he reached up and ran his fingertips over a spot on his neck just below his ear, the place where Kitt had always kissed him. Catching himself, he glanced at her and saw that her brown eyes had gone almost black. She wasn't hearing the clink of silverware or smelling the fajitas. She was far away in that barn...on top of those hay bales...with him.

Despite all his best intentions, Michael responded to her. Kitt had been his wife for no more than a year, but they had shared such a deep, passionate love. "Remember, Kitt?" he asked across the forgotten meal. "Remember how we talked for hours up there? We made such great plans for ourselves—"

"You sure are wordy, Michael Culhane," Kitt cut him off as she slid out of the booth.

He nodded, aware now of the restaurant and the changed woman and the long years between them.

"Words are my business," he told her.

"There's something to be said for silence." She grabbed her purse and took out her keys. "I'm going back to the motel. I have to double-check the list of monuments I ordered, and there's a stack of papers waiting to be filed. Maybe you can find a way—"

"I'll go with you." He rose and took the check from her hand.

"Give me that," she snapped, snatching the paper from his fingers. "I'm paying for my own dinner."

"I figured you would. I just wanted to see how much to leave for a tip."

Michael watched Kitt stalk to the cashier's desk, and he knew she felt as off balance as he did. Everything he did was systematic and calm. How could he have gotten caught up in talking about the barn? How could she have sat there almost in a trance as he rambled on and on about things they both had long ago chosen to forget?

Kitt sucked in a breath of chilly night air as she started the pickup. For some reason, her knees felt weak, and she hated that. It was Michael's fault. Not one of the men she had known in the past fifteen years had been able to embarrass or even tease her. Not one had encroached on her methodical, orderly approach to life. They respected her intelligence and skill. They admired her. She was an equal, a colleague. She was Dr. Tucker, fellow scholar—not some starry-eyed girl staring at owls in a barn. Michael sat beside her in the truck, his big body filling the cab. His knees pressed up against the dashboard and his elbows didn't seem to know where to land. He smelled like he always had—warm and masculine.

She rolled down the window.

"That oil refinery puts out quite a perfume," he remarked after a minute. Looking like a tangle of white Christmas lights, the collection of industrial buildings stood out against the darkness. It made Kitt think of some weird science fiction city, all pipe angles and jets of white steam and ever-burning flares. The unreality of it as she sped past seemed to match the skewed sense of proportion in her brain.

She was riding in a pickup with Michael Culhane. The flat darkness of the highway engulfed them, and she stared out at her headlight beams. Michael and Kitt in a pickup. At sixteen, she was snuggled up against him as they spun down dusty farm roads. He'd have one hand on the steering wheel, his arm cocked on the open window. She would lay her head on his shoulder and let out a breath, perfectly comfortable. He would take the stalk of hay from his mouth and lean over to kiss her. And she would laugh.

Without turning her head, Kitt glanced at Michael in the darkness. His arm stretched along the back of the seat, his fingers tapping the red vinyl. Perilously close to her shoulder.

"Remember that old Chevy pickup I used to have?" His voice only added to the unreality.

"No," she said quickly.

"Yeah, you do. It was white. Gray seats. A gun rack on the back window. I used to take it around the farm after school and check on the cattle. Remember the time we got a flat tire and I couldn't figure out how to work the jack? And then you—"

"No. No, I don't remember that. I really don't remember much of anything from those days, Michael. To tell you the truth, I keep my focus squarely on the here and now."

"You never were a good liar, Kitt."

They rode on without speaking. She kept her eyes fastened on the road. Maybe she had been lying. But she was not going to think about the past. It was over. She didn't know why he had to bring it all up. What had he thought he could accomplish? Remembering that year only made her angry. And when she got mad, she withdrew. So if he hoped to get her to feel all those old emotions again, he was dreaming. She felt nothing. Nothing.

"Okay, we'll talk about the here and now." He pulled a miniature recorder from his coat pocket and clicked it on. "Tell me about the dig. What have you found? Anything interesting?"

She wheeled the pickup into the motel parking lot. "Nothing much. A lot of violent deaths. A lot of...of babies." She switched off the ignition and dropped her keys into her purse. "I've decided to call a press conference tomorrow afternoon at two. You can come to that."

She threw open the door. He clamped his hand down on hers, pressing it into the cool vinyl seat. "Where will this conference be?"

"At the new cemetery where we'll be reinterring the caskets. Chisum Memorial Cemetery. It's just the other side of Catclaw Draw."

"I'd like go out to the project site and take some pictures in the morning."

"It's against Bureau regulations."

"Why?"

He hadn't taken his hand away. It felt warm and strong. "You haven't been vaccinated."

"Wrong. I'm up to date on everything. You know, covering the border, international travel."

Kitt stared into his eyes. The orange-and-blue neon sign over the motel office sent flickers of color across his face. He wasn't smiling.

"Regulations," she said softly.

"I'd be quiet as a mouse."

"Is causing conflict part of your job description, too?"

Michael's fingers closed around hers. She tried to pull back but not hard enough. He lifted her hand, turned it over and uncurled her fingers. As he ran his fingertip across her palm, she recalled the way he once had touched her, so gently and with such love.

"I suppose stirring things up a little is part of my job." His voice was low, raspy.

She closed her eyes. "You used to be so quiet. I never could get you to say what you were thinking."

"I learned how to talk. Some people think I'm quite wordy now."

He searched her eyes, almost as though he was looking for the girl he'd once known. Kitt held her breath, aware of a mingling sense of sadness, emptiness and loss she hadn't felt for years. At the same time, she knew the ache inside her came from a deep longing for what had been and what was so badly missing now. But it was Michael Culhane who caused that ache.

She drew her hand away and slid out of the cab. "I need to notify the local media about the conference. Excuse me."

"Good night, Kitt."

She got out, leaving him in her truck. Aware he was watching her, she stepped into the dark room, sat down on the bed and pressed her hand between her knees. The hand he had held. The one that tingled even now.

"I'd like room 118."

The motel owner held out his hand, and they conducted the transaction in silence. Credit card, license plate number, key. Michael studied a poster on the paneled wall.

Visit New Mexico: Land of Enchantment

He walked down the sidewalk to the room he had requested. It was next to Kitt's, and he suddenly wasn't sure why it had seemed so important to be that near. Her curtains were drawn, her lights off. She was making all those phone calls in the dark?

Michael let out a breath as he inserted the key. He felt more wrung out now than during the past two weeks, which he'd spent trailing a couple of DEA officers between El Paso and Juarez for a feature story on drug trafficking. Of course, it wasn't every day a man ran into his ex-wife.

In the room, he pulled off his boots and flicked on the television across the room. When he tossed his jacket onto a chair, the recorder clunked against the wooden leg. He took it out and set it beside him as he stretched across the bed. Long day. Longer night ahead.

Against the background jabber and sporadic laughter of a talk show, Michael's thoughts churned. He had not expected to see Kitt again—ever. All these years, he had stayed as far away from Clovis as possible. Now he felt chagrined at his image of the woman he had pictured still living there:

She would have stayed in the Tucker family's fine brick house for a couple years, drowning her sorrows in the luxurious life and eventually forgetting all about Michael and their baby. Then she had met some fellow—probably a junior vice president in her daddy's bank. They had married and moved into another elegant brick home. She had a couple of kids....

Michael shook off that thought. He had been so wrong about her. Kitt had not given birth to any more babies. She wasn't a housewife or a Junior Leaguer or a country clubber. And she wasn't Mrs. Michael Culhane, either.

She was Dr. Tucker. She had more education than he did. What a thought! A chuckle of amazement tickled the top of his stomach. Miss Priss, the belle of whatever society Clovis had to offer, now worked outside in the sun supervising big archaeological projects. She created charts and compiled reports. She ordered people around and gave briefings to the news media.

As much as he knew about her, Michael realized there was a lot more he didn't know. And he wanted to find out everything. She said she lived alone, but had she ever married again? Were her parents still alive? Did she still like pecan pie better than anything else in the whole world? Did she still sleep with her sheet over her head in case spiders dropped onto her face? Was she still ticklish behind her knees…?

At the sound of a cough through the wall, Michael sat up and clicked off the television. He could hear Kitt's muffled voice as she spoke on the phone. Calling reporters about her press conference the following day. Or talking to someone else? A man? Michael frowned at the idea, then chastised himself for caring.

Why had he antagonized her at dinner? Why had he insisted on bringing up their past when she clearly wanted to forget everything?

He had told her the truth—conflict was part of his life now. Hardly ever did he have a conversation without digging into somebody's secret pain. He probed everyone from senators to little Mexican boys selling roses on the Avenue of the Americas bridge. He never let simple answers be enough. That was why he was good at what he did—that was why he'd won awards and commendations, and that was why he expected to land an overseas assignment by the end of the year.

But did he have to touch Kitt's pain? The facts were clear. She didn't want him. She didn't want the memories of their life together. She'd rebuilt her world without him. She was her own person now, separate and strong.

Michael closed his eyes and lay back on the pillow. Why had God allowed their meeting? Did Michael have unfinished spiritual business he needed to work through? He had done everything he could to heal and to find forgiveness for his past. He believed he was a new man now, made right and whole in the eyes of the Lord.

So what was he supposed to do about the woman in the room next door? Did God need to work on Kitt instead? Even if that were true, it wasn't up to Michael to bring about her restoration. His calling was to follow Christ, not pester his ex-wife.

Still, he at least ought to inquire about her spiritual health. Or would that be the surest way to alienate her completely? Finally he resolved that tomorrow he would keep his distance. He'd cover the press conference and let the skeleton with the gold teeth rest in peace. He would write up a story, send it in and head for Albuquerque.

But for now, he thought…for right now, he was going to let himself remember Kitt Culhane. Sweet young Kitt, that skinny girl who ran through the milo with him and laughed about life and kissed him with such intense love. Kitt who was lying on her bed on the other side of the wall. A beautiful, intelligent woman who shivered when he touched her fingers in the pickup truck.

He flicked off the lamp and pushed the button on the little recorder. It whirred softly.

"Tell me about the dig. What have you found? Anything interesting?" His voice sounded professional. A little cocky. There was a pause.

"Nothing much. A lot of violent deaths. A lot of…of babies."

Kitt lay curled in her bed with the sheet over her head. She felt hot, a little sick. Maybe it was the Mexican food. Maybe it was the fact that she'd peeked out her curtain and watched Michael move in to the room next to hers.

Everyone she had phoned would be coming to the news conference. Reporters from the *Catclaw Draw Daily Call*, the *Carlsbad* paper and a couple others planned to drive out to the site. Several radio stations and a TV crew were coming, too. With Affiliated Press covering the story, most news outlets in New Mexico could pick up the story and run it.

Kitt considered getting up and compiling a few more notes. But she already knew what information she would give out and what she wouldn't. Michael was going to be disappointed. It would be several days before she had Dr. Dean's final report on the last few skeletons. The skull with the two gold front teeth would remain classified information for now.

The comforting murmur of the television next door suddenly stopped, and Kitt stiffened. She could hear a bedspring squeak. A loud thud sounded on the wall near her head. She imagined Michael's headboard swaying as he settled into bed.

She pulled the sheet more tightly over her head as the sound of his voice filtered through the wall. He was talking to himself. No, it was a woman! Unreasonable fury surged up through Kitt's chest, and suddenly she recognized the voice as her own. The recorder. He was listening to her.

Kitt jammed the pillow over her ears and tucked the sheet all around herself. A little cocoon. Dr. Kitt Tucker was wrapped in a cocoon of sheets and pillows all because her ex-husband was a few feet away.

Grow up, Kitt. Other women saw former husbands all the time. They chatted amicably and worked out details of their lives—trading children back and forth, discussing their work, their interests, their new loves.

But Kitt had no other loves. It was hard to admit that after all these years the best she'd been able to manage was a man who had run off and left her all alone in a tiny, freezing trailer. Left her with empty arms and an empty womb.

Now she lay like some half-dead mummy. She was thirty-two and single and still alone. Wasn't this supposed to be the best time of her life? Wasn't she supposed to be having fun, friendships, an active social life?

Instead, she felt like a petrified old prune that had fallen behind somebody's refrigerator. She felt barren inside. As empty as a pitted prune.

She closed her eyes, willing away the shadow of despair that tried to creep into her heart. After her baby's death, depression had caught her in its claws and nearly devoured her. She wouldn't allow that again.

But how could she stop thinking of the moment when Michael had held her hand in the pickup? Even now, just remembering, she felt her heart begin to thud. Surely after all these years she couldn't be aching for a man so long ago erased from her existence. But if not Michael, then what? Or who?

In a sudden swift movement, she pulled the pillow into her arms and squeezed it tightly. She clenched her fists and held her breath, willing away the thought of him.

"Tell me about the dig," his voice said through the wall. It was the twelfth time. She had counted. "What have you found? Anything interesting?"

"Nothing much. A lot of violent deaths. A lot of...of babies."

Chapter Three

❧

Kitt leaned over the sink and peered into the mirror. A couple sandbags were sitting beneath her eyes. Any genteel woman would hurry to the refrigerator for cucumber slices, she thought. But there was no time for that sort of luxury. The sun was up, the day still cool, and work waited.

She grabbed a hank of hair and began brushing at the bottom, working her way up. Michael had left his room a half-hour earlier. She'd heard his door close as she lay staring at the purple light of dawn on her ceiling.

The recording of their voices had run on for what seemed hours in the night, stopping at the end, rewinding, starting again. Somewhere in the early morning his room had gone silent. She had waited, tense and listening, imagining him asleep. But within a minute his television had come on.

So Michael had wrestled with his own private demons last night. She was glad. He deserved every toss, every turn, every painful memory.

She began braiding her hair, starting at the top of her head, her elbows crooked up high behind her. She felt tired, emotionally drained. One more day, she thought, and Michael would be gone again. She would just have to get through this day—through the press conference—and she could get back to living her normal life. She lowered her arms, swung the braid around and started working on the bottom half.

She looked like she always did, minus the sandbags. Tall, a little thin, not exceptionally pretty but good enough. She wore a white sleeveless T-shirt beneath her old plaid work shirt. The same faded jeans she'd had on the day before were buttoned to her waist and cinched with a worn leather belt. Her steel-toed black workboots were cushioned by thick cotton socks. All in all, she decided as she came to the end of the braid, she was definitely not a genteel lady. But she was herself.

She clamped the end of the braid between her teeth like a lariat and rummaged through her cosmetics bag for an elastic band. She remembered a sack of day-old powdered-sugar doughnuts lying beneath the seat of her pickup. She would grab a cup of coffee in the motel lobby on her way out, and that would take care of the morning meal.

"Kitt!" A hammering began on the turquoise door.

She swung around, her teeth sinking into her braid.

"Kitt, I've got breakfast."

Dropping the braid, she stared at the door. "I'm in a hurry to get to work."

"It's fast food."

"Very funny, Michael. Listen, I'm trying to get dressed."

"Let me in, Kitt."

"I've got my own breakfast in the pickup. I told you I'd see you at the press conference."

"Kitt."

She walked to the door, aware that her braid was slipping apart.

"G'morning." He shouldered past her, his arms heavy with a large white sack. At the table, he began unloading. Steaming scrambled eggs in disposable containers, orange juice, English muffins, jelly, hot black coffee. She watched his big shoulders moving beneath his blue oxford shirt. He looked every bit the journalist. Khaki pants, loafers, argyle socks. Notebook jammed into his back pocket. She wondered if he'd left the recorder in his room.

"I usually eat doughnuts for breakfast," she said.

"Unhealthy, you know."

"Eggs have cholesterol."

"And protein."

His eyes dark, Michael eyed her up and down as she stood by the open door. Suddenly uncomfortable about her scuffed black boots and the worn-out knees of her jeans, Kitt realized her long hair hung over her shoulder, half braided. She pushed it behind her.

"You look beautiful," he murmured. "I like those jeans better than the fancy boutique dresses and shiny high heels you used to wear. You could be a farmer's wife."

"I'm an archaeologist," she told him as she shut the door and stepped to the table. It gave her a perverse pleasure to see that he was wearing his own set of sandbags. His face looked a little pale, too. A sleepless night would do that to a person. Michael's hair looked fresh, though. Newly washed, springy, it fell over his forehead and ears.

"I have to be at the dig at seven." She sat on the edge of the chair and picked up a plastic fork.

"You'll be there."

He joined her at the table, bowed his head for a moment, and then took a swig of coffee. Kitt studied him in surprise. Had Michael Culhane actually *prayed* over his breakfast? Sure, he had grown up in a churchgoing family, as had she, but religion was never a part of their marriage. They'd had too much else going on to complicate their lives with worship services and Sunday school. After their baby's death and the divorce, Kitt had turned to other means of healing. A therapist and medication had helped her through the depression. School had filled her hours. And time had gradually softened the sharp ache inside her.

Michael had told her he joined the army shortly after he walked out of their home. She had no doubt the discipline and rigors of the military helped him cope with their losses. Succeeding as a soldier must have given him a sense of satisfaction after such an abysmal failure at marriage. But had Michael turned to God, too?

Curious, Kitt thought about asking him. Sometime in the night, after listening to their voices over and over, she almost believed they could be cordial. Even friendly. After all, she was here and he was here, too. Maybe it was time to take care of unfinished business.

On the other hand, that opened the terrifying possibility of another encounter with the pain that had debilitated her. Better to keep a quiet distance and let him go on his way after the press conference.

"So I thought I'd spend the morning checking out the town of Catclaw Draw," he said. "Talk to the local editor—see if there are any other stories that might be worthwhile."

She hoped he had forgotten about Black Dove and his two gold teeth. That mystery was better left buried in the New Mexico soil.

"There'll be three or four newspapers represented at the news conference," she said. "You won't be getting a scoop, you know."

Michael shrugged. "A century-old cemetery is not exactly scoop material. So how does one go about digging up a site like that anyhow?"

"The same way one digs into a big breakfast. Maybe a little slower."

He paused in lifting a forkful of eggs as the hint of a grin turned up the corners of his mouth. "I learned to eat fast during the Gulf War."

"Ah. Well, it's mostly contract work. I design the project, and then I farm out various aspects of the job."

"So you *are* a farmer."

"Very funny." She would almost swear he was flirting with her. That comment about her looking beautiful...and now this teasing tone....

"On most sites, I only plan and oversee the work," she told him. "But with something as small as this cemetery relocation, I can get involved personally.... Aren't you going to get out your notebook, or turn on your recorder or something?"

He shook his head. "This is just for me."

Kitt took a swallow of tea. Odd that he had remembered how she liked it—piping hot, with milk and sugar stirred in. It felt so strange to sit with him like this, eating breakfast together as they once had. Talking over their plans, sharing thoughts. Keep it light, Kitt, she reminded herself. Just get through the day.

"How do you design a project like this?" Michael was asking. "Are all the graves clearly marked?"

"Hardly. With the elements and neglect, the headstones are crumbling." She leaned back in her chair, trying to relax. "Planning a project like this one is fairly straightforward. I examine the area to be flooded. I search for missing pieces in the historical picture—the archaeology and anthropology of the site. I issue my findings to the public. Private companies or universities submit proposals to detail how they would handle the project."

"Like a bid?"

"Sort of. With my input, the Bureau picks the best one and awards a contract. Once the work starts, I act as administrator."

"It seems like the main job is opening the graves and

moving the remains. What kind of report does the Bureau want from you?"

This felt better. Now they were talking like two professionals. She could handle it until he left this afternoon.

"I write up three kinds of summaries," she explained. "One is an interpretation of the project. Another is for archaeologists. A third is for the general reader. There are a lot of history buffs around here."

Michael leaned forward, elbows on the table. "You might look like a farm girl, but you know your stuff."

"I've been at it a lot of years." She should get up now and head out the door. Instead, she heard herself say, "What about you? You're pretty comfortable with your career, I guess."

"There was a time, early on, when professionals like you intimidated me. I'd be trying to get a story out of them, and it was awful. I could tell they were experts in their field while I knew next to zip. But it didn't take long to figure out that my skill was getting people to communicate what I needed to understand—along with a lot of other things they might have preferred to keep under wraps."

"Don't try that on me."

He smiled. "Kitt, remember how we used to just sit around and talk? We used to be able to tell each other everything. You would get me to open up to you about stuff I couldn't share with anyone else."

Kitt was staring at the mulberry trees through the window as she tried to make herself think about anything but the man across the table from her. Anything but the past.

The project. Everyone would be driving to the site by now. Dr. Dean was probably asking where she was. The summer students would start climbing into the pits. The bulldozer would roar to life.

But she couldn't dispel the image of a gangly young man leaning across the table, his hands working a sweat-stained ball cap around and around. His mouth twisted as he talked about his father—about the pressure to succeed, about the pressure to stay quiet and to be obedient at all times. He talked about his mother and her old rocking chair. He talked about the farm and his dreams.

"I remember," she answered.

"Remember the time you told me how your father despised me because I was beneath you? I was nothing but a farm boy who'd never amount to anything?"

She nodded, fingering a stain on her jeans. "Michael, please—"

"I want to talk about what happened between us, Kitt. I want to talk about the baby."

She pinched the denim fabric. "No, Michael. It was a long time ago. It's over now."

"I want to talk about it."

"Well, I don't!" She heard her voice lose its professional detachment. She was that girl again, that broken, hopeless child.

"I want to know what happened," he demanded.

"You know what happened. You were right there! The baby died inside me. She just died. That was it. We went home to the trailer and three weeks later you walked out the door and didn't come back."

"Kitt, I need to tell you—"

"I don't want to hear it, Michael. It doesn't matter anymore, can't you see that?"

She got to her feet and he leaped up. He grabbed her hand. "It does matter. You mattered to me!"

"If I mattered to you, then why did you run off and leave me?" Snatching her hand away, she backed up against the bed. "Don't try to fix it now, Michael. It's been too many years. We've gone on. We've turned out okay in spite of it. I want to stay okay. Talking about what happened and going over everything again is not a good idea."

"You want to heal, Kitt. I can see that in you. You want to heal as badly as I do."

"Tearing the scab off an old wound is not healing. It's re-injuring." She tried to compose herself. Surely he had to know she was right and they should drop the whole subject. "Listen, this was a weird thing, us running into each other. It caused us to start thinking of things we haven't thought about in years. I'm sorry, Michael. If you'll excuse me, I'm late for work."

"Okay, Kitt," he said. "You're right. Skip it. Sorry I brought it up." He shrugged and walked to the table. "See you at two, if I can make it."

She pushed her hands into her pockets. "If you can make it?"

"Things are starting to pile up. I really didn't have time to take Burton's place on this story anyway. I'm thinking about heading up to Albuquerque this afternoon. You can send me the report when you finish, and I'll write the piece on the relocation from that."

"Okay." She suddenly felt deflated. It had been strangely good to get angry, to shout at him. But she'd gotten her way, just like that. The subject of their past was closed. Now he would walk away from her again.

It seemed too soon. There was more anger inside her. And other things she hadn't even known were there. Tears…she could feel them trying to well up. Fear…fear of letting go, fear of taking hold. And longing…she had discovered that in the night. She knew it now, watching him in the early morning light. He was big and handsome. He smelled good. His eyes kept calling to her.

She forced a smile and slung her bag over her shoulder. "Hey, thanks for the breakfast."

"You're welcome. I'll clean this up and shut your room for you."

"Bye, then."

She stepped out into the sunshine. The pickup started with a cough. The steering wheel felt hot under her frozen fingers and she gripped it tightly as she drove.

Hod stood beside one of the opened graves, peering into its depths. "I told you not to come back," Kitt said more harshly than she intended.

The old man glanced up in surprise. His face in the morning light looked even more ancient than she remembered. Unshaven chin, hooked Roman nose, stringy white hair that needed a thorough washing. He smelled of perspiration and liquor and woodsmoke.

"I had to come," he said simply. He had lost most of his teeth, and his words were hard to make out.

"I told you before, it's against regulations."

"I'm here to see the twilight."

"Oh, don't start in on that twilight business." She felt grouchy, impatient. Her hair was unbraided. Her stomach was half empty. And she had a headache. "If you have some reason for being here—"

"The gold."

"There's no gold here, Hod. None. This is a cemetery."

"Yep." Gnarled hands straightened the patched black wool suit he wore. "My father's gold mine. He took me there when I was nine years old."

"Well, a gold mine certainly would be interesting. But I can assure you, there's not one here."

"I know that. The mine is on a mountain. Rocks all around. A pine tree bent by the wind into the shape of an *L*."

"Okay, and this is a cemetery, Hod. Flat ground. No mountains. These holes are graves. Human remains are buried here."

"Yes. Mothers and fathers."

Kitt took off her hat and began coiling her loose hair into a knot. "Mothers and fathers?"

"What's your name, young lady?"

"Kitt Cul—" She jammed her hat onto her head. "Kitt Tucker. Dr. Kitt Tucker, and I'm responsible for keeping people off the site."

"Dr. Tucker, please let me stay."

"I'm sorry, Hod. I can't do that." She felt like the wicked witch.

His shoulders hunched, the old man turned toward his battered truck.

"You all right this morning, Dr. Tucker?" Dr. Dean laid a hand on Kitt's arm. "You're looking a little worn."

They walked toward the nylon tent. The dew on the long grass was drying swiftly as the sun rose higher in the pale blue sky. The Pecos River, winding between cottonwoods, scrub oak and salt cedar, whispered between the silences of the morning. Locusts sang. Clumps of small white butterflies drifted up from cow patties, then settled again. Bees darted among purple-tipped alfalfa blossoms. A mockingbird wheeled overhead, its black-and-white wings flashing in the sunlight.

"Thanks for getting things started for me," Kitt said as she stepped through the tent door. "I had a late night. I've called a news conference this afternoon over at Chisum Memorial."

"You finish up with that reporter from Albuquerque?"

"I guess so." Finished was right. "Find out anything more on that skeleton with the gold teeth?"

"Nothing else was in the grave. He had a knife tip in his scapula. Two inches long."

Kitt nodded, fiddling with a set of calipers. "I saw that."

"Just the gold teeth and the knife tip and the newspaper clipping. He didn't have a casket, so there won't be any wood to help us date the age of the grave."

"Did the skeleton itself tell you anything about the man?"

"I haven't started the measurements. Just looking, I'd say

he was an old fellow, which is strange considering most of the men in here died young and violently."

She glanced up. "You don't think his death was violent?"

"Hard to say. The knife tip in his shoulder didn't kill him, and there were no bullets in the fill dirt. Course, someone could have slit his throat or knifed him in a vital organ, and we'd never know it... The skull appears somewhat odd."

"In what way?"

"It's the teeth."

"Gold teeth are unusual in a location where most of the people were poverty-stricken."

"Actually, I'm not talking about that. This man's teeth look different to me. He's definitely not Negroid or Mongoloid. His features appear to be Caucasian—but the incisors are shovel-shaped. I'll let you know what I think after I complete my examination."

"Thanks." Kitt set the calipers on the table. As an archaeologist, she had the job of piecing together the puzzles of history. She had always enjoyed developing hypotheses based on the information that came out of dig sites and the old Muddy Flats cemetery interested her in that way. She had imagined putting together the final reports she had described to Michael—the charts and diagrams, the factual findings and her own conclusions.

But faced with this strange, gold-toothed skull, she felt uncharacteristically reticent. She wished she hadn't dug it up. She wished it didn't have those gold teeth. She wished Dr. Dean had said it was obvious the man was just another of the poor pioneers of early New Mexico.

It was Michael's doing, she thought as she stepped into the glaring sunshine. If he hadn't latched on to the ridiculous notion that the skull fit the description of Black Dove...if he hadn't pestered her for an interview...if he just hadn't come at all...

* * *

Kitt spent the morning as she had for two months—sitting at the edge of grave pits drawing outlines for the summer students. She watched them trowel the dirt and remove the collapsed coffin lids. She helped one young man pick soil away from a skeleton, then sift the remaining dirt with a screen. They found three tin buttons and a bullet in the chest area. Another violent death.

But instead of engaging in the usual banter that kept the whole group informed and feeling like a team, she lapsed into deep silence as she worked.

Michael had been right, she realized. She did want to find a healing. Somewhere inside herself she wanted to understand what had happened. Why had everything fallen apart so quickly? Why had they been chattering best friends one minute and mute adversaries the next? Why had their passion suddenly died? Why had Michael left her all alone in that battered, windblown trailer?

She wasn't going to get the answers now. While her career was built around digging up the past and finding answers to unsolved riddles, she would never understand what had happened in her own past. She would never know why she and Michael had come apart at the seams.

Holding up the sole of a boot that a student had just uncovered, she turned it back and forth. The leather had worn partly away to form a hole in the center. The sun shone through tiny holes where thread had once laced the sole to the upper. On the left side the heel had eroded, leaving a sort of triangular wedge.

"Looking at that heel, I expect the poor fellow had bandy legs," the summer student said. "Probably a horseman. A cowboy. He must have done some walking, though, to have worn out the sole that way. Or maybe he inherited the boots from somebody else. Isn't it pretty unusual that they left this guy's boots on when they buried him, Dr. Tucker?…Dr. Tucker?"

Kitt's eyes darted to the young man. "That's right, Sam. Very unusual. The people in the Muddy Flats area were so poor they passed their shoes from person to person."

"How about that fellow with the gold teeth you uncovered yesterday, Dr. Tucker? He wasn't like the others we've found here. Two gold front teeth…he must have been pretty rich."

"I expect so, Sam."

"Rich enough to have gold teeth—but not rich enough to have a coffin or a stone marker. What do you make of that?"

"Maybe nobody liked him. Or maybe he was a stranger passing through Muddy Flats when he died. He might have had a disease. Or maybe he was some kind of outcast."

"Like an Indian or something. What do you think, Dr. Tucker?"

She shook her head. "We'll see."

Kitt shaded her eyes as she looked out across the group of reporters. An attractive young female reporter had come from the *Catclaw Draw Daily Call*. A thin blond fellow represented the *Carlsbad* paper. Old Hod sat beneath a distant cottonwood, his hat in his hand. Michael was not present.

She hadn't expected him to be. After lunch, she had gone to the motel to change clothes. She spent some time going over what she wanted to present, and she talked with her supervisor at the Bureau. They set the site's closing date for the following week. The gray car that had been parked outside Michael's door the previous night was gone, his room silent.

The two o'clock sun was blistering at the Chisum Memorial Cemetery. Recent graves stood out against the irrigated green grass, their stone markers topped with wreaths and bouquets of bright artificial flowers. A pair of large oak trees cast a welcome shade over one section. A canopy had been stretched over a new grave. Beneath it stood a woman and a little girl holding hands, staring down at the spaded dirt.

Kitt shifted her attention to the area that the Muddy Flats cemetery would occupy. It had been her idea to re-create the original setting and atmosphere of the historical cemetery—shaggy kochia grass sprouting from bare brown dust, sandstone rocks, prickly pear cactus, stands of yucca. If a few rattlesnakes and horned toads moved in, that would be fine. The Muddy Flats graves would return to their previous state, with nature as their landscaper and caretaker.

"On behalf of the Bureau of Reclamation, I'd like to thank you all for coming out this afternoon." Everyone quieted as she began speaking. "Within four to six weeks, the old Muddy Flats cemetery will be relocated directly behind me in this open field. The headstones are being restored. New markers will be placed on every previously undesignated grave."

The reporters had begun taking down her words in their notebooks. Some had recorders. Hod kept turning his hat in his hands. Kitt brushed her palm across the back of her damp neck.

"I'll go over what we're currently doing out at the Muddy Flats site, and then some of you may have questions." She opened her notes and began her prepared remarks. "A contractor from Catclaw Draw is working for us. At each grave his crew digs until the first signs of remains are discovered. We've found that the skeletal material at the site is in remarkably good condition due to the clay soil. Photographs of the remains are taken while they're still in place. Our physical anthropologist, Dr. John Dean of Northern New Mexico University, will use these photographs in his report. The bones and other remains are then removed from the pit, put on a board and taken into Dr. Dean's tent. There he performs fifty-eight examinations on each skeleton, including tests for signs of disease. We've done six to eight skeletons a day…"

She faltered as a gray compact car sped through the cemetery and pulled to a halt just beyond the ring of reporters. Michael Culhane got out.

Kitt was focused on her listeners as Michael approached. When her gaze locked onto him, his heart thudded heavily. He took a place at the back of the group.

"The remains are put into metal boxes," she was saying. "We also add the coffin material and other archaeological artifacts found in the grave. At this point in the project, we've finished excavating all the marked graves, and we've placed a numbered lath at each one. We then moved the soil fill from the surrounding area and started trenching to see if there were any unmarked graves."

Michael took out his recorder and switched it on, grateful he stood head and shoulders above the other reporters. He had her clearly in view.

"We have found thirty-seven graves to this point," Kitt continued as she looked at her notes. "Of the fourteen males from ages eighteen to forty-five, ten suffered violent deaths. There are lots of infants buried at Muddy Flats—some no more than four weeks old. Childhood diseases such as diphtheria and whooping cough are probable causes. Married women normally had a baby every two years, and the children were difficult to nourish...."

Michael studied Kitt as she addressed the small group. Her voice sounded tight and professional. She spoke in a clipped way, as if she were analyzing the data while she relayed it. But he knew just by watching her what was going on beneath that cool facade. He knew she was thinking about those babies. He'd heard her voice on the tape recorder all night long.

It hadn't taken much time that morning to make a decision about something that had been playing in the back of his mind since she'd reentered his life. He was going to find the real Kitt again.

Sitting in the quiet of the local library, he had outlined a rough plan. Even put it down on paper in his reporter's notebook. The plan was off to a good start already. And with the help of a few history books, he now had a modus operandi—a method of procedure that involved a certain gold-toothed Shawnee war chief. The only weakness in his plan was the ending.

Michael had no clear idea of what he hoped to accomplish by drawing Kitt out of her silence. He supposed that just the healing they had talked about that morning would be enough. Kitt thought she knew him well, but there were a few things she didn't understand. She believed he was still the boy who found it hard to talk, the youngster who took suggestions as orders. The good boy. She didn't know what the years had done to him.

He was blunt now. Met things head-on. Like a bulldog, he would latch on to a problem and not let go until he'd solved it. He put puzzles together just like she did. And the way their lives and their marriage and their love had fallen apart was the biggest puzzle he knew. He had his teeth in it now. He wanted answers.

God must have brought them together again to finish the healing process. Michael's healing, if not Kitt's. She appeared to need no healing, he noted as he listened to her voice. She was stunning in the afternoon sunlight, her long brown hair drifting loose. She had changed into an outfit that would have turned heads even in Santa Fe—a white cutwork blouse, an Indian broom-pleated skirt of purple cotton that hung almost to her ankles, silver hoop earrings, a leather belt and sandals. Five silver bracelets marched up one arm. She looked like a Gypsy and sounded like a professor. The combination was intriguing.

"Yes, there have been a few surprises," Kitt was saying. The reporters had begun to ask questions. She appeared relaxed and seemed to be enjoying herself. This was her domain. "The myth of the tall, rugged John Wayne-type cowboy certainly has been dispelled at Muddy Flats. Most of the men were barely over five feet tall. The women, of course, were tiny as well."

"What sort of artifacts did you find in the graves, Dr. Tucker?" a short, blond man asked. "Can you give us some details?"

"We found little, actually. These people had very few possessions. Only two men were buried with their boots on, and just six of the graves contained shoes. We found copper and brass buttons, like you might see on a pair of jeans today. There were some denim scraps. We also found buttons of shell, bone and glass. The buttons rarely matched. Lots of nails, all square. Some of the coffins had handles. One infant had worn a pin engraved with the word *Baby*. We did find…we did find safety pins in the infants' graves. It was a difficult thing to see…."

Michael watched her face as she paused to collect herself. Her eyes drifted to the ground and studied a clump of dry grass beside her foot. He felt an impulse to go to her—but then she was speaking again, her shoulders straight and her chin high.

"We found hardly any jewelry. Three males wore cufflinks. One pair was made of onyx with a matching collar stud. One woman had a necklace of bone and glass tubular beads."

"What about wedding rings?" Michael asked.

He saw Kitt's hand tighten on her notebook. "Five. Two were made of iron. Two were a gold alloy. One was a kind of hard rubber."

"Did you find any valuable items in the graves, Mrs. Culhane?"

Kitt's expression darkened as she focused on Michael. "I'm afraid you've mistaken me for someone else, sir. My name is Dr. Tucker. And no, we found nothing of any real value in the graves—small brooches, the head and arms of a ceramic doll, scraps of black broadcloth, a piece of folded newspaper."

"What about the skeletons themselves? Did you find anything unusual or interesting about any of them?"

The other reporters had turned to stare at Michael, their faces hostile. Who was this jerk? they seemed to be thinking. After all, this was a cemetery relocation, not a major crime scene.

"As a matter of fact," Kitt said briskly, "we were able to substantiate some of the legends that have been circulating around the Catclaw Draw and Muddy Flats areas for nearly a century. The grave of William Jackson, who was said to have been shot at close range by his father-in-law, contained many pieces of buckshot. Another man, by the name of Johnny Southern, was rumored to have been shot in a duel. We found a slug in his grave near the heart area."

"Anything else?"

Kitt looked steadily at Michael. "One elderly man whose grave was unmarked had two gold teeth and a knife tip embedded in his scapula."

"Where?"

"The scapula. It's the shoulder blade."

"I mean the teeth. Where were they—in the front?"

Kitt clenched her jaw. "Yes. In the front. The two upper incisors were made of gold."

"Would you say, then, that what you found in the Muddy Flats cemetery confirmed or dispelled the written and oral history of the area?"

"Without a doubt, it confirmed it. I had believed, actually, that the local stories were exaggerated. I thought the tales of the old Wild West were largely myths. But based on the number of violent deaths in the cemetery, I would have to say that the legends are probably quite accurate."

"You've changed your mind, then?"

Kitt stared at Michael. "Yes, I would say I've changed my mind."

"So you would agree that you—as an archaeologist and a

historian—have a responsibility to change your opinion about something if it can be proven different than you had thought? Let's say, for example, you turned up evidence that made you question a piece of information you had always believed. Would you then feel obligated to pursue that evidence until you were satisfied with its authenticity—even if it disproved what you had assumed was true?"

Michael was studying her, his eyes locked on her face. He knew her well enough to see she felt angry, cornered. But he had strong reasons for wanting her to admit that the gold-toothed skull was unusual—that it bore further investigation.

"What are you driving at, sir?" she asked. "Are you referring to something specific?"

Michael grinned, acknowledging her tactic. She *knew* Black Dove was buried in Guadalupe Y Calvo just as certainly as she knew that Michael Culhane was trying to get a rise out of her. So she had turned the tables on him. He wouldn't want to reveal his suspicions about Black Dove. Reporters were notoriously protective of their scoops.

"Just a simple question about archaeological technique," he responded. "Does a historian have a responsibility to try to solve an archaeological puzzle—even if the solution proves the historian wrong?"

"Yes," she said. "Generally speaking, that would be true."

"Thank you, ma'am."

"Are there any more questions?" Kitt glanced around. "Then if you'll excuse me, I need to close down the site for the day."

Flipping her notebook shut, she started toward the Bureau pickup. Michael caught up to her before she had taken five steps, his long-legged stride eating up the distance between them.

"Black Dove's out there, you know," he said, placing his palm flat against the door so she couldn't open it.

"Black Dove is in Mexico. Guadalupe Y Calvo. Just go look at a map—you'll find the town."

"I studied a map this morning in the library. Guadalupe Y Calvo is there. But Black Dove isn't. I checked some history books, Kitt. I'm sure he was buried at Muddy Flats."

"Go read Dr. Oldham's research notes, if you're so sure about that. He substantiated everything. There are interviews, military records, the whole bit."

"I'm throwing down the gauntlet, Kitt. Pick up that puzzle piece like the good archaeologist you are. Try to prove that Black Dove isn't in the grave at Muddy Flats."

"I don't have time, Michael. I have to finish this project. There's no point in chasing some insignificant historical figure whose final resting place has already been documented."

"Come on, Kitt," he said with a smile. "Take the challenge."

"You know, you're obnoxious, Michael," she told him. But her voice was soft. "It's no wonder they haven't made you an overseas correspondent. You'd probably start another war."

She took the door handle and pulled it. Michael bent his elbow. Dipping her knees, she stepped beneath the bridge of his arm and got into the truck. He leaned through the open window, his arms crossed.

"You don't work on Saturdays, do you?" he asked. "I'll pick you up at nine. We'll take a drive. I have a load of things on Black Dove to go over with you. Those librarians are thorough."

"I'll be busy tomorrow, Michael." She started the engine.

"Nine o'clock," he said.

Kitt rolled her eyes, let out a sigh and stepped on the gas. As she drove away, Michael saw an old man near a cottonwood tree tip his hat.

Chapter Four

❧

Kitt slammed the dryer door a little harder than necessary. A young woman with pink plastic rollers in her hair looked over the top of her gossip magazine. Heaving the plastic basket into her arms, Kitt walked across the Laundromat. The sickly sweet perfumes of fabric softener and detergent mingled with the scent of over-dried clothes. She dumped her clean laundry onto a linoleum table. Someone had left a pile of religious tracts next to a wadded gum wrapper. Kitt shoved her hand into the warm pile of clothes and pulled out a T-shirt.

It was still light outside. A few stores were open—a card shop, a boot repair store, a newsstand. The laundry was next to the movie theater. Both faced the main street, as did most of the other businesses and restaurants in town. There was only one show at the theater, and it cost a dollar to get in. Shoppers walked by, glancing surreptitiously at their reflections in the laundry's window. Cars carrying teenagers cruised past, "draggin' Main."

Memories of her own high school years brought a soft smile to Kitt's lips as she folded her laundry. The same scene had existed in the small New Mexico town of her youth— kids cruising an endless loop from a hamburger joint at one end of the street to a convenience store at the other.

The in crowd hung out together in one group—cheerleaders, football players. Their status symbols had been heavy, gold class rings with wads of tape to make them fit girlfriends' fingers, expensive cologne, enough hair spray to deplete the ozone layer, souped-up cars with noisy engines.

The "stomps" rodeoed and belonged to FFA or 4-H or both. They exhibited projects at the county fair and didn't mind hosing down a hog or rubbing lanolin on a cow's udder. They had their own symbols—pickup trucks, roper boots, cowboy hats, five-inch silver buckles on braided leather belts.

There were other groups, of course. Rebels with black jackets and funky haircuts, "brainiacs" with arms full of books, computer geeks with blank gazes from playing games all night, shy wallflowers who didn't fit in anywhere.

The kids had inherited their parents' traditions along with their prejudices. And by the looks of Catclaw Draw's main drag, the subcultures were still intact. Hardly anyone crossed group lines.

But Kitt Tucker had. She was supposed to hang with the rich kids. Her father was president of the bank, after all. They lived in a large brick house in Colonial Park. Her parents had given Kitt a brand-new red sports car when she turned sixteen, and her mother made sure she wore the latest styles. She went to society functions, and she even spent one summer at a camp back East to learn proper etiquette.

None of that had kept her from Michael Culhane. The moment she moved to town and set foot in the high school, they had been drawn to each other like magnets.

That's when the arguing had begun. Her parents railed at

each other. Why had they moved to this podunk town? her mother wanted to know. Couldn't her father have gotten a better job? Kitt's father was quick to shout back. Why couldn't her mother have raised a daughter who knew how to behave? He'd worked hard to become bank president, and he wasn't about to see his daughter marry some poor cotton farmer.

Michael's parents had argued as well—mostly with him. Why wasn't he getting his chores done? Was he too good for the common folk now? Who did he think he was, anyway? He'd better get his backside into the field and onto a tractor before he got a licking he'd never forget. He'd be better off with the young people he'd grown up with in Sunday school. Didn't he know someone such as Kitt Tucker—a girl who drove a sports car and wore short skirts and makeup—was bound to be fast?

Kitt shook her head and pulled a pair of socks from the pile of clean laundry. It hadn't mattered a bit—all that fighting. She and Michael had spent every spare minute together anyway. Their time together formed the sort of memory a woman took from the shelf now and then, dusted off and studied for a minute. The last thing she had expected was for that memory to come barging back into her world, big as life, twice as handsome and with more of that old magnetic pull than ever.

She thought back to the sight of him standing behind the cluster of reporters that afternoon. Sunlight had caught the blond streaks in his hair and carved shadows beneath his cheekbones. In his blue oxford shirt with the sleeves rolled to the elbow, he wore an air of self-assurance and reliability—the sort of man's man whom employers respected, coworkers envied and women pursued.

Even now, in the laundry, Kitt realized she had already grown used to the squareness of Michael's jaw. In less than a day, she had replaced the memory of her rangy, loose-limbed teenaged husband with this broad-shouldered, hard-chested reporter. He had grown tall, and it felt almost normal to look up into his face. How strange to lose the boy and accept so swiftly the man he had become.

Only one thing about Michael Culhane remained the same. His blue-gray eyes. They followed her movements as they always had. They studied her mouth as it formed words. That deep-set gaze raked through her hair and across her face, just as she remembered. Though Michael's outer self projected confidence and professionalism, he also wore—not far beneath the surface—the natural physicality of a leopard on the prowl.

She hurled the sock ball into the empty basket at her feet. The woman in curlers lifted her eyes over the magazine again.

Throwing down the gauntlet, indeed. Of all the nerve. Kitt flung a second sock ball into her laundry basket. How dare that skeleton have two gold front teeth? Worse, she now had to factor in Dr. Dean's unsettling assessment of the remains.

"I've finished going over that skeleton of yours, Dr. Tucker," the physical anthropologist had said that afternoon when she returned from the news conference. "Quite a fellow. He was six feet tall, powerful and handsome. I'd make him about sixty-five at death, but his body had held up remarkably well. He'd lived a violent life—broken femur, two broken ribs, knife tip in his scapula. He had been active right up to the end."

"Thanks, Dr. Dean." She had almost hoped that was all.

"One more thing. There's no question about his race, Dr. Tucker. Other than the two gold teeth, his six remaining front incisors were shovel-toothed. He was a Native American."

To her dismay, Kitt realized she was caught in a true dilemma. Michael had been right that afternoon at the conference—remains that so closely matched the description of Black Dove should be given careful consideration. It was her job. Her responsibility. But more than that, these tantalizing clues might add up to something truly fascinating. She felt the old tingling thrill at the thought of tracking down and fitting together the pieces to an intriguing puzzle.

If only she could send Michael Culhane packing. Head him back to Albuquerque where he belonged. Kitt hurled a third sock ball into her basket. She glanced at the woman in curlers. Though her eyes had lifted from the magazine, they were riveted to the laundry's door where Michael leaned, a grin of triumph on his face.

"Hey, Kitt. I spotted your truck on my way to dinner. How goes the laundry?"

When she didn't answer, he strolled across the room. She grabbed a pair of jeans and began the futile exercise of smoothing their set-in wrinkles. Twenty-four hours ago, she fumed. Just twenty-four hours ago, her life had been calm, purposeful and orderly. Now she had an ex-husband who was determined to dog her like a bloodhound, a gold-toothed skull that refused to rest in peace and a misbehaving heart.

"There's a street festival two blocks down." Michael rested one hip against her table and crossed his arms over his chest. "The high school rodeo association's putting it on for the state championship finalists."

"How about that."

"Want to go?"

"I understand you're having trouble with this fact, Michael, but I'm not in high school any longer. And you're not a rodeo cowboy."

"The event is open to the public. It's a family thing with square dancing and fiddlers."

Kitt hadn't been to anything like a street festival in years. But the thought of funnel cakes, popcorn, country music and couples swirling across scattered hay made her feet itch. She could almost smell the hot apple cider.

"I'll help you finish your laundry, and then we'll go to the dance. I was always good at laundry, remember?" He heaved himself up on the table and picked up a red T-shirt. "What was that place called? You used to hate it. The idea of washing your clothes in a machine that somebody else had used was disgusting. 'Oh, Michael,' you would say. 'This makes me sick.'"

"U Washem…that's what it was called." Kitt shook her lowered head, a grin playing at the corners of her lips.

"Ah, the old U Washem Laundry. Those were the days."

Michael was folding a shirt on his thigh just the way he always had. Beneath her brows, Kitt watched his big hands smooth over the cotton sleeves and down the front. He began to fold the shirt in half.

Quickly she pulled her thoughts back to matters at hand. She should tell Michael about Dr. Dean's conclusions. Though everything would be in her final report, it was only fair that Michael know now, when it interested him. But if he were aware that the gold-toothed skull belonged to an Indian, he'd have even more reason to hold her to his challenge.

Oh, why had Michael noticed her car? Kitt mused as she sorted through her clean laundry. It was so uncomfortable to perform this remembered ritual with him. She could feel that her back was ramrod straight and her shoulders rigid, but she couldn't make herself relax—as if, by holding her breath, she could wish him away.

But he was enjoying this. He was smiling at her, and his eyes had softened at the edges. Their blue-gray was not so much the color of steel now—more the shade of a lake in winter. A ladybug had ridden into the laundry on his shoulder and she could tell he didn't know it was there.

If he just weren't so close, chatting comfortably and smelling like the boy who once had turned her heart. If his hair didn't look all soft and shiny. If his arms weren't brown and thick with muscle. It was that jaw, most of all. That square, hard, man's jaw.

"Nice slacks, Kitt," he said, handing her a pair of faded, frayed blue jeans.

"If you're going to fold, fold," she said.

Their eyes met, challenging. "So you never got married again, Kitt?"

"I was barely married to you, and it just about destroyed me. Why would I ever want to do that again?" She shook her head. "Michael, I thought you were going to Albuquerque."

"Later. What about dating? You do that a lot?"

"Some. You?"

"Some." Michael picked up another T-shirt. "Anything special with any of these men?"

Kitt watched him spread out the fabric and try to smooth it into shape. It occurred to her that he was nervous. Maybe even a little jealous. She almost wished she could describe some delectably handsome, wealthy professor who was courting her. No such luck.

"I travel a lot," she said softly. "There's not much time to get involved."

He nodded. "I'm on the road two or three weeks a month. No stranger to U Washem laundries, that's for sure."

She laughed. "I can't believe I keep having to do this. When I landed the job with the Bureau, I promised myself I'd never go in one of these places again. I went straight out and bought a washer and dryer. They're still practically new."

"You should see my apartment. I'm hardly ever there. Looks like a mausoleum. In the living room, I've got a lawn chair and an orange plaid couch handed down from Grandma Culhane.

A frying pan and a stewpot in the kitchen. My folks gave me the old bed I had when I was a kid."

"You still sleep on that awful thing?"

"And it still sags in the middle."

"Well, with you and your brother jumping up and down on it like a couple of monkeys." Kitt stared at her hands, unmoving on the stack of folded laundry. What on earth was she saying? Why was she even speaking to the man who had caused her so much agony?

"I'm sorry, Kitt," Michael said, reaching to touch her arm. "I know you don't want to talk about the past. It's just that seeing you again brings it back. We did have some good times, you know. Really good times."

She swallowed. "It's not easy for me to think about it. I do better when I stay in the here and now."

"I admire what you've done with yourself, Kitt."

"Thanks. I'm comfortable with who I am."

"I realize you'd rather not go into everything that happened, but I do want to apologize for what you went through when I left." He hesitated for a moment, then he let out a hot breath. "I'm sorry I walked out on you."

"Why did you leave me, Michael?" She lifted her eyes.

He shook his head. "I thought you hated me. That you blamed me for the baby. For giving you the baby…and then for her death."

"You didn't cause our daughter to die."

"You were so silent. From the time we found out she would be stillborn, right through to the birth…"

"Michael." Kitt heard the panic in her voice. She wasn't ready to talk about it. She couldn't go back over that time. "I'm sorry…I can't…"

"Come on, honey." He slid off the table and put his arm around her shoulders. "Let's walk over to that street festival. It'll do us good."

"I really don't feel like doing anything, Michael."

"Then we'll just watch."

* * *

As Kitt let Michael lead her out into the evening, he thanked God for softening her. Though the pain between them was still raw, they both needed this. With her arm tucked in his, Michael felt some of the ache lessen. They set the laundry baskets in her pickup cab and wandered down the street.

A group of square dancers was in full swing. A flatbed truck formed the stage for two fiddlers, a guitarist and a banjo player. Beside them on a bale of hay, a young man in a red-checkered shirt called the steps. Couples of every age whirled around the street, their boots keeping time. Hay bales lined the sidewalks for those choosing to sit out a dance. Against the brick wall of the local bank stretched a long table with lemonade, steaming hot apple cider, hot dogs and popcorn for sale. A church youth group was running a cakewalk for a missions project, and the local senior center had set up rocking chairs for the elderly. With no alcohol allowed and a couple policeman strolling the premises, the whole town seemed to have turned out for an evening of good clean fun.

Michael settled Kitt comfortably against his side as they observed the dancers. Even though her purple skirt and soft white blouse didn't quite fit in with all the blue jeans, cowboy boots and silver buckles in the crowd, he was glad she was wearing them. The fact of the matter was, Kitt was the best-looking woman at the party—and he felt an odd sense of boyish pride to have her on his arm.

But this Kitt was so different from the trusting, light-hearted teen who had loved him with such passion. There was a new depth to her, a serious, secret side that he was learning to understand and respect. If she didn't want to talk about their baby and all the things that had happened, he would let it rest for a while.

She turned to him, her brown eyes glowing. "Want some lemonade?"

"I'll get it."

"No, let me."

As she stepped toward the long table, her hair brushed against her shoulders. She was all swaying movement—hair, skirt, body. Picking up two paper cups of lemonade, she reached in her skirt pocket and pulled out some loose change. Laundry money. Her arm looked slender as she paid for the drinks.

Seeing her from a distance, Michael was struck again at how beautiful a woman Kitt had become. Strapped sandals curved around delicate ankles, and heavy silver bracelets hung on her wrists. Her waist was almost too thin. If it weren't for the maturity in her eyes and voice, he wouldn't have put her much over twenty.

As the square dancing ended and the musicians began to play two-steps and waltzes, Kitt rejoined Michael. She stood at his side and they sipped lemonade. Though their arms barely brushed against one another, he imagined he could have counted every single silky hair from her wrist to her elbow without looking. He could feel the hem of her skirt swaying against his pant leg—and it suddenly came to him that these weren't old feelings renewed.

This was not nostalgia.

Kitt was desirable for who she was at that moment. And he knew if he had just met her for the first time, he wouldn't be feeling a bit different.

"Dr. Tucker!" A sandy-haired youth waved from the other side of the street. Kitt waved back.

"It's Sam," she said softly. "One of the student workers out at the site."

The young man began weaving through the crowd, his eyes pinned on Kitt. Michael glanced at the woman beside him, uncomfortable with the gnawing irritation he felt at the smile she had directed at Sam.

"I didn't know you'd be here." She spoke to the intern

with genuine pleasure in her voice—a tone exactly the opposite of what she'd been using with Michael for the past twenty-four hours. "Are the others here?"

"Jake and Matt are. Ashley's coming later."

"Great! Sam, I'd like you to meet Michael Culhane. He's with the Affiliated Press out of Albuquerque."

Sam stuck out his hand and Michael shook it.

"So—would you like to dance, Dr. Tucker?"

Kitt's eyes darted to Michael for an instant. Without waiting for any sort of response, she stepped into the street.

"See you later, Michael!" She waved as if he were a pet flea she was setting free.

The next moment, she was spinning around and around in the arms of some kid named Sam. Some scrawny, long-legged boy in a ball cap. And she was laughing! Her head flew back. Her hair swung low and whisked away from her back. Worst of all, they kept perfect time—his hand settling right at her waist, and his skinny legs following the beat right next to hers.

Michael downed his lemonade and crumpled the cup. You weren't supposed to care who your ex-wife danced with. You weren't supposed to admire the turn of her ankles and the swish of her hair. And you sure weren't supposed to wish it was you holding her tight instead of some baby-faced yokel.

But the fact was, he did care. He cared a lot.

Michael tossed his cup into a trash can and started through the crowd. In half a minute he had caught up with Kitt, politely freed her from Sam, and taken her in his arms.

"Michael—that's rude," she said. But a smile crinkled the corners of her pretty eyes.

"I imagine ol' Sam can find someone else to dance with."

"She won't dance as well as I do."

"True." Michael drew her closer, reveling in the scent of her hair. As they stepped and turned, she kept her eyes on his face, and in the growing darkness he couldn't help focusing on her lips.

"You told me you didn't want to dance," he said.

"I changed my mind."

"We dance well together, Kitt." His voice was ragged, the emotion too close to the surface. He wove his fingers through hers, pressing their palms together.

"I couldn't have asked for a better teacher. The two-step wasn't something they taught in my etiquette classes."

Michael tried to disguise the shiver that ran down his spine as her sweet voice danced through his heart. Her breath was warm and smelled of lemons, and in his arms, she felt lithe and so feminine. When the song ended, she started to move away. But Michael kept his arm behind her back as the next number, a waltz, began.

"When I first saw you last night," he murmured against her ear, "I had the idea that we might call a truce in the hostilities."

"That sounds all right." She gave a small shrug. "I mean, okay to a certain extent."

"But right now, I'm thinking something different."

"Like what?"

"I'm thinking how good this feels and how much I like talking to you and seeing you smile. And I'm thinking, Kitt, that maybe we could settle the past. Heal the old wounds."

"I guess that might be possible. Maybe. But I do have the project to finish, and I know you need to get back to Albuquerque."

"And what I was thinking was…that we might work ourselves up to the point of being friends again."

"Well, I suppose we're probably past the hostility. But I really don't want to go back over what happened."

"I think you do."

"No."

"Fifteen minutes ago you asked me why I left you. You want to settle this as much as I do."

The song ended, and they stepped apart. As Michael walked beside her across the hay-strewn street, Kitt spoke in a low voice. "If we talk," she said, "we'll have to relive it. Michael, it hurt so much. I don't want to go back to that."

"Listen, I'll be staying in Catclaw Draw this weekend and into next week," he told her. "The bureau chief wants me to cover the state rodeo finals and write an update on the nuclear waste storage plant near Carlsbad. It's Burton's territory, but he's still—"

"Still down with the flu," Kitt said with a wry smile. "Good old Burton."

"Hey, I'm beginning to think a lot of my buddy Burton. We can credit his flu bug for our happy reunion."

"I'm not sure I'd call it that. And as for taking the time to talk, I'll have to decline. I have a lot of work to do."

"Regarding a certain gold-toothed skull?"

Before Kitt could answer, the fiddlers ended their set. "We'll take a ten-minute break, folks," the singer announced, "and then we'll be back to wake ya'll up. Don't run off, now!"

She turned to Michael. "Well, that turned out to be fun. Thanks."

"My pleasure. Want a hot dog?"

"No, thanks. You really wouldn't believe the stack of papers waiting for me at the motel. I'd better get going."

"Had supper, Kitt?"

"No, but—"

"I'll buy you a hot dog and we'll stroll. Come on, two old pals, right?"

"Michael, please don't push me."

"I'm not pushing, Kitt. I never push. I simply issue strong invitations. And I can tell you really don't want to go back to that motel room."

"Oh, is that right? How can you tell?"

"Honey, the moon is in your eyes," he replied in a playful tone. "The music's in your blood. And you're with the most handsome, charming fellow you've been with in a very long time."

"A little vain, are we?"

"Just truthful."

"Go get me a hot dog, Prince Charming." She gave his shoulder a swat, and he set off for the refreshment table.

Not long after, they were wandering down the street, eating hot dogs, drinking sodas and gazing into store windows. Michael felt the knots that had started in his stomach the night before slowly begin to untie. They talked about nothing—whether hot dogs needed only mustard, or ketchup, too. They meandered into a card shop and Kitt bought a couple postcards.

"Are you enjoying the festival?" the shop clerk asked as he slipped the cards into a bag. "You with the rodeo?"

"No, we're just visiting Catclaw Draw," Kitt answered. He was a nice-looking blond fellow with a friendly face. Probably a hometown boy.

"Your first visit? Where are you staying?"

"We're over at the Thunderbird Motel."

"Honeymooners?"

"Oh, no—" Kitt began.

"Sort of—" Michael overlapped.

The young man glanced from one to the other.

"No, we're definitely not—" Kitt began again.

"More like a reunion than a honeymoon," Michael said.

"We get a fair number of honeymooners passing through," the young man explained. "Carlsbad Caverns, you know. Well, if you do make it a honeymoon someday, come on back through Catclaw Draw."

"We'll do that," Michael said.

"Enjoy the evening."

The temperature had dropped with the sunset, and Michael slipped his arm around Kitt's shoulders as they exited. "Nice fellow," he said.

"You gave him the wrong impression, Michael. That wasn't necessary."

"Just being polite."

The fiddlers were working up the crowd with another song when Michael and Kitt rounded the sidewalk onto the street. Little girls were dancing with their daddies while babies dozed in strollers. Sam and three other young bucks leaned against the bank wall, watching as Michael led Kitt back into the fun. Linked arm in arm with a long line of dancers, they kicked up their heels and stepped out with fancy footwork, circling the moonlit street. The faster the fiddles hummed, the swifter the lines wove around and around. Pretty soon Kitt's heart was thumping double time and the bank wall tilted and spun at a crazy angle.

Laughing, she glanced up at Michael. He was smiling at her. His hair bounced with every move; his long legs skillfully kept the rhythm. The lines grew swiftly shorter as couples dropped out, gasping with laughter and exhaustion.

Michael could outdance every high stepper in the place, Kitt realized. Trade in that blue oxford for a denim work shirt and those loafers for a pair of cowboy boots, and he would put every rodeo cowboy on the street to shame. As it was, he appeared more like some Wall Street type gone mad—shirttails flying, pens jiggling in his shirt pocket, notebook flapping out his back pocket. She grinned, heady with secret bubbles that seemed to burst up inside her and made her want to giggle out loud.

She was having fun! Different from the satisfaction she felt attending museum openings or art gallery showings or the Santa Fe Opera. Different from the quiet pleasure of dinner with a colleague or shopping at the Indian market. This was something she hadn't felt in years. It was pure silliness and excitement. As she swayed at Michael's elbow, she felt like a little girl again. Her hair danced around her shoulders, and her feet were light as air. Her breath came in short gasps intermingled with laughter.

The fiddles sang as if they might burst into flame. Faster, faster. Kitt whirled around and around. Michael's feet became a blur. Faster, faster. And as suddenly as it had begun, the song ended. The crowd broke into a roar of clapping and cheering. Kitt sucked in a deep breath. She glanced around. She and Michael were the only ones left in the street.

A crooked grin tugged at one corner of Michael's mouth as his eyes met hers. "Well, I'll be," he said.

One of the fiddlers stepped up to a microphone. "Now ain't these two showed all you cowboys how it's done?"

Laughter rippled through the crowd. "Let's hear it for the city boy and his gal!"

As the clapping began again someone called out, "Give her a kiss!"

Kitt swung around, fairly certain the voice belonged to Sam.

"Give her a kiss! Give her a kiss!" The crowd took up the chant.

"I reckon you'd better oblige the folks," the fiddler said, leaning over the mike. "Pucker up, you two!"

When Michael put his hands on Kitt's shoulders, she went instantly stiff, all the fun evaporating in an instant. Happier in her own regimented little world, she wished she hadn't allowed him to lure her away from her laundry and her piles of papers. Surely there wasn't a chance he would kiss her here in front of this rowdy crowd—and risk destroying what little harmony they had built.

Looking into his eyes, Kitt saw the wariness as he drew her protectively closer. No, he wouldn't do it. She knew him well enough to read that clearly in his eyes. Like some Old West sheriff, he hovered near, ready to guard her from the whistling, hooting cowboys.

But she didn't need protecting, Kitt knew suddenly. At this moment, in the suspended and almost imaginary world of the street festival, she felt as alive and eternal as a teenager. And she wanted that kiss.

"Thanks for the dance, Michael," she said, rising on tiptoe and sliding her arms around his neck. Before he could react, she brushed her lips lightly across his.

For an instant, Michael stood rock-still. As she moved to back away, his hands closed around her waist, locking her in place. Their eyes met, brown and blue-gray, challenging, consuming.

"Kitt?" he murmured.

She lifted her chin, as hoots and hollers reverberated across the street. The fiddles struck up a new tune. Dancers wove past, feet kicking out another two-step. Somebody's elbow jostled Kitt, but she barely felt it.

They stared at each other. Kitt suddenly couldn't remember why she had kissed Michael. She wasn't a teenager who could live forever. He wasn't a strapping, gawky farm boy. He was every bit a man. And she was every bit a woman. And they were capable of anything.

The thought scared her half to death. "Listen, Michael," she began.

"Kitt—" His voice overlapped hers.

"No, let me talk—"

"I just wanted to say—"

They laughed a little sheepishly.

"I've got to get back to my room, Michael."

"I need to interview the organizer of the rodeo for a few minutes."

They understood each other.

"Thanks, Michael."

"See you in the morning, then?" He stroked her cheek with the tip of his finger, then headed off in the direction of the refreshment table.

Kitt started down the sidewalk toward the laundry. But her feet didn't want to maintain the steady pace she had set for them. Before she knew it, she was running. Skipping. Dancing the two-step.

Laughing deep in the pit of her stomach, she flung open the pickup door and slid in. She sat catching her breath, head thrown back on the seat. Then she picked up a handful of folded laundry and tossed it into the air. She started the engine and drove to her motel with a single pink sock perched on her head.

Chapter Five

❧

For miles, the road west of Catclaw Draw stretched out flat as a sleeping kitten's belly. Occasional pronghorn antelope lifted their heads and studied the passing gray car. Yuccas covered in thick, cream-colored blooms stood tall amid swaying kochia and grama grass. Lack of rain had left everything a dusty brown that lightened to yellow in patches. Gray-green prickly pear cacti struggled to peek over the top of the grass. Purple thistles provided the only spots of bright color. Straight fences followed the highway, enclosing herds of black cattle. Meadowlarks, mockingbirds, quail and doves flitted overhead or perched stoically on the barbed wire.

As though someone had scratched the kitten's belly, the road slowly began to ripple and rise. The Sacramento Mountains materialized straight ahead, with the snow-capped Sierra Blanca peak shining like a crown above them. Salt cedar and mesquite gave way to piñon and juniper. Grass grew knee-high and green. As the car climbed into

the mountains, Ponderosa pines rose higher, finally towering overhead. Sparrows and blue jays played among their
branches. Chokecherry trees flourished in ravines. Bright
orange Indian paintbrushes dipped and danced along the
roadway.

Kitt kept her eyes on the window, so aware of the man beside her that she had to force herself to concentrate on anything but him. When he had met her that morning outside
the motel, Michael looked completely different than he had
the two previous days. His hair was damp from his morning
shower. A navy T-shirt molded to the hard planes of his chest.
The short sleeves of the cotton knit shirt hugged the muscle
in his arms. He wore faded jeans with a hole in one knee, and
white running shoes. The gray car with its leather seats and
briefcase on the floor may have said "professional," but his
body—tanned, fit and catlike—was every bit the athlete.

Already, Kitt was half sorry she'd agreed to his suggestion
for a picnic. Not only did Michael look great, he smelled as
he always had—an outdoorsy scent tinged with spice. Not
overwhelming, but clean and masculine. His presence filled
the compact car, leaving Kitt feeling ill-equipped to handle
her emotions this morning. Her sleep the night before had
been interrupted with bouts of worry, mingled with confusion and giddy happiness.

Nerves stretched almost to the breaking point in the sleek,
metal-and-leather prison of his car, Kitt made up her mind
to stay detached. She would get him to reveal the information he had compiled on Black Dove—though no doubt it
was nothing she didn't already know. They would spend a
pleasant morning together, perhaps ease some of the pain
that had built at the end of their disastrous marriage. After
that, she could see him on his way and get back to her work
and her life.

"Sunflowers." Michael's voice interrupted her thoughts.
He gestured with his chin.

Kitt leaned against his shoulder to crane out his window. Yellow blossoms crowded the banks of the Rio Peñasco. A pretty scene stretched along the road, looking like one of those quaint but sweetly artificial paintings on café place-mats—winding rivers, flowers, pine trees and blue, blue sky. Black-and-white cows dipped their noses into blue-green grass. A mounted man galloped a horse across a narrow wooden bridge.

Michael pulled the car into a picnic site along the river. Wild sunflowers grew in thick patches right up to the water's edge. Red hot pokers, tiger lilies, peonies and blue flag irises nudged places for themselves among the lush green grass and limestone rocks. Box elder trees towered beside walnuts. A trumpet vine with red-orange flowers climbed a cotton-wood tree.

Kitt chose a spot of mingled shadow and sunlight beneath a huge old cottonwood. Michael cleared away fallen branches and spread a motel blanket. He had ventured out early to a convenience store to round up lunch meats, ap-ples, potato chips and sodas. They ate in silence, Michael tossing pebbles into the river and Kitt listening to the rus-tle of green leaves overhead.

"Hod—this strange fellow who keeps appearing at the site—likes to sit under the cottonwoods out at the ceme-tery," Kitt said. "He'll pick up a fallen stick and whittle it for a while without even looking at what he's doing. Then he'll drop that stick and pick up another one and start over."

"Who is he?"

"Just some old man who mutters to himself a lot. He told me he's been looking for a lost gold mine all his life. His fa-ther showed it to him once when he was a boy, but he for-got where it was."

"Poor guy. Does he think you're going to dig up his lost gold?"

"I'm not sure. Dr. Dean guessed he might have a relative

buried in the cemetery. He's very persistent about coming around. I think I finally ran him off for good yesterday."

"What a meanie."

Kitt glanced quickly at Michael, who grinned disarmingly.

"It's for his own safety. Besides, I'm opposed to strangers wandering around out of curiosity. I won't have the site turned into a circus."

"One old geezer isn't much of a circus."

"I know. Maybe I should have let him stay." Kitt studied Michael as he leaned back against the trunk of the cottonwood tree, palms cupping his head. She looked away. "If you want to know the truth, I kind of like Hod. Dr. Dean thinks he may be close to a hundred years old. I bet he could tell some stories about the past."

"Speaking of the past, what about that gold-toothed fellow you dug up? Are you going to give me that interview?"

"You came to the press conference, Michael."

"But you promised Affiliated Press an interview. A private interview. Really, Kitt, your selective professionalism surprises me."

Unable to prevent herself, Kitt glanced back at Michael. He was resting against the tree with his eyes closed and a little smile that was almost a smirk on his mouth. What was he getting out of this conversation? She knew his agenda wasn't entirely the gold-toothed skull. Yet nothing really productive could come from a truce between them. Not unless he was still suffering deeply from the breakup of their marriage. The mischievous expression told her he was having too much fun for that to be true.

"What do you mean by 'selective professionalism'?" she asked. "I always follow protocol."

"Always? First you break Bureau rules by letting an outsider on the site. Then you refuse an interview that you had originally scheduled—never mind that the reporter drove all the way to Catclaw Draw to cover the exciting cemetery relocation story. And then—"

"The reporter drove only thirty miles from Carlsbad for the story, and he was on his way to Albuquerque anyway. And if the relocation story is so dull, why doesn't the reporter go on back to Albuquerque where he belongs?"

"And worst of all, you blatantly choose to ignore an intriguing trail of clues leading to the identity of the unknown gold-toothed skull in the Muddy Flats cemetery."

"I am not ignoring the clues, Michael."

"Then why don't you pursue them?" He opened his eyes and fixed her with his blue-gray gaze. "Are you afraid you're going to look bad when part of your paper is proven inaccurate? Or are you trying to protect Dr. Oldham? Or are you just afraid to take my challenge, because you would have to work with me?"

It was unnerving the way the boy who used to twist his Cummins cap around and around when he tried to talk had become so clever with words. More unnerving was the way he was able to see right through her.

"What are all these clues anyway, Michael?" she asked. "All I know is that a poor guy in an unmarked grave in a New Mexico cemetery had two gold teeth."

And he was a Native American, she added silently.

Michael stood. "I'll get my file."

Before long, they were poring over photocopied newspaper clippings and passages from books. The pickings were fairly slim, but enough to excite the historical treasure seeker in Kitt.

"The first we hear of Black Dove is just a mention in this article on James Kirker, the white scalp hunter," Michael explained. "Black Dove, it says, was a Shawnee from Ohio who was run off his land by white settlers. He and a band of displaced Shawnees joined up with Kirker in 1836 at Bent's Fort. I assume Black Dove must have been with Kirker during the following years, but I couldn't find records of Kirker's activities until 1840. That's when he went to the town in Mexico where you think Black Dove is buried."

"Guadalupe Y Calvo."

"So what happened during the lost years? What did Black Dove do while he was hanging around with Kirker from 1836 to 1840?"

Now Kitt leaned against the ragged cottonwood trunk. "That's easy. Records of Kirker's activities played a large part in my report. He left Bent's Fort with Black Dove and the other Shawnee and Delaware Indians who formed his gang. A couple of fellows named Robert McKnight and Stephen Courcier hired them to protect the Santa Rita mines in southwestern New Mexico."

"The copper mines?"

"That's right. Santa Rita was owned by the Mexican government, which used Indian labor to dig deep pits in the ground. The conditions were primitive and cruel. The Mexicans sent the copper in mule trains from Santa Rita down to Chihuahua City to be minted into coins. But along the way, Apaches often attacked the caravans, stole the copper and massacred everybody. Finally the mines had to shut down."

"So McKnight and Courcier got the bright idea of hiring a gang of thugs—Kirker, Black Dove and the others—to protect the copper trains?"

"Exactly. In essence, Kirker and his men were bounty hunters. They ambushed and scalped the Apaches. The Mexican government paid them by the scalp."

"Interesting to think of a white man scalping Indians. History usually recorded it the other way around."

"History sort of forgot about James Kirker."

Michael sifted through his file until he came to a photocopied picture. "This is supposed to be a daguerreotype of some of Kirker's men. Which one is Black Dove?"

Kitt glanced at the familiar portrait. "No one's ever proven this is really Kirker's gang. But it does seem to fit the description. They were mostly displaced Shawnee and Delaware Indians, but he also had a few Frenchmen, Englishmen and maybe a Hawaiian or two."

"Hawaiians? You're kidding?"

"No. And there was a large African-American fellow named Andy who ran with Kirker. This one is supposed to be Black Dove."

She tapped the chest of a towering figure dressed in a strange combination of beaded Indian buckskin and mountain man fur and flannel. It was his face, however, that drew an observer's attention from the rest of the motley crew. Black Dove stood tall, powerful, light-skinned and strikingly handsome. He had a high forehead, prominent cheekbones, a Roman nose and malicious black eyes.

"How did he get the gold teeth?" Michael asked, his attention fixed on the photograph.

"Supposedly when he was a kid, he got into a fight and bit off the other boy's nose. As punishment, his two front teeth were knocked out by order of the chief. They say Black Dove never opened his mouth to speak again—until he was able to get his hands on some gold and have those new teeth fitted."

"Sounds like one mean dude." Michael glanced at the river for a moment and narrowed his eyes. "It's possible to enhance photographs by computer, you know. A group of researchers studied some photos of a fellow who claimed to be Billy the Kid. Remember that? They compared the photographs of the guy with the one authentic shot of Billy and proved that they were two different men. So here we've got a photograph of Black Dove—and at the cemetery, we've got a skeleton. With computer enhancement, it shouldn't be too hard to match them up."

"Not if you've got a research grant, government permission and a bundle of money—and can find anyone who's interested in an obscure Shawnee with two gold teeth. I hate to say this, Michael, but we're really the only ones who care much about old Black Dove. Us, and maybe Dr. Oldham."

"True, he's not exactly a major historical figure. But he is interesting, and there may be more to him than we know. If he was buried in the Muddy Flats cemetery, somebody in Guadalupe Y Calvo invented the death Dr. Oldham was told about." Michael set the photograph on the stack of papers. "So Kirker, Black Dove and the gang spent several years scalping Apaches for the Mexican government. Why did they quit and move to Guadalupe Y Calvo?"

"Problems. They were quite successful at killing Apaches. Kirker became famous. Men called him the king of New Mexico—the scourge of the Apaches. The Santa Rita mines were profitable again. But then the Apaches began attacking Chihuahua City itself. So the Mexican Society for War Against Hostile Indians asked Kirker to protect the city. He promised to eradicate every Apache from the face of the earth, and he might have done it. But he got greedy. Kirker kept all the cattle he took when he raided Apache villages—no matter whose brand was on them. That made him very unpopular. Also, his success was an embarrassment to the Mexican army, who really should have been controlling the Apaches. When a fellow named Conde became governor, Kirker lost his contract."

"I bet the Apaches were happy about that."

Kitt nodded. "And they went right back to attacking Chihuahua City."

"So that brings us to Guadalupe Y Calvo." Michael rummaged around in his papers. Kitt studied the top of his head as he bent over his portfolio. Sunlight tipped the golden strands of his hair and made it gleam. His brow was furrowed in concentration. His farm-boy hands, still strong, riffled through the papers with a surprising gentleness.

The fact of the matter was, Kitt realized suddenly, she was having a wonderful time. In some ways the passing hours reminded her of the old days in the Clovis High School library—she and Michael poring over old books and papers. They had always shared this love of lore.

But Michael had changed in many ways. This discussion wasn't just a way to pass the time. The Black Dove scavenger hunt had potential to become a scoop for him, and Michael was pursuing it with all the skills he had honed through his years as a reporter. His news nose was on full alert. It could be something really good. The tingle along Kitt's spine told her the same thing. His research skills and news sense—combined with her knowledge of history and ability to solve puzzles—might lead them to something worthwhile. Not to mention the pleasure both would take in the chase.

A wariness filtered over her as he slid a page from his file. It was too easy, too much fun to be with him again.

"From what I read on the Internet, the town of Guadalupe Y Calvo sounds like a strange place," he was saying. "Sort of a Shangri-la sitting southwest of Chihuahua in the Sierra Madre mountains. I had a hard time finding the place. Did you know there are six or eight cities in Mexico called Guadalupe? And then there's the Guadalupe mountain chain in New Mexico and Texas."

"Our Lady of Guadalupe is the patron saint of Mexican Indians. There's a famous shrine to her in one of those Guadalupes you looked up. Tourists flock there."

"Tourists must not go to Guadalupe Y Calvo much, because I could hardly find anything about it. Here's a short reference that says, 'Guadalupe Y Calvo sits at an altitude of almost ten thousand feet. It can be reached only by air. The town was settled by Englishmen who began mining gold and silver there in 1835. Most of the houses bear a strong resemblance to thatch-roofed English cottages. No roads lead into Guadalupe Y Calvo, and no wheels have been on its streets—not automobile, truck, wagon or cart.' That's it. That's all I could find."

Kitt tapped her chin, thinking. "Dr. Oldham corresponded with the priest there, but we never knew the place was remarkable in any way. No roads. No wheeled vehicles. English-style cottages. That's odd."

Michael scribbled something in his notebook, then he lifted his head and met Kitt's eyes. "So we know Black Dove moved to Guadalupe Y Calvo with Kirker and his men. Why?"

"Apaches again. This time the Apaches were raiding gold trains that left the little mountain town bound for Chihuahua City. That fellow, Robert McKnight, had a part interest in the gold mines at Guadalupe Y Calvo. He hired Kirker, but it wasn't long before the Mexican government came calling again. They wanted Kirker back in Chihuahua City. This time they promised him a lot more money for each Apache scalp."

"Did Black Dove go with Kirker?"

"For a while. When Kirker and the men got to Chihuahua City with the first set of scalps, the governor told them he could pay only ten percent of what he had promised. Black Dove was furious. Legend has it that he painted half his face red and half black. Then he marched into the governor's office brandishing his tomahawk. Black Dove threatened to scalp the governor—and I imagine he would have."

"Our pal Black Dove didn't have much respect for human life."

"The governor buckled and gave him the mules and horses that were his due. Then Black Dove decided he'd had enough, and he left Kirker. Some of the Indians stayed with Kirker until his death, the records show. But Black Dove went back to Guadalupe Y Calvo and again hired himself out to protect Robert McKnight's gold trains. We don't have any more records of Black Dove's life, but Dr. Oldham was told that he died and was buried in Guadalupe Y Calvo. We have no reason to doubt it."

"You *had* no reason," Michael corrected her. "Now you've got that pesky skull. But there ought to be records in Guadalupe Y Calvo of Black Dove's burial in the church cemetery."

"Dr. Oldham wasn't able to get them. But think about it, Michael. If the town hasn't even progressed to the wheel, they might not have kept many records. Although…even very old churches usually have something…."

"We could call."

"I doubt there would be phones."

"Write."

"Go ahead, Michael. But I can guarantee you're not going to get anything more than Dr. Oldham did. He's the best there is at digging up records."

"You respect him a lot."

"Yes, I do. He's efficient and careful. He wouldn't miss something like that. Besides, I saw his notes. I read everything he had. There are no records of Black Dove's death."

"Of course there aren't. Because he's buried in New Mexico in the Muddy Flats cemetery. Or was, until you dug him up."

"Oh, Michael!" Kitt felt a chuckle well up in her chest. He was smiling at her, his hair rustling over his forehead.

"The facts are clear, Dr. Tucker. On the one hand, you have a very distinctive-looking Native American named Black Dove. He was tall, he had a Roman nose—and he had two gold teeth. That fact is mentioned by more than one contemporary source. Most important, you have no records of Black Dove's death. On the other hand, you have a mighty suspicious-looking skeleton with two gold teeth."

Kitt swallowed. "Okay, I'd better tell you…the skull belonged to a Native American. Dr. Dean gave me the news yesterday afternoon after he'd finished his examinations."

"Kitt—" Michael bit off his exasperation. "What else?"

She picked a blade of grass and twirled it in her fingers. "Dr. Dean said the man was tall and physically fit even at an advanced age. He had several healed bone fractures—indicative of a violent life. And he was handsome."

"Why didn't you tell me?"

"Why would someone like Black Dove ever have come to Muddy Flats, New Mexico, Michael? Why? Just answer that one question and I promise I'll take up your challenge. I'll find out what really happened to him."

Seeing him start to respond, she quickly added, "And you can help me."

Michael tossed a stick into the river. They had sat in silence as Kitt thumbed through his file, her dark brows drawn together. He broke a second stick and tossed the pieces into the rushing water. She was trying to be skeptical, he realized. But she was losing the battle. She wanted to find out about Black Dove as much as he did. And not just because it was a fascinating story. It would mean working with him—sorting out clues, time in the library…time together.

He took a moment to study her. Dressed as she was in a white shirt and shorts, she might not be taken too seriously. But he knew that clever mind of hers was working over the facts—and probably more efficiently than his had.

Why had she kept to herself Dr. Dean's conclusion that the skull was from a Native American? There could be only one reason. She badly wanted to pursue the mystery—but alone. Yet she had told him about the clue after all. She had let him in.

"I think I know why Black Dove came to Muddy Flats," Michael said.

Kitt lifted her head, her dark eyes pinning him. "Why?"

"He was a man on the run. He joined up with Kirker in the first place because he was an outcast. He had been humiliated by his chief. He felt like a failure, and he didn't care if he died hunting down Apaches. He didn't have anything to live for."

Michael hooked one arm over his knee and absently tapped a stick against the folds of the blanket. "It was kind of like when I left you, Kitt. I was a wild man. I thought your love for me had died with the baby, you know?"

Fighting the emotion those memories evoked, he looked up at her. Kitt reached out to touch him, as if to tell him to stop speaking. As if to comfort him.

Michael knew he didn't need to tell her this, and maybe she wasn't ready to hear it. But it was time. At some point in the night, he had been staring at the ceiling, trying to pray and think and understand her impulsive kiss at the street festival. And all at once, snatches of Bible verses started coming at him like bullets in the darkness. *For this cause shall a man leave his father and mother, and shall cleave to his wife.*

They are one flesh.

What therefore God hath joined together, let not man put asunder.

Zing…zing…zing…each bullet striking his heart. Where had they come from? He had glanced at the television, wondering if it had been tuned to an evangelist. What cause was it that permitted a man to leave his father and mother? How did two people become one flesh? If God had joined him to Kitt, why were they now asunder? What had happened to them, and why?

Restless and confused, Michael had gotten out of bed and turned off the TV. He couldn't stop thinking about how he had held Kitt that night, and how she had stood on her tiptoes to kiss him. The years and the pain seemed to vanish as if they'd never even been there.

But then another Kitt took the place of the beautiful girl dancing through his mind. This one sat in a rocking chair, her stomach swollen and her eyes haunted. For hours on end, she did nothing but rock back and forth, staring at the floor. When he tried to touch her, she jerked her hand away and wept.

Had he and Kitt been good enough only for the happy times? Had their baby daughter's death inside Kitt's body killed their marriage, too? Maybe that was what had put them asunder. Maybe that terrible loss had torn their one flesh into two again.

If so, who could they blame?

Themselves? Each other? The doctor? Their parents? God?

While a soldier in the Gulf War, Michael had fought two battles. In his personal struggle, he had finally chosen not to fault God. Blaming himself for the tragedy, he had turned to the only source of strength he could find in the blackness. Maybe he was naive, but he still didn't believe God had intended their baby to die. Even if God had allowed that umbilical cord to wrap and tighten around her tiny neck, surely He wanted good things for her parents. There must have been some purpose in the Lord permitting such a terrible thing to happen.

During the night, pacing the carpeted motel floor, Michael couldn't deny the strong sense of truth still beating in his chest. God had been there in the room with him. His Holy Spirit lived inside the man who trusted Him—a man still so far from spiritual perfection that during a time of crisis, he discovered he had forgotten to pack his Bible and couldn't remember his pastor's phone number and wasn't able to think how to pray beyond, *Help me. Help me, Lord.*

Now despite talk of a gold-toothed skull and questions about a mysterious Shawnee, Michael knew again the pressure that had been propelling him forward ever since the motel door had opened on Kitt Culhane two nights before. It was a spiritual shove. A holy kick in the behind. Almost as though God had been shaping and molding him for this moment by a mountain stream ever since he walked out on Kitt years ago.

Determined to obey the prodding of the Holy Spirit no matter what the end result, Michael reached out and took Kitt's hand in his. "Kitt, I need to tell you why I left you that day," he said. "I blamed myself for what happened. I decided if I was out of the picture, your parents would take you back home. You'd be yourself again. You'd be where you belonged. You could have the life you deserved."

When she didn't respond, he continued forcing out the words. "I didn't want to live without you, Kitt. But I believed you didn't love me anymore. I was sure you resented me for what happened. We had married against our parents' wishes, and then you got pregnant right away. Your family all but disowned you. My dad wouldn't speak to me and threatened to fire me from my work on the farm. My mother predicted nothing but misery for us the rest of our lives. You cried so hard about how your parents were treating you. We barely had enough money to buy food. And even though things were good between us, when the baby died—"

"Michael." There was a note of panic in her voice.

"I'm sorry, honey. I won't talk about it." He hung his head for a moment, fighting the urge to take her in his arms. "But I want you to know what happened to me. After I left, I stayed with my uncle in Amarillo for a while. I couldn't think straight. I drank a lot. I tried to find a job. I tried to rodeo. Nothing worked. I wanted to die. So I enlisted in the army. Soon after basic training, they shipped me to the Persian Gulf, just in time for Desert Storm. That was fine with me—maybe I'd go out in a blaze of glory."

He looked at the river, his thoughts momentarily far away on sandy plains. His fingers were laced through Kitt's, and he realized he was holding them too tight.

"God found me there," he said, shaking his head. "I don't know how, because I wasn't looking for Him. I just wanted it to stop hurting."

"Oh, Michael." Kitt's voice was filled with sorrow. "I never hated you. I didn't blame you for what happened."

"Maybe not. I sure thought so, Kitt." He gave a dry laugh. "Well, I didn't die in the Gulf War, so I had to keep going. I think God knew that's all I could manage. By the time I got out of the army, I had learned how to be a reporter and do the job pretty well. At some point I guess I decided to keep on living."

"And now you're here," she said.

"With you and that skull. I figure it may have been the same with Black Dove. Maybe he joined Kirker because he had nothing to lose. The Apaches couldn't do him in, and after a while he got good at his job."

"So why do you think Black Dove came to Muddy Flats?"

Michael released his grip on Kitt's hand, but he didn't let go. "I imagine Black Dove had had about enough of trying to get himself killed," he told her.

"You think he was heading off to start a new life for himself?"

Michael looked into her brown eyes. "I think he was going home."

Chapter Six

❧

The motel blanket felt suddenly too small for both of them, and Kitt got to her feet. She waded through a patch of sunflowers to the riverbank. Crouching, she dipped the tips of her fingers in the icy water. A silvery trout hung motionless in the shadows.

Sensing movement in the sunflowers, Kitt glanced to the sandy shore beside her. Michael's running shoes appeared side by side on the damp bank.

"Wish I had my fishing pole." His voice above her held a wistful tone.

She picked up a yellow aspen leaf and set it in the river current. It washed downstream a few yards, then hung up in a snag of fallen logs and driftwood.

"So did I answer your question?" he asked.

She stood. "About Black Dove's motivation for being in Muddy Flats? I suppose it's a possibility that he was on his way home to Ohio. But most of the Shawnee had been run out of that state. There wouldn't seem to be much reason for him to go back."

"Maybe he wanted to find out what happened to his people after he left. And if he was headed for Ohio, he might have passed through Muddy Flats. There was a town there in the 1870s, wasn't there?"

"Barely. The village itself didn't come into being until 1875. But a few settlers had already moved into the area."

"If Black Dove went through, he might have stayed. He might have lived in Muddy Flats for a few years and then died there."

"That's a huge leap of supposition, Michael. It's remotely possible, I guess."

"You agree we might have found Black Dove's grave?"

"It's unlikely, but maybe."

Michael flipped a stone into the river. "So are we going to work together on this?"

Kitt shoved her hands deep into the pockets of her shorts. "I know I said I would let you help me, but that seems unnecessary. You have your work in Albuquerque, and this sort of thing is really part of my job description. I could do the research by myself and send you my findings for your story."

"Or I could do the research by myself and send you my findings for your files."

Her focus darted to his face. "But I'm going to follow the clues, Michael. I have to. It's what I do."

"It's what I do, too."

She studied his face and attempted to read the messages there. He had that stubborn set to his jaw. His nostrils flared slightly, and his eyebrows narrowed. Michael Culhane was hardheaded, all right. But those blue-gray eyes held a tenderness he no longer tried to hide from Kitt. He had changed so much since his youth, and she wasn't sure why. Only moments before he had shown her the soft side of himself, the exposed underbelly of his pain. He had let her glimpse his soul.

It hurt to go over old memories. It hurt her…and it hurt him. But Kitt was glad he had filled in the gaps. She hadn't known about the army or Desert Storm. She hadn't known why he left her in their little trailer that day. She hadn't understood for fifteen years. Until now.

A wave of sadness and relief and overwhelming peace flooded through Kitt with frightening strength. Suddenly she realized she couldn't trust herself with Michael. She didn't have a plan in place for this—for what to say or how to act. Where once she had nurtured a hard, cold lump of bitterness toward him, now she felt only soft warmth…and longing. She had no idea what to do with it. She could hardly breathe. Couldn't speak. Most of all, she knew she couldn't let herself cry.

Over his shoulder, Kitt spotted a hiking trail. Words burst out of her. "Look, Michael, there's a little path. Come on, let's see where it goes."

Without waiting for him to respond, she took off running. She glanced behind as she crossed a redwood bridge. He was staring after her, his mouth opened in surprise. Grateful to have burst free of the suffocating emotional tidal wave his confession had triggered inside her, Kitt raced around a rocky outcrop toward a scraggly pine tree.

"Kitt, for goodness' sake, girl!" Michael started after her. "You didn't give me an answer."

Catching sight of his navy T-shirt just below her on the path, Kitt gave a little cry and began scampering higher. The path narrowed as it wound among a stand of towering juniper, cedar and pine trees. Her sandals slipped on the thick layer of fallen needles as she ran. She had started with a good lead, but now Michael was right behind her.

"Come back here, you," he called.

"You can't force me into doing things, Michael Culhane. I won't be pinned down like that." She darted behind the gnarled trunk of an alligator juniper, ran a few yards and rejoined the path after leading him off in the wrong direction.

Kitt ran on in silence, aware that he was searching for her somewhere in a thicket of yellow-green cedar bushes. The scent of piñon hung heavy in the crisp air. She tilted her head back, letting her hair flip against her shoulders as the path took her alongside a gurgling tributary. Sunlight, yellow and thick as butter, filtered down through the pine branches to cast patches of warmth on her face.

"Gotcha!" A form leaped out from behind a massive tree. Strong arms closed around her and pressed her up against the trunk. "Can't pin you down, huh? Can't corner you, huh?"

"Michael!" She laughed, pushing at his shoulders. "The bark is poking into my back."

He grinned. One hand was propped on either side of her head, effectively locking her in place. "Too bad."

"Now who's the meanie?"

"Sticks and stones," he said. "Okay now, Dr. Tucker. The moment of truth. Will we work together or not?"

"Is this how it would be—you bullying me and pushing me around?"

"It doesn't have to." He brushed a strand of hair from her cheek. "You could give a little, Kitt."

"Oh, Michael, I don't have anything left to give. It's all gone. I lost myself years ago, and I'm empty inside."

"No, you're not." He lowered his head and let his lips drift across her mouth. As he drew back, a shudder ran through her. His kiss…her husband's kiss…so familiar and yet so unexpected.

"You're beautiful," he said. "Still sweet and warm."

"You're wrong about me." She couldn't allow this. So much hard work had gone into excising him from her life. First her daughter, then her husband. Both dead to her. Both thrust from her body and soul with such labor.

How could she even consider allowing him to take a single step back in? Placing her hands on Michael's biceps, Kitt gave a push. He didn't budge.

"It could be like this between us again, Kitt," he murmured. They waited, looking into each other's faces, each allowing the other the opportunity to back away.

When his lips touched her cheek and then found her mouth again, she went limp. He wound his fingers through her long hair, and she slipped her arms around him. Despite every warning siren that screamed inside her brain, Kitt ran her hands across his solid shoulders, up through the soft curls at the back of his neck and into the thick mat of warm, golden brown hair on his head. Lost somewhere in the past and somewhere in the present, she couldn't think beyond the moment.

This was Michael, her Michael. Her husband and best friend and lover. And as she sagged weakly in his arms, it came to her that she would give herself to him. She had known him again for less than two days—and she would, without thought of consequences, do this heedless thing.

Michael lifted his head, his mouth damp and his eyes caressing her face. "Kitt," he said in a low voice. "It's that same old power between us."

"I know. Oh, Michael, I'm so scared."

She closed her eyes and laid her head against his shoulder as he held her close. The pine trees overhead dripped sunlight on them. Kitt knew what they both were thinking. This was a mistake. Another of their mistakes. There was a power between them—but, in the end, it was a destructive power. It was too much, too strong. It had consumed them once before.

"I don't ever want to hurt you again, Kitt," he said, his breath warm on her cheek. "I don't ever want to make you cry like you cried when your parents turned away from you. I don't ever want to make you withdraw from me again, like you did when our baby…when she stopped moving."

Kitt knew they were both afraid of what could happen between them. Half of her wanted him to keep holding her, to be as they had been together so long ago. The other half wanted to run. Run as far away as she could get. There was no doubt which half was the sensible one.

She stepped out of his embrace. He pushed his hands into his pockets and stared up into the pine branches. They were both silent for a long time, letting the moment pass. Kitt bowed her head and folded her hands across her stomach.

"I don't think normal divorced people act this way around each other," Michael said finally.

Kitt looked up and smiled. "So who says we were ever normal?"

"I feel like I used to back in the old days."

"You were skinnier."

He chuckled. "Ah, Kitt, this is so crazy."

"You know it can't happen, Michael. I mean, if we worked together on this Black Dove business, things would probably get way too tangled."

"It might be all right."

"Not in the long run."

He let out a long breath. "But I'm going to follow those clues, Kitt."

"So am I."

"Together, then?"

She shook her head. The future could hold nothing for them. She knew that. There was too much baggage. Too much pain. Yes, they still had some of the old feelings for each other. But physical desire hadn't been enough to hold their marriage together, and it must have no place in any cordial relationship they might build for the future. Surely such impulses could be kept under rein by two professionals, couldn't they?

"Together—but with rules," she said at last.

"I know the rules. The same ones we had before we married."

Kitt eyed him. "We were good kids—churchgoing and

moral. We both committed ourselves to abstinence, and we kept our promise. But we weren't strong enough to go on that way very long, and so we wound up getting married."

"We got married because we wanted to spend the rest of our lives together."

"Well, it was too soon. We were too young. We still needed those rules."

Michael reached out and ran his hand over her shoulder and down her arm. "Yeah, but now we're adults."

"Adults who were once married to each other. Who nearly destroyed their lives. Who can't trust themselves, let alone each other."

"I trust myself," he said. "It's because I don't have to rely on my own strength. I may have been a church boy back in the old days, but I didn't know God the way I do now. I live for Christ, Kitt. Not for myself. Not for what I want but for what He wants to do in me."

She considered his words. So that's what was different about him. Michael had turned to God for help after their baby died and their marriage fell apart and he didn't get killed in the war. Well, she hadn't. God didn't love her enough to protect her daughter's life, so why should she rely on Him for anything? He had abandoned her, so she, in turn, had walked away from Him to find her own strength. She sensed that God was still around, looking down on her and watching as she built a life for herself. But did He care? Did He ever do anything to help her? Doubtful.

Michael believed he could rely on his Christianity to keep him whole and at peace despite Kitt's presence in his life. But she didn't trust God for a moment. Not any more than she trusted Michael. Or herself.

"So Jesus is going to protect you, Michael?" she said, slipping her arms around his neck and standing on tiptoe to press her lips against his. Without hesitation, he instantly caught her close and returned the kiss. Taken by surprise, she was swept into the moment. And then, just as swiftly, she pushed him away.

"You see," she said, gasping for breath. "The old rules were lousy, Michael. They didn't work back then, and they sure wouldn't work now. And as for this newfound faith in God—"

"Okay, okay." He groaned and rubbed his eyes with both palms. "Maybe I was wrong."

"This isn't some sort of game. It's real life, and the consequences are deadly serious."

Kitt stared down at her feet as she waited for his response. In the past, their desire for each other had torn them from their families. It had made them reckless. Unwise. It was still unwise.

"All right, you win." He flicked a pine needle into the air. "We found a loophole through the old rules back then, and we'd probably look for one again. But I do trust God, and I believe He can keep me strong. I just have to do my part. I shouldn't be alone with you, Kitt. It's not wise. The temptation is too strong."

Kitt watched a wisp of cloud drift overhead. She imagined God looking down on them and shaking His head. The same two kids, playing with fire. Making up rules. Pretending they had control of their own destinies. These kids had made a lot of mistakes. They'd paid for them. They'd grown and learned. And here they were again. Thinking up rules. Heading back into the fire as if they hadn't learned a thing.

Kitt thought about arguing with God. It was really Black Dove they were interested in. Meeting each other again and deciding to work together were circumstances beyond their control. But she knew the argument didn't hold much water. It wasn't really Black Dove. She and Michael were still drawn together like magnets. Somehow their lives were woven into a circle. The circle had begun fifteen years ago, and had been broken. Now it was time to complete what they had started. They would finish their circle. Tie up their loose ends.

And then they could go on with their separate lives. She told God that. But He still shook His head. Two kids. Chasing each other around. Making up rules.

"Okay," she said. "Let's hear these new rules."

He crossed his arms over his chest. "They're going to be strict. We'll work together in a professional manner. Associates. This Black Dove thing shouldn't take long to resolve anyway. While we dig for answers, we'll speak to one another as coworkers. Not as former marriage partners."

"Nothing about the past, Michael?"

"We can talk, but no touching. No physical stuff." He paused. "We'll be friends."

Kitt considered. "Colleagues."

"What steps do you think we should take in our research?"

She tried to concentrate. A spot of sunlight shone on the tip of his nose. His hair was rumpled. He didn't look anything like a newspaper reporter or a research colleague. He looked exactly like Michael Culhane, her husband.

"To begin with," she said, summoning the remnants of her former persona, "we'll go over Dr. Dean's report on the skeletal remains. I'll call Dr. Oldham in Albuquerque and ask him to send me his files on Black Dove."

"I've already done that."

Her heart faltered. "When?"

"I called him yesterday evening. Nice guy. But he's not going to send his files."

"Why not? That doesn't sound like Dr. Oldham." She felt slightly betrayed that Michael had already contacted her former professor. It was as if he had gone behind her back. But she had withheld the key detail in the physical anthropologist's report—at least for a time.

"Dr. Oldham was skeptical about the idea that Black Dove could be buried at Muddy Flats," Michael said. "Called it a wild-goose chase and referred me to the paper he wrote with you. He insists Black Dove is buried in Mexico. I don't think he believes you're in on this with me."

"I'll call him myself. Dr. Oldham is careful. That's why he's so good. He taught me to protect my sources, my research—and, above all, my sites."

"Okay, we'll compare Dr. Dean's notes on the skeletal remains with Dr. Oldham's research on the historical records of Black Dove. What next?"

"We'll go to the museum at Catclaw Draw and talk to the historian. He knows everything there is to know about the town of Muddy Flats, and he's trustworthy. I'm confident he wouldn't tell anyone about the skull with the gold teeth."

"And after that?"

"What do you think? What would you do next?"

Michael studied Kitt's face. "You know, don't you?" he asked.

She looked away. Hadn't they talked about it a hundred times in the high school library? They had picked out their favorite New Mexico figures. Billy the Kid. Geronimo. Kit Carson. John Chisum. They had followed those men's lives in the history books and the old records. But they had always talked about their grandest dream of all…the ultimate adventure.

Michael smiled. "I would follow Black Dove's trail. And so would you."

"I couldn't do that. You know I have to deal with those ditches."

"We would go every place Black Dove went," Michael continued, repeating the plan they had conceived so long ago. "We would walk in his footsteps and touch the things he had touched. We would find out where he lived, what he ate, what he wore. We'd look up every scrap of paper in every file that had ever been kept on him. We'd relive his life in the West. From the beginning."

"The beginning." Kitt repeated the words. "Santa Rita. The copper mines at Santa Rita."

The Catclaw Draw Historical Museum occupied one of the oldest houses in town. Trimmed with wooden curlicues and fanciful gingerbread, its imposing Victorian facade loomed over a vast green lawn. An American flag fluttered in the afternoon breeze.

"Before starting the cemetery project, I spent hours here," Kitt told Michael. "The curator assisted me in my research. It feels almost like coming home."

He paused on the walkway and eyed the two-story structure. "Strange-looking building."

"It's constructed of artificial stone," she explained as they climbed the wooden steps to the porch. "The stone was manufactured about a hundred years ago. Several homes in Catclaw Draw were built of it, but most of them have been neglected. It's a shame to see how their owners have let them get so run-down."

Again Michael was struck with the incongruity. Kitt's professional voice and far-ranging historical knowledge coming from a slender figure in a white blouse and shorts. He had better get used to it. She might look like a mere girl, but she thought of herself as she really was. A mature, intelligent, accomplished woman. She expected him to see her that way, too. They had made an agreement.

On the ride into town they had worked out their plan. This Saturday afternoon they would start their research at the museum. Sunday, each would be alone. Michael would visit the local church, while Kitt finished her paperwork. Though he had asked her to join him at the worship service, she said she had too much to do. It was the first time he really began to see that she had changed not only physically and emotionally, but spiritually, too. While the other alterations seemed for the best, Kitt's indifference to God disturbed Michael more than he cared to admit.

They had decided that on the following Monday and Tuesday Kitt would wind down her project out at the site. Wednesday they would head for the western mountains of New Mexico—and the copper mines.

"Michael Culhane, I'd like you to meet Charles Grant." Kitt indicated the burly, bearded redheaded fellow who stood at the foot of a staircase. "Charles runs the museum. Michael is a reporter with Affiliated Press."

Michael stuck out his hand. "We're trying to track down some information on a Shawnee by the name of Black Dove. He might have spent some time at Muddy Flats."

Charles Grant was a strange mixture of the Jolly Green Giant and Dickens's Ghost of Christmas Present. If he'd chuckled a deep "Ho, ho, ho," Michael wouldn't have been surprised. But when Charles began to talk there was no mistaking this man for a caricature.

"Black Dove." His voice rumbled. "The name rings a bell. Let's take a look at my files."

They worked their way through the rooms of the house—past glassed shelves filled with antique teacups, tiny button boots, crocheted gloves. They skirted the kitchen that still bore the implements of a bygone era. Iron corn bread molds, corn-drying hooks, coffee grinders. The museum smelled of old things—faded wallpaper, dried leather, a dusty velvet Belter settee—as though this were somebody's great-grandmother's house that had been shut up for years.

Charles directed Michael and Kitt to sit on an old oak church pew in his small office. Their host spun across the floor in a wheeled metal chair that looked like it had lost most of its springs. He whirled around, pulling out drawer after drawer. He stacked files on top of files. Books on top of books.

"Now, Muddy Flats is lush and fertile in the 1800s,"

Charles began. When Michael pressed a button to record the interview, he noted that the historian spoke in the present tense, as though Muddy Flats were still a vibrant community. His big freckled hands moved as if he could see and touch what he was telling them about.

"Muddy Flats is at the juncture of seven rivers, you see. They're not dried up, like these days. They're flowing—I mean, really flowing. Oliver Loving and Charles Goodnight pass this way on their trail ride to Fort Sumner. The trail later is called the Goodnight-Loving trail. They're attacked by Indians along the way. But that doesn't stop them. They open up the trail and the cowboys start to follow."

"When does the first settler arrive in Muddy Flats?" Kitt asked, speaking in the present tense, too.

"Well, there's a Mexican settlement when Goodnight and Loving pass through. But it's not until 1867 that a fellow by the name of Reed—Dick Reed—establishes a ranch and trading post at Muddy Flats. Then old Tom Gardner comes on the scene and starts another small ranch and a farm. That's around 1870."

"Around 1870." Michael felt victorious. "So there *are* people at Muddy Flats. When Black Dove comes along, he finds people living there."

He was back in another century, too.

"There's really no village, though, until five years later," Charles continued. "By the 1870s, at least thirty men and their families are living at Muddy Flats. Texans, mostly. Some are former Texas Rangers. They're all rugged frontiersmen. In the mid-1870s, the population's up to three hundred folks."

"What does Muddy Flats look like?" Michael asked. It was hard to imagine three hundred people building homes and working farms in a place where no one lived now. A place that was nearly a desert and crawling with rattlesnakes and scorpions.

"Muddy Flats is quite a little town," Charles said. "Most of the homes are made of adobe brick. There's a saloon. A general store. A saddle and boot shop is run by a fellow from Germany. A guy named Jim Woods does the horseshoeing and blacksmithing. Dee Burditt is the pharmacist and drug-store owner. Another family runs the hotel and restaurant. Supplies are brought in from Pecos City, Texas or from Fort Sumner. A round trip by ox team to Fort Sumner takes six weeks. They go only once a year. The post office is established in June of 1877. There's even a stonecutter. You know about him, Kitt."

"He carved many of the headstones in the cemetery, Michael."

"What about a doctor?" Michael asked.

"No doctor. Kind of hard to imagine, isn't it? All those people. No wonder you've found so many babies in the cemetery."

Michael glanced at Kitt, uncomfortable at the thought of what she had been forced to do by her job. He spoke again quickly. "Do you have a list of all the people you mentioned?"

"Kitt compiled one. The names I have are scattered throughout a lot of references." Charles dug around in a file. "This is what Kitt came up with. I think she's been very thorough. Of course, a lot of people are not on here, because no census is ever taken in Muddy Flats before the town dies."

"What kills it?"

Charles shook his head, almost as though he felt a physical ache over the death of the little village. "Overgrazing. Erosion. In 1882, Muddy Flats is the second largest settlement in southeastern New Mexico. Five years later there's a drought. Two years after that, devastating floods. Cattle drown by the hundreds. By 1890 artesian water is discovered to the north around Catclaw Draw. Wells are drilled. A new county is formed—but Muddy Flats is not chosen as the county seat. People start moving out of town. The good grass dies. Brush, mesquite, catclaw and greasewood move in. The seven rivers dry up. That's it. Muddy Flats is dead."

The three of them sat in silence. Michael felt the watchful presence of the past. Muddy Flats had been alive for a few minutes while Charles talked. He had almost been able to see the blacksmith's fiery forge, hear tinny music coming from the saloon, smell the aroma of baking bread.

Michael noted that Kitt was scanning the list of Muddy Flats residents she had compiled earlier. A pine needle stuck out of her sandal buckle.

"What about Native Americans?" he asked Charles. "Any around this area?"

"The Apaches stir up trouble near Muddy Flats for at least thirty years. Fort Stanton is built in 1855 to try to control the situation—but Apaches are successfully raiding cattle from the 1860s to the 1890s. Nobody can stop them, not even a wealthy cattle baron named John Chisum. He can't keep them from stealing his cattle. Nobody can stop the Apaches. They're fearless. And tricky, too."

"Are we talking about Mescalero Apaches?" Michael asked.

"Yep. They're all over this place in the 1800s."

"Any record of Fort Stanton calling in anyone besides the military to deal with the problem?"

"You mean someone like James Kirker and his scalp hunters? Nope. No record of anyone coming for that purpose."

Kitt glanced at Michael. He knew they were thinking the same thing.

"I suppose there's a remote possibility that Black Dove might have moved to Muddy Flats to help control Apache raiders," she said. "He was an expert. Probably the only one left. By then, Kirker was dead. He had died in California almost twenty years earlier."

"If the military had brought in someone like Black Dove,

Fort Stanton would have it on record," Charles said. "But I've never seen anything like that."

"I'll call them on Monday morning and see what I can find out." Michael made a memo in his reporter's notebook.

Kitt tapped the list of Muddy Flats residents she had compiled. "As you mentioned, Charles, some people buried in the cemetery aren't on here. We've found so many unmarked graves. A lot more than we expected. Why do you suppose that is?"

"Even though the town died, the Muddy Flats area has been ranched for years," Charles explained. "Not every grave would be marked. Plows will go by and turn over a stone. Cattle come along. I told you about those Boy Scouts who tried to clean up the cemetery a few years back."

Kitt winced. "Good intentions, I guess."

"No telling what destruction those twelve-year-olds caused," Charles said. "I found out about it after the fact."

"You can't change the past—I've learned that over the years," Kitt said, her brown eyes darting to Michael's face for a moment. Then she returned to her notes. "Let's sum up what we have. Black Dove was a Shawnee with two gold teeth. He's reportedly buried in Mexico, though we have no official record. He was a scalp hunter, accustomed to hunting down Apaches. Apaches were causing trouble around Muddy Flats. The Muddy Flats cemetery contained the remains of an Indian with two gold teeth. If he came to Muddy Flats at all, Black Dove would have been nearly fifty. Pretty old to ride around scalping Apaches."

Michael watched as Kitt pondered the information. Her little notebook was propped on her knees. Her hair fell like a brown satin sheet over one shoulder.

"Kitt told me she had to be cautious with a cemetery relocation not to offend any next of kin living in the area," Michael said. "Do you know of anyone whose ancestors lived at Muddy Flats? Anyone we could talk to who might know some of the history of the old town?"

Charles rubbed his rough red hair. "There are a few distant relatives. A bunch of folks ranch up in the mountains near Ruidoso. But they've all written down their stories. It probably wouldn't do you any good to talk to them. Let's see…around Catclaw Draw, you've got a few families. I can give you the names. Most of the old folks have already been in to let me get their stories on tape. We're working to produce transcripts of what they remember. You can go through those files if you'd like."

Michael nodded. "Any artifacts from Muddy Flats?"

"If you can believe it, not a thing. It's like the whole town vanished. When people left, they took everything with them. A few years back a woman called to say she had a plate from Muddy Flats. But when we analyzed it, the plate turned out to be modern delftware from Holland. The foundations of an adobe house used to stand out there by the river, but someone plowed them under. You wouldn't believe how hard it is to protect historical sites."

"Yes, I would," Kitt said.

Charles grinned and slapped his huge palms on the desk. "Well, gotta close up, now. Michael, you come on back Monday, and we'll go over those transcripts. But as to anyone really old…" He frowned for a moment and tugged on his thick beard. "Come to think of it, there is one fellow. Lived around Catclaw Draw all his life. Most people think he's a little loco. But the fact is, he's as sane as you or I. We talk a lot. He's been searching for a gold mine his papa took him to see when he was a kid. It's up on a mountain somewhere, near a pine tree bent into the shape of an upside down L. This fellow knows a lot about Muddy Flats. You'd almost think he'd lived there. Name's Hod. Ever hear of him?"

Michael gave a laugh. "Good ol' Dr. Tucker, here, just ran him off the project site."

Kitt gave Michael a disparaging look. "He'll be back," she said. "I've tried to run him off before. He just keeps reappearing. He tells me the twilight is coming and he has to be there to see it."

"The twilight…" Charles let out a low whistle. "No kidding. He tells you that?"

"What? What does it mean?"

Charles lifted his red eyebrows. "It means old Hod's about to find his papa's lost gold."

Chapter Seven

❧

Hod didn't come back. Kitt watched for him all day, glancing at his spot beneath the cottonwood tree as she worked in the sweltering heat.

She hadn't seen Michael, either. Just as he'd promised, he treated her with cool detachment. From the moment they left their picnic site, Michael had assumed the role of a congenial colleague. He spoke to her civilly but never touched her. He smiled occasionally, but he never gave her the look she had seen in his eyes at the street festival or on the mountain. After their trip to the museum, he had taken her to the motel. And that was the last she saw of him.

Saturday night she had eaten alone at a restaurant. Sunday morning, on the spur of the moment, she decided to drop in at a nearby church for the worship service. She hadn't been to church in years, and as she sat wondering if Michael might show up, the atmosphere brought back poignant memories. She had half expected him to walk through

the door just like the old Michael—all Sunday spit and pol-
ish in a white shirt, black tie and shiny shoes. He would sit
behind her with his family, his long legs finding her feet
tucked beneath the pew in front. His loud tenor would ring
out behind her, clear as a bell. But Michael probably wasn't
a tenor anymore. And he hadn't come to this church.

As the service drew to a close, Kitt recalled his comments
about the changes Christ had brought to his life. In spite of
all he'd been through, Michael had chosen to trust God and
rely on His strength. Kitt felt certain God had turned His back
on her, but Michael had reached for Him and clung to Him.

And there he had taken refuge and found strength.

Kitt wondered where God really was in all this. During
the end of her marriage, He had seemed so far away and indifferent. Eventually, she had stopped looking for Him at all.
She had learned to place confidence in herself rather than
in the invisible Divine. She managed her own life and de-
rived satisfaction from what she accomplished. In those
painful, empty years, she had learned to live without her
baby, her husband and God. She was all she needed, and she
was enough. At least…it had seemed that way once.

God and cemeteries and Michael and their little baby and
the past. Everything seemed to be wound together in a tight,
painful knot that twisted inside her stomach.

Kitt carried a heavy pine box to the trailer bed and set it
beside others for transporting to the new cemetery site. The
recently constructed coffins were small and square, but each
contained every item found in its corresponding grave—not
only skeletal remains, but also scraps of fabric, jewelry, coffin wood, spent bullets. A small fragment of each original
coffin had been kept aside for further testing and examination. These slivers of wood would be enclosed in the central historical monument identifying the new cemetery.

The orange sun settled low over the dry grama grass as

Kitt dusted off her hands. Dr. Dean was straightening up the items under his yellow nylon tent. A group of summer students had gathered around him to say their goodbyes. Most of them would leave for their hometowns that evening.

Only three graves remained to be uncovered the following day. Kitt and two students would excavate them. Then she would close down the site. Stakes would be pulled up, the contractor's mobile home would be towed away, the earth would be smoothed over. Within a few months, the blue-green water of the new lake would begin to seep up and erase all trace of their work. The desert would be covered by twenty feet of water. Speedboats and skiers would skim across the lake's surface. Muddy Flats would be no more.

"Bye, Dr. Tucker." Sam held out his hand. A breeze ruffled his blond hair. "I've enjoyed working for you."

"Thanks, Sam. You've done a great job. I'll send you a recommendation."

The other young men and women stood awkwardly around her for a moment. They had become like family in the few short weeks of working together. Sharing their excitement over discoveries, mulling questions, consoling one another at disappointments. There wasn't one of them she didn't like and respect. As if on cue, they began hugging her, murmuring words of appreciation. And then they wandered away like scattered ducklings, driving their dusty cars through the withered grass.

Kitt's cell phone sang out as she pushed through the turquoise door of her motel room. At the sound she instantly thought of Michael and hated herself for the hope that welled up inside her. She heaved her leather purse onto the bed and flipped on the light as she dug into her jeans pocket.

"Kitt Tucker," she said. The metal case felt clammy in her hand.

"Kitt, how's it going down there?" It was Dave Logan

with the Bureau. She berated herself for wishing otherwise, like some schoolgirl with a crush.

"I'm shutting down the project tomorrow," she told him. "The new site looks great."

"Good job, Kitt. Dr. Dean has nothing but praise for the way you've handled things."

Kitt felt a sense of satisfaction at Dave's words. She had always been appalled at the typical method by which historic cemeteries were moved. Usually a relocation contract was awarded to some operator who came in with shovels and backhoes. The graves were transferred swiftly, with no thought for next of kin or archaeological significance.

"Muddy Flats is special. I'm proud of the way we worked it, Dave," she said. "We completed everything on time and we made several interesting discoveries."

"I saw the story Affiliated Press did on you. Nice photo."

Kitt felt a chill creep down her spine. "I didn't know a story had been written yet."

"I've got it right here in the *Journal*. Fellow by the name of Michael Culhane wrote it. Came out in yesterday's paper."

"How did it sound?"

"Good… There's only one thing."

Kitt sat on the chair. Her boots felt heavy. "What's that?"

"Well, it's nothing much. But a man named…let's see…Oldham. Dr. Frank Oldham—a retired history prof at NNMU—called me yesterday. He tells me this Culhane fellow is curious about that skull with gold teeth you mentioned the other day. Dr. Oldham says Culhane claims to be working with you on this. He says Culhane thinks you may have found the grave of a famous Shawnee named Black Dove, and he requested Dr. Oldham's research notes. What's going on, Kitt?"

Kitt sagged back into the chair. She hadn't been able to reach Dr. Oldham on the phone the day before. Now Michael's bulldog tactics had upset him, and had gotten the Bureau involved as well. Thanks, Michael.

"Don't worry about it, Dave." She began unlacing her boots. "Everything's under control. The skeleton has some interesting similarities to the description of Black Dove. I'm planning to look into it. Culhane insists on following the leads, too. He thinks he's got some kind of story." She paused, wondering what information Michael had chosen to reveal to the public. "Did the article mention the skeleton with the gold teeth?"

"No." A silence was followed by the sound of Dave letting out a long breath. "Kitt, are you planning to research this along with the reporter? Because you know how the press has treated us in the past."

"No, it's nothing like that. During my vacation, I thought I would—"

Three rapid knocks on the door drew Kitt's attention. Michael's figure, tall and shadowy, was outlined against her curtains.

"Hang on just a second, Dave. Someone's here." She headed across the room. Michael's back was to her when she opened the door.

"Moon's out," he said. Turning, he smiled at her. "Mind if I talk to you for a minute?"

"I'm on the phone."

"I'll wait." He motioned to a bench outside her room.

Kitt sat near him and began working her boot off as she tried to end the conversation with her boss. "Dave, just don't think twice about this thing. There's no problem. I'll be able to wrap it all up quickly."

"What if you have found Black Dove's remains? What ramifications would there be for the Bureau? Would we have to reexcavate that skeleton?"

"Absolutely not. We've gathered all the information we could possibly need. I removed everything from the grave, and Dr. Dean examined the remains thoroughly."

"There won't be any problem flooding the site then, will

there? I mean, we won't have a bunch of historians putting up a fuss over this, will we?"

"No, Dave. I'm sure you won't have any problems there."

Michael had stretched out his legs, one foot crossed over the other. He wore a yellow T-shirt with the name of a sports shoe company on it. His fingers were laced over his belt buckle. He slowly tapped it with his thumbs while he watched her.

"Kitt...I know this is really none of my business." There was another long pause. "Dr. Oldham tells me that Michael Culhane is your former husband."

Kitt dropped her boot onto the ground. "That's true."

"Well, we—Sue and I—we're concerned about you, that's all."

Kitt could picture Dave's sweet little wife hovering in the background as her husband continued. "Dr. Oldham said you had told him about your marriage back when you were working together. I was surprised, because I didn't realize you had ever been married. Sue said you had told her once, but you never mentioned it again because it had been a long time ago. Dr. Oldham remembered your husband's name— you know how he is with details. Anyway, while they were on the phone, Dr. Oldham asked this Michael Culhane fellow if he knew you, and he admitted you had been married."

"Yes, but now I'm just a source for an article. No big deal."

"Kitt, if you need any help down there, or any advice or anything—"

"No, really. I'm fine."

"Here, Sue wants to talk to you."

Kitt glanced at Michael. She could see the golden halos in his eyes. He hadn't moved as he waited, relaxed but alert. His face was expressionless.

"Kitt, honey." Sue Logan's kind, almost childish voice came through the phone. "Now you just listen to me for a minute. That man hurt you an awful lot—you told me so that afternoon when I had you over for tea, remember?"

"Yes, Sue. But—"

"You told me he just up and walked out on you less than a year after you got married. He left you alone in a little trailer with no money and no job. And if it hadn't been for your parents rescuing you and sending you off to school, well, I hate to think of it. Now, I know you're a mature woman, but we all love you here and we just don't want to see you hurt again. When Dave told me you were working on some kind of a project with that man, my heart went out to you, honey. You know what this man could do! You loved him so much. He might play on your sentiments. He could—"

"Sue, really—"

"Now, that marriage is over, honey. You've done so well for yourself. Why don't you just come on back to Santa Fe and work on those ditches like you'd planned? We'll go shopping. Did you know there's a new exhibit at the folk art museum?"

"Sue, listen. Please understand. Everything is all right. Tell Dave that I'll be in Silver City for a couple of days at the end of this week, and then I'll be back. We'll go to the exhibit, okay?"

"Okay." The word was a defeated little sigh. "You've always been stubborn. Kitt, honey...be careful."

"I will."

Kitt folded the phone and dropped her other boot to the ground. "Sue and Dave Logan," she said.

"Sounds like they're worried."

"We're friends as well as colleagues. We've known each other a long time."

"Guess I'm the bad guy."

"Surprise, surprise. There's still time for you to back out and head for Albuquerque."

"My boss is expecting a follow-up article. Besides, I couldn't let you down like that." His mouth curved into a faint smile.

"You didn't tell me you had already written your first story."

"I'm efficient. Besides, my article just gave the bare bones." He winked. "I'll do something bigger when I have more on the Black Dove angle."

Kitt could see Michael wasn't about to back out. "Dr. Oldham called the Bureau," she told him. "Dave Logan is suspicious of you."

"You didn't get in touch with Oldham yet?"

"He was out when I called."

Michael shrugged. "Oldham thinks I'm some kind of treasure hunter. He's afraid I might stir up unfounded interest in the story, and then looters will start destroying sites."

"Treasure hunter? Why would he think that?" Kitt rubbed the soles of her feet. There was no treasure involved—unless you could count a couple of gold teeth.

"He was afraid I thought there was treasure involved. And then when he found out my name, he put two and two together about us. You have a lot of loyal friends, Kitt."

"I do," she said. "I place great stock in faithfulness."

The curve went out of Michael's mouth, and he looked at his thumbs. She could tell her retort had stung. But just his presence beside her on the bench had brought out the old hurt again.

"Maybe you're right," he said in low voice. "Maybe I should head back to Albuquerque."

"I won't stop you."

He was silent for a moment. "I guess I deserved that."

"I'm sorry. I didn't mean to hurt you."

"It's okay. If we spend time together, the past is bound to come out. And I want it out. I want to heal. Pain always comes with healing. And some of the pain belongs to me."

Kitt watched him from her perch at one end of the wooden bench. The old Michael had never been able to speak so freely. Back then, his words had come at a price, and he had revealed the depth of his emotions for her very slowly. Now he had little trouble expressing what he wanted, needed and felt.

"I came over to ask you a favor, Kitt," he told her. "I've spent a lot of time today at the museum, and I've also interviewed a few people. I'd like to go to the site with you tomorrow and talk to the old man."

"Hod didn't come back."

"I think he'll be there tomorrow."

"I ran him off, remember?"

"I put out the word in town that tomorrow is your last day. Hod spends a lot of time wandering the sidewalks, and he's in and out of the shops. Everyone knows him. I figure if he really believes you're going to find something out there, he'll show up."

Kitt drew off one sock and began rubbing her bare foot. "Michael, did you really have to go spreading the news that tomorrow was the last day? I mean, now who'll drop by? I had hoped to finish those last three graves and wrap up everything without being disturbed."

He shrugged. "Had to get hold of Hod one way or another. He could be the key to all this."

"Why couldn't you just find out where he lives and go to his house?" She pulled off her other sock and wiggled her toes. "You don't need to interview him at the site, do you?"

"Nobody could tell me where Hod lives. They think he stays out west of town, but no one's ever been there. So can I come to the site?"

"Persistent, aren't you?" She tugged the band from her braid.

"Persistence is a quality I value." He was smiling again. "Persistence. Faithfulness. They're pretty much the same, aren't they?"

"No."

"I think they are." He took the elastic band from her

hand. "So are you undoing your hair in front of me because you always used to, and you remember how much I like it? Or are you undoing it in front of me because you want to drive me crazy as punishment? Or is it because you finally feel comfortable with me—"

"I took out the band because I'm getting in the shower in a minute."

"Oh, boy," he lowered his head and rubbed his hand over his eyes. "Okay, this is not good."

Kitt grabbed her boots and stood quickly, aware she had inadvertently trod on dangerous ground. "You can come to the site tomorrow since we're basically finished. I'll put you in charge of entertaining all the interested citizenry who show up thanks to your news broadcast around town."

He looked up, let out a breath and nodded. "You've got yourself a deal."

"Great, then." She placed her hands on her hips as he stood, blocking her path to the door. "I'll go inside now, if you'll move."

He leaned one shoulder against the doorframe. "So do you think I'll be able to get anything out of old Hod?"

She tilted her head to one side, a wry smile tickling the corners of her mouth. Michael, Michael, Michael. Despite his big talk about relying on God, he was still the same bad boy, wasn't he? She studied his tall, male form for a moment, his shoulders nearly filling the frame, one hand hanging loosely at his narrow hips. A wisp of sun-gold hair had fallen across his forehead and was brushing the top of one eyebrow. She felt an urge to reach up and tuck it in place.

She pushed her loose hair behind her back. He was right, of course. She had begun undressing without even thinking about it. It seemed natural having him nearby, his deep-set eyes watching her as she took off her boots and socks.

"All I've been able to get out of Hod is a lot of rambling nonsense about gold mines and twilight and a tree bent in the shape of an *L*," she said, keeping her tone light. "Charles Grant thinks Hod is perfectly sane, and maybe he is. You'll just have to see for yourself, if he shows up tomorrow."

"I wonder what he thinks you're going to find out there at that cemetery." Michael knitted his fingers together, as if he needed to find something to do with them. "He doesn't think his father's gold mine is around there. He told you that."

"I think Hod is just a curious old man," Kitt was saying when she saw Michael's hand reach for her braid.

With a gentle tug, he drew her toward him. She came, a little hesitantly, and he began to unbraid her hair. "For three days I've listened to you through that thin motel wall," he said. "I've heard you leave for meals, for work. Yesterday, you went to church."

"For old times' sake."

"And I couldn't go." He shook his head. "I didn't want to be near you. Didn't trust myself. When I knocked on your door just now, I was half afraid you wouldn't want to talk to me…and half afraid you'd let me inside. I'm glad you didn't."

She had jammed her hands into her jeans pockets while he absently fiddled with her braid. "I thought God was running your life," she said.

"He is, but…" Michael ran his thumb down her braid, loosening the long brown plait. She had woven it wet after her morning shower, and her hair was all crinkled and wavy, each curl picking up glints of light from the motel's neon sign. As if mesmerized, he sifted it through his fingers, arranging it around her shoulders.

"Michael," she said. "I need to go."

"Yeah." He moved to one side and lowered his hand. "Sure."

"I don't think this is going to work."

"Why not?"

"You're touching me. It's against the rules."

"Just your hair…"

"Michael, you have to know I'm never going to be able to

forget our past." She looked away, battling unexpected emotion. "It doesn't matter whether we have long, heart-wrenching talks. It doesn't matter if we have huge fights. It doesn't even matter if we get to be friends. I just…I just can't forget it all. The past has become a part of me. It made me into what I am today."

She leaned against the doorframe opposite him. "I mean, you can take me on a picnic and wind up kissing me. Or you can stand there and unbraid my hair…"

Michael nodded, his blue eyes shadowed. "I hear a great big *but* coming."

"But the truth is, no matter how much we might have loved each other once, and no matter how much we might still be drawn to each other, the truth is, the past is always going to be there. And it's more than just that you hurt me or I hurt you. It's that *life* hurt us, you know?"

"Death hurt us."

"God hurt us. He cheated us."

"No, Kitt—"

"Every time I look at you, I remember it all, Michael. You're locked up with that part of my life. The only way I got over it was to erase you."

"Now that I'm back, you feel the pain again." He ran his fingers down her cheek. "But that means you didn't erase me, Kitt. You just put me and the baby on a shelf and chose not to look at us."

Kitt focused on the cars cruising the street in front of the motel. "I guess I don't know how to erase. I don't know how to forget."

"You think the only way you're going to get back to being you is for me to go and climb on the shelf again where I belong. That's what you want, isn't it? You want me to leave."

Kitt stood silently for a moment, watching Michael fight to compose himself. He looked almost childlike in the soft light, and she ached to slip her arms around him. Instead, he took both her hands in his and held them loosely. They leaned against the door frame, their toes almost touching.

"When I was in Saudi Arabia, I had a lot of time to think it all over, Kitt," he said, his voice a shade deeper. "I knew I could never forget what happened to us. I knew it would always be a part of me. I realized that there were two ways I could look at it. Either God had meant for us to be together, but our parents, our youth and the death of our baby forced us apart. Or He hadn't wanted us to be together in the first place, but we had just gone ahead and blindly forged our own disastrous future."

"Which did you decide was right?"

"I came to the conclusion that we weren't meant to be together in the first place. It had been a mistake from the beginning. But the sickness in my heart all those months in the Gulf tried to convince me otherwise. In the end my brain won. I finally accepted that you and I had paved our own path to destruction. I couldn't deny the truth. I hadn't bothered to ask God what He wanted before I married you, and what happened was the natural consequence of my selfishness."

"It was God's vengeance on us."

"No, Kitt. God allowed those painful things in order to bring us back to Him."

"That's ridiculous. Who would want to go near a wrathful God?"

"I did. And I found His love and forgiveness waiting for me. I found His grace—blessings I didn't deserve."

"You didn't have me, though."

"You're standing here right now, aren't you?"

A wash of shock ran down Kitt's body. Was Michael actually saying he believed God had brought them back together? Did he think there was some way they might pick up the pieces of their marriage and rebuild it?

"Listen, we agree that you can't ever forget the past," she

told him. "And you certainly can't pick up where you left off. Especially when it turns out as badly as it did for us. So you just put it away and go on."

"That's what you do."

They looked into each other's eyes. Michael squeezed her hands, his thumbs pressing against her palms. Then he straightened and stepped away from her. She locked her hands together as she watched him leave. As he reached for the handle of his door, she turned and started into her room.

"The thing is, Kitt," he said.

"What?" She swung around, a note of unconcealed hope in the word.

"The thing is, I think I was wrong back there in the desert." He faced her again. "I'm beginning to see that we were meant to be together after all. God planned everything for our good, just the way He promised me He would."

He stepped into his room, shut the door and left her standing openmouthed and openhearted by the bench.

"Here he comes." Kitt gestured with the point of a trowel in the direction of the cottonwood tree.

A battered pickup, minus a windshield and trimmed with rust, rumbled up the dirt road and pulled to a halt. The door creaked open. Hod settled his felt hat lower on his forehead and slid to the ground. As he ambled through the grass, Michael imagined his legs, scrawny and as thin as a sparrow's beneath his wool trousers. Hod pulled out a yellowed handkerchief, lifted his hat and mopped his forehead.

"The old fellow has definitely seen a few years," Michael said.

"Dr. Dean thinks he may be nearly a hundred. I'll try to talk to him."

"Let me. He might think you want to run him off."

Michael jogged away from the pit Kitt had been excavating since just after sunrise. He had enjoyed the time with

her, even though she was quiet and more restrained than she
had been the day before. As she worked, she had explained
the process of exhuming historical remains, as well as the
technical and legal aspects of her work. His appreciation of
her skills had deepened. She even let him dig beside her,
dusting the top of a caved-in coffin lid they had uncovered.

He brushed his palms on his jeans as he approached the
elderly man.

"I ain't leaving." Hod crossed his arms and puffed up his
chest. He was wheezing from the exertion of his walk. "You
tell Miss Priss that I'm here to stay today."

"You can stay. It's all right. She's just finishing up."

The faded blue eyes crinkled with pleasure. "Good." He
pushed Michael aside with one hand and tottered forward.

At the lip of the pit where Kitt was working, Hod paused
and bent over. "I'm staying."

"That's fine today, Hod." She shaded her eyes from the
midday sun. He seemed to be smiling, his few teeth poking
askew from bare gums.

"I'll watch right here." He hunkered at the edge of the
crumbling ground and peered down at her.

Michael knelt beside him. "Dr. Tucker tells me your name
is Hod."

"Right."

"Hod… Hod what?"

"Ain't that good enough for you?"

"I guess it'll have to do."

The old face assumed a solemn gaze as Hod watched the
lid of the coffin come slowly into view.

"Lived here long, Hod?" Michael asked.

"Long enough."

"I hear you know more about Muddy Flats than just about
anyone."

"Who told you that?"

"A friend of yours. Charles Grant over at the museum."

"Muddy Flats died about the time I was born."

"So you were born here?"

"Not here." Hod scowled, his bushy white brows drawing together. "This here's a cemetery. You don't birth babies in a cemetery. No, sir."

"Were you born in Muddy Flats?"

"Over there." Hod pointed west with his chin. "House I still live in."

"Did you know a lot of the people who lived in Muddy Flats?"

"You sure are an all-fire nosy feller." Hod blotted his forehead with the old handkerchief.

"Just curious."

"Curiosity killed the cat."

Michael sighed. Kitt was carefully removing the coffin lid. It had sunk in the center, as she had told him all the coffins did. There was not much dirt underneath. He could see the top of a skull.

Then Hod surprised him by answering his question. "I did know one citizen of Muddy Flats. My papa. I knew him for ten years before he died. He's the one that showed me the gold mine."

"I've heard about that gold mine of yours."

"Papa took me up there one fine day," Hod said. He spread a gnarled hand across the sky. "Blue as a robin's egg. Big, rocky mountain. We climbed all day, see. Got there late in the afternoon. My papa said, 'Boy, remember this tree in the shape of an upside-down L. Don't you forget it now. I'll write down the directions.' But, you know, I was just a kid. I went down in the mine with him and saw all the gold. Sure enough—you don't believe me?"

"I believe you."

"Bars on one side. Raw nuggets in saddlebags on the other side. All piled up in a long skinny room of that cave."

"Cave? I thought you said it was a mine."

"I did."

"Well, was it a cave or a mine?"

"It was a cave."

Michael scratched his head. Kitt was picking at the skeleton with her trowel and chopsticks. The skull was completely free of dirt. Other bones showed now, too. She dusted a little bit, dug a little bit, then sat on her heels and studied the remains.

"I didn't pay no heed to that mine of my papa's," Hod said. "I just went on playing and fooling around. I was tossing rocks down a hillside and watching them roll along until they hit the bottom. You know how a boy'll do."

"But he left you directions to the place?"

"Not that I could ever find. Papa up and died one day not too long after that. He lay there in the field and held my hand and he said to me, 'Boy, I know you'll be all right. You got that gold. It's all I have to give you, but it'll keep you rich and healthy all your life.' It was then I realized that I couldn't remember where the mine was, see? And I didn't have no directions. But Papa had passed on."

"So you started searching for the mine?"

"'Course I did. Papa had wanted me to have it. It was all that he had to give me in the world. I wanted to find it again not so much for the gold as for the fact that Papa give it to me. That house and that gold mine. It was all he had to give. I kept the house, but I lost the mine."

A tug of sadness pulled at Michael. He could picture the little boy, holding his father's hand as the old man lay dying. It was plausible that Hod had spent his whole life searching for the lost legacy.

"Didn't your mother remember where the gold was?"

"Mama died when I was born." Hod sniffed and looked away. "Never knew her, myself. Papa told me she was the prettiest sight he ever saw. Tiny little ankles. Wide-spaced green eyes. Finished off his roving days right then and there.

'Son,' he told me. 'Find you a good woman like your mama was, and don't never let her go. You hold on to her no matter what troubles come your way.' 'Course I never did find me no woman. I know I never saw my mama in real life, but I got a picture. Weddin' picture of her and my papa. I never knew her, but I loved her all the same."

Michael nodded. For all his rambling, old Hod did sound pretty sane. "Do you remember seeing the smelting furnace down in your papa's mine, or outside on the mountain slope?"

"Smelting furnace? What's that?"

"That would have been where your papa melted the nuggets and formed all those gold bars you saw. There would have been a big furnace and piles of cinder slag all around."

Hod pulled at his chin, his blue eyes narrowed. "Nope. No furnace. Papa didn't mine the gold right there in that cave, see. He brung it there. Brung it in on mules. He stashed it there in the cave."

"So it wasn't really a mine after all. It was a cave." Michael felt a twinge of excitement.

"That's what I told you. Why don't you listen, boy?"

"Michael—" Kitt's head appeared over the lip of the pit. "Hand me that screen. Help me do some sifting, would you? I've found the most interesting thing down here."

Chapter Eight

❧

Michael climbed into the pit and handed Kitt the sifting screen. The skeleton was completely exposed now, but he could tell nothing more than that the person had been fairly short.

"Look at this, would you?" She crouched in the dirt at the foot of the grave.

"What is it?"

"Beads! Hundreds of them." She lifted a handful of dirt mixed with shiny, multicolored seed beads. "They're beautiful."

Michael knelt beside her. "What are they made of?"

"Glass, I think." She rolled the beads around in her palm. "They must have been sewn onto her skirt. Can you imagine the work?"

He picked up a few beads and rubbed the dust away. "I'd guess there are more than a thousand here."

"This is by far the most beautiful thing we've found. And take a look at this."

She leaned toward the spot where the woman's hand had rested on her breast. A gold ring set with an emerald encircled one tiny bone of her left hand. Michael couldn't help feeling that the whole thing was a little morbid. This had been a living, breathing woman once. But Kitt seemed to be concerned only with its archaeological significance.

"This is the most valuable jewelry on the site," she was saying as she carefully picked away dirt with her chopstick. "Look at the size of her emerald."

"You're sure it was a woman."

"Oh, yes. See the facial structure." She paused and gazed at the skull for a moment. "She was beautiful. Someone loved her very much to have given her that ring. And her dress must have been costly, too, with all those beads."

In an instant, the detached scientist had evaporated, and Kitt's voice was full of melancholy. Michael began to see he'd been mistaken. She brought more than just a trained eye to her work. There was a tenderness, too. A feeling and empathy for who these people had been and what their lives had meant.

"I can't believe this woman didn't have a headstone," she said softly. "We never realized this grave was here. It was completely unmarked."

"How did you find it?"

"After we had excavated all the marked graves, we did a lot of trenching. We found quite a few unmarked sites. But they were generally the graves of men. By the number of bullets we found in the fill dirt, you could surmise that they must have been men who had just been passing through Muddy Flats. They'd probably gotten into fights in the saloon, or something, and been shot. Some didn't even have coffins."

She turned to the ring and stroked it for a moment. "But this woman. Someone cared for her a great deal. Look how she was buried with her hands folded. And she has on the prettiest shoes. Not even boots. See, this is patent leather. You can tell they were high-topped shoes with heels."

Michael picked up another handful of beads. "I wonder why she didn't have a headstone."

"Nobody would carve one for her." The voice came from above them at the top of the pit. Kitt and Michael lifted their faces into the late afternoon sun. Hod was gazing at the skeleton, his face lined with sorrow. "She had a wooden cross once. I guess somebody stole it. Or maybe it just rotted away. But nobody would carve the stone for her."

Michael glanced at Kitt. She was staring at the old man. Hod folded his handkerchief and brushed it beneath one eye then the other. He took off his hat and held it in his lap for a minute, turning the brim around and around.

"Hod," Michael spoke up gently. "This grave. Is this…is this—"

"The twilight has come." Hod settled his hat on his head and gingerly rose to his feet. "And now the night will follow."

With that, the old man ambled away.

Michael looked at the skeleton at his feet. A chill prickled up his spine. He felt like he was standing on hallowed ground.

"Did I hear him talking about…" Kitt's words faltered. She knelt on the dirt.

"I'm going after Hod," Michael said. He heard the pickup cough to life and begin chugging away into the distance. "I think this woman was his mother."

The Bureau of Reclamation truck sped down the highway toward Catclaw Draw. Michael stared out the window while Kitt drove in silence. Determined to accompany him, she had given the excavation assignment to her two remaining assistants. Dr. Dean would photograph the grave's contents and set the skeleton on a tray to measure. Then he would sift the soil to retrieve each and every one of the thousands of seed beads.

"You really think you should have left the site, Kitt?" Michael angled his head toward her.

"I can't go casually digging up the remains of someone's mother and then just leave it at that." Her fingers clenched the steering wheel. If only she'd known that was why Hod had been loitering around the site. She would have spoken with him more seriously. She would have taken his feelings into account.

"If you're relocating a historical cemetery," Michael said, "you would hardly expect to find a survivor just one generation removed. I mean, it is an archaeological dig, Kitt. You would assume that the remains would be those of distant ancestors."

"You can never assume anything. Dr. Dean guessed Hod was old enough to have known someone buried in the Muddy Flats cemetery." She shook her head. "What did Hod tell you about his mother? I was concentrating on my work."

"He said he never knew her. She died giving birth to him."

Kitt gave him a quick glance, then swallowed. "Dr. Dean will be able to tell us whether the remains fit that description."

"How much can you tell from a collection of disjointed bones?"

"If the woman died in childbirth, her pelvic girdle will be expanded. Dr. Dean will be able to give us that information. He can also tell us her approximate age, her height, a composite physical description and her general physical fitness. That should give us a fairly good idea whether she was Hod's mother."

"What are you planning to do when you find Hod?"

Kitt's heart ached as she drove. It wasn't just an old man's suffering that troubled her. She could almost see a woman giving birth—a young woman with wide-set eyes, a gold and emerald ring on her finger and a skirt embroidered with a thousand glass beads. She was picturing a tiny baby—alive. And a beautiful mother—dead.

"I'm going to talk to him," Kitt said. "I feel I should go over the Bureau's policy again, and I feel I need to make an apology. Hod was acting so strange. All that about the twilight and the gold mine. He must have been very distressed about the whole thing."

"He told me he still lives in the house where he was born. It's somewhere west of Muddy Flats. Should we try to find it?"

"Let's look for him in town first. He may have gone to see Charles Grant."

"His father died when Hod was ten."

"After showing him the gold mine?"

"Turns out it's not a mine after all. It's a cave. Hod's father brought the gold in on mules and stored it there. There was no smelting furnace or anything. Part of the gold was in bars and part of it was in nuggets."

"So you really believe what Hod was saying about the gold?" Kitt again glanced at Michael. He was stretched out across the seat, but she could sense his tension. His blue-gray eyes scanned the highway.

"I do. I think Hod is telling the story as he remembers it."

Kitt swung the pickup into the museum parking lot. "The question remains how well Hod remembers anything."

Charles Grant stood on the porch, fumbling with keys as he locked the museum. At the sound of the truck, he turned and waved.

"Any sign of old Hod around here, Charles?" Kitt called.

He shook his head. "Try *Mi Rincon* down on Main. It's the local tavern where he hangs out. Usually there by now."

"Any idea how we could get out to his house if he's not there?"

"What's going on?" Charles headed down the sidewalk toward them.

"He was behaving oddly at the site this afternoon," she explained. No need to mention the grave. "I'd feel better if I could check on him."

"He lives in an adobe house out west of town's all I know. Take Prickly Pear Road and head in that direction. You'll probably see his old truck. Need some company?"

"That's okay. Thanks anyway." Kitt gave Charles a little smile before pulling onto the street.

Mi Rincon sat on a shaded lot at the edge of Catclaw Draw. Though it was just after five, cars and trucks already lined the street in front of the small tavern. Sure enough, Hod's pickup had been badly parked at the side of the bar. Kitt heaved a sigh of relief and glanced at Michael. He gave her a thumbs-up sign and climbed out of the truck.

Curly wrought iron covered the windows of the flat-topped little building. A neon beer sign flickered in one window. A bouquet of faded plastic flowers peeked over the sill of the other. The tavern's name had been painted across the white stucco wall in shades of blue and pink. From inside, the jumbled sound of a poorly recorded mariachi band filtered into the yard. A skinny dog with big brown eyes lounged on the front step.

"*Mi Rincon,*" Michael murmured as they stepped through the door. "My hideaway."

Kitt leaned against a cool white wall for a moment, waiting for her eyes to adjust to the gloom. The smell of heavy Mexican beer mingled with the scent of lemons, cigarette smoke and perfume. A bar lined with patrons stretched from one end of the room to the other. Waitresses in white peasant blouses and flower-embroidered red skirts wandered back and forth chatting with customers. Two couples danced in one corner, keeping a beat with the blaring *rancheros* music.

"There he is," Kitt whispered, elbowing Michael.

Hod slouched in a far booth, alone. His hat sat forlornly on the table beside an empty beer bottle. His eyes were trained on a second bottle that he was twisting around and around in his palms. Michael and Kitt wound their way past the tables and slid into his booth. He didn't look up.

"Hod," Kitt said softly, leaning across the table. "Hod, it's Dr. Tucker from Muddy Flats."

Hod kept turning his beer bottle.

"Talk louder," Michael whispered, leaning against her.

She cleared her throat and began again. "Hod, it's Dr. Tucker from the Muddy Flats cemetery. Are you all right?"

"She sewed him up, see," Hod mumbled. "Her being a seamstress and all. It was a natural thing."

Kitt glanced at Michael.

"He come into town with that wound, but nobody would touch him. 'Course they wouldn't. Scared to death of him. All of 'em was. But not her. She wasn't scared. Took him in and sewed him back together."

"Hod—"

"It was her as stitched them beads on the dress. He told me. I do recollect that part real good. He brung the beads to her, see. As a present for sewing him up. She wouldn't take no payment."

"Are you sure your mother was buried at Muddy Flats, Hod?" Kitt asked.

"Papa buried her, all by hisself. 'Course, I forgot where the grave was after somebody stole the wooden cross. Or maybe it rotted away. I forgot just where it was he put her, see. Just like I forgot where the mine was. I do recollect a good many things. But them two things I forgot. I forgot where it was Papa put her, and I forgot where it was he took me that day."

"But you do remember her burial was at the Muddy Flats cemetery?" Kitt wished Hod would at least look at her. The empty bottle on the table attested to the fact that the old man was pretty far gone, and it was going to be hard to reach him.

"Only place around in them days was the Muddy Flats cemetery," Hod said. He took another swig. "Muddy Flats town was about gone by then. Papa said it didn't bother her much. Her family took off west and left her without even a fare-thee-well. She didn't mind them livin' in the house all by theirselves. She was happy with my papa, see."

Kitt reached toward the old man. "Hod, listen, by tomorrow we should have a fairly good physical description of the woman in the grave. If you'd like, I'll be happy to share that information with you. I want to apologize for not consulting you more closely. If you'd mentioned that your mother was buried in the cemetery, I'm sure the Bureau—"

"She loved him in spite of everything," Hod said. He shook his head. "Oh, Papa told me they had their hardships all right. Him so old and her just a girl, really. Him a stranger and her a local gal. Her family had disowned her, see. Booted her straight out of the house. But she and my papa got married anyway, so it was all right."

Deeply moved, Kitt slid from her place beside Michael and slipped in next to Hod. Her braid fell over her shoulder as she took the old man's hands.

"Hod, I'm having new headstones carved right now in Carlsbad. The ones for the unmarked graves will read 'Unknown.' But if we can show that the woman in the grave is your mother, I'll be more than happy to have her name inscribed. And if you have any more information, such as her birth date—"

"I was birthed out in that big house, you know. Papa told me he done everything he knew how to do for her. She was just a tiny little thing, see. Like a little bird. Not near big enough to have a baby. I guess I killed her."

"No, Hod." Kitt squeezed the old man's hands. "You didn't kill her. It wasn't your fault that she died."

She felt strange and detached suddenly. The music seemed to be pounding in her head. Michael stretched out his hand and touched her arm. Hod sank down in the seat, his body heavy against hers.

"If I could have found that gold, see, I'd have been okay. It was my papa's gold that he brung with him when he come to Muddy Flats. He had it when he met my mama. He was going to take care of her. But she died. And then he died, see. And I forgot where everything was."

Hod placed his calloused hands on top of Michael's, and the three of them sat there, hands clasped across the narrow table, waiting, listening. The mariachi record ended and a country-and-western band started up. More people filtered into the bar, men in straw cowboy hats, women in tight jeans. The sky outside the iron-barred window had darkened to cobalt.

Hod sniffled. "I do reckon we could carve her a headstone. *Sweet intercessor 'twixt God and man, gone on wings to plead for us there.*" He hung his head and sighed. "Papa always wanted one to say that for her. 'Course he never had a headstone, neither. I never knew exactly where they buried my papa. They took me away. Gave me to some family in Carlsbad to raise. But I come back to our house, see. As soon as I could get away, I come back to our home. I ain't never been gone again, 'cept to look for the gold mine."

Hod's head swayed as he spoke, finally coming to rest on Kitt's shoulder. He closed his eyes. She gazed down at the wreath of wrinkles lining his face. His eyelashes were white. The yellowed handkerchief lay on his lap.

"Kitt." Michael whispered her name. She lifted her eyes. Their three hands, stacked cuplike, still lay on the table, Hod's on top. "Is he all right?"

"She sewed him up, see," Hod mumbled. "She was a seamstress."

"I think he's falling asleep." She looked around the tavern. One of the waitresses was leaning against a pole, smiling at the three in the booth. Kitt smiled back, a little uncertainly. The woman lifted her shoulders from the pole and sauntered across the room.

"Drunk?" she asked.

Kitt shrugged. "Or asleep."

"He's drunk." She clucked her tongue. "Every night, same

thing. Two beers, and he's out. We usually drag him to the couch over there and let him sleep it off. He gets up some time in the night when he's sober again and drives home. You want I should call Juan?"

"No," Michael said. "We'll take him home."

"You friends of his?"

"Sort of. He comes here every night then?"

"Every night, regular as clockwork. Sits right in that booth. Reads the newspaper. Drinks two beers. Falls over on the table and we drag him to the couch. He's too old to be drinking, you know. And you should get his windshield fixed, if you're his friends. He's too old to be driving a truck like that."

"How old do you think he is?" Kitt asked quietly. Hod was snoring softly against her shoulder.

"He's over a hundred. We have a party every year around Christmastime. Let's see…I think he told us he was a hundred-and-five last Christmas. But with Hod, you can't be sure. Everybody likes the old guy. But he tells some stories—I mean some real stories. So how you know old Hod?"

"I met him out at the Muddy Flats cemetery," Kitt explained. "I'm relocating the graves there."

"No kidding? I heard about you. So you want a beer or what? We got margaritas and everything. You name it."

"No, thanks. We'll just take Hod home. Any idea how to get to his place?"

"Nobody ever goes out there. Everyone thinks it's kind of haunted, you know. Like ghosts and everything. The stories that old guy tells—I mean like his papa was some kind of traveler who married this young seamstress, and when she died he went crazy with grief. It's like everybody Hod knew died some strange way. But he just keeps on living and living." She leaned down close to Michael. "Hod says he's not allowed to die until he finds his papa's gold mine. You ever heard that one, huh? He ever tell you that story?"

"Not that one."

The waitress threw back her head and laughed. "I guess he's gonna go on living forever. Because he sure ain't having much luck finding that gold mine." She shook her head and chuckled again. "So, you sure I can't bring you a drink? We got nachos, too. With jalapeños."

Hod dozed against Michael's shoulder while Michael drove the old man's truck through the darkness, west toward the last remnants of sunset. Kitt followed in the Bureau vehicle as Prickly Pear Road dwindled into nothing more than a rutted track. Thick dry grass swished against the sides of the pickup. A barn owl lifted into flight from a fencepost.

Michael followed the road until it forked. Guessing the more traveled ruts might indicate the way to Hod's home, he turned south and Kitt trailed behind. Before long the silhouette of a flat-roofed adobe house appeared like a wraith out of the darkness. No lights shone, and he might have driven past it but for the moonlight glinting on the glass pane of a window.

As the two trucks pulled up in front of the house, Michael realized it was much larger than he first thought. A long wooden porch wrapped around three sides. The building seemed to ramble on and on in a disorganized way, as though no one had thought it through before starting to build. Grass grew high. A honeysuckle vine had climbed a wooden post and hung over the steps, nearly blocking the porch entrance.

"I'll carry him," Michael whispered when Kitt appeared at his side. She stepped back, and he gently eased Hod into his arms. "He's as light as a feather. I bet he doesn't weigh more than a hundred pounds."

Hod shifted against Michael's broad chest, burying his cheek in the crook of the younger man's arm. Kitt pulled the honeysuckle to one side, and Michael bent low as he stepped onto the porch. Two old rocking chairs sat on either side of the open front door.

"See if there's a light," Michael said.

Kitt ran her hand over the rough adobe wall in the entry hall of the old house. There was no switch. But she did find an oil lamp and a book of matches sitting on a pine table beside the door. The lighted room revealed a long, flagstone-floored hallway, lined on either side with stacks of newspapers and old books.

"This place is a fire waiting to happen," Michael murmured as he carried Hod down the hall. "Take a look at this living room, Kitt."

Holding the lamp aloft, she sidestepped between the rows of papers. Michael paused in amazement. The living room was a portrait of chaos. An old ruby velvet couch, an upright piano, an elaborate étagère and two dusty chairs were half buried in faded, yellowing newspapers. Maps lay scattered like wood shavings. Books formed mountains on the floor. The one bookcase in the room had been completely buried, as though someone kept trying to put books on the shelves even after there were no more shelves in sight.

"I'll bet there's some valuable old stuff in here," Kitt said as Michael appraised the newspapers. She beckoned. "Come on, I'll help you find a place to put him."

They passed room after room in the sprawling house, and each was filled almost to bursting with reading matter. Michael saw at once that Hod's home was valuable for more than just the materials he had collected over the years. The furniture belonged to another era—and though covered with dust and cobwebs, it appeared to be in good condition. Elegant dishes lined the kitchen cabinets. Tea sets etched with gold. Darkened silverware. Creamy white pottery. But then there were newspapers stacked in the sink, and only one leg of the table was visible beneath another mountain of paper.

The bedroom, oddly enough, was neat as a pin. A massive brass bed stood at one end, weighting down a pink-and-red flowered hooked rug. Tables lined with old photographs in silver frames marched along the walls. In one corner, a vanity with flower-printed drapes seemed to be waiting, untouched. Silver-backed combs, brushes and mirrors had been artfully arranged. Perfume decanters and atomizers—their contents long evaporated—sat in two tidy rows.

"Do you suppose this is his room?" Michael asked, as he settled Hod on the intricately patterned quilt. "It looks like some kind of a shrine."

"I think he sleeps here. Look, his clothes are in this wardrobe. But he obviously does most of his living in the rest of the house."

"Obviously." Michael studied Kitt as she wandered mesmerized around the room. She looked like some sort of a ghost herself, with that lamp. She drifted over to where Hod lay slumbering peacefully on the bed. Kneeling, she set the lamp on a table and began unlacing his worn leather shoes. She pulled them off and placed them side by side, their heels even with the side of the bed. Then she loosened Hod's collar and drew two old quilts over him.

"Look how the wrinkles on his face have relaxed and gone smooth," she murmured. "He seems younger now. Almost beautiful." She reached out and stroked the lock of white hair on his forehead.

Michael knew they saw Hod in the same light. A living link with the history. He had been born in a century long past, and in a strange way he had held on to that time—a house with no electricity, probably no plumbing. A house filled to the brim with relics that recorded the first automobiles, the first washing machines, electric typewriters, men walking on the moon. Hod had lived through too many wars, a depression, flappers and hippies…it was hard to imagine the tumultuous changes the old man must have witnessed.

Michael lit another lamp, and shadows came to life. Studying Kitt as she knelt beside the bed, he felt they were all connected—as though in the tavern with their hands stacked together, he and Kitt and Hod had formed a sort of bond.

Lifting the lamp, he walked slowly around the room. And then Kitt joined him, gazing into the faces of Hod's past. There were old lithographs, daguerreotypes, faded photographs. But no children. Only adults—women in long white dresses with leg-of-mutton sleeves, men in starched white collars and checkered suits. Who were they?

Kitt turned the frames over, looking for inscriptions. Those she found shed no light on their subjects' identities. They were written in black ink, in a beautiful, feminine hand. "Aunt Rose in the garden." "Cousin Sylvia having tea with Maria." "Anna Emmaline's twenty-first birthday." "Uncle Andrew outside his new law office."

"I wonder what happened to all these people," Kitt said softly. "Maybe some of them were in the Muddy Flats cemetery."

Michael wanted to put his arm around her and pull her close. He sensed they both felt the undeniable passage of time. Loss was palpable in this room. Sadness darkened its corners and hung like a mist in the windows.

Michael had made peace with death. It had happened somewhere in the emptiness that followed the loss of their daughter, the end of his marriage and his own spiritual rebirth. Death came, ending a person's brief span of time on earth. Yet it did not triumph. Christ had defeated death, and with that victory, He had taken away Michael's fear.

"Life goes on," he said.

Kitt lifted her head. "Does it?"

"Forever. I have no doubt."

"Have you forgotten the skull with the two gold teeth? Whoever he was looked awfully dead to me."

"You dug up his skeletal remains," he said. "That man's spirit lives."

Her eyes clouded. "Don't be naive. You saw our baby, Michael."

"Yes, and I saw friends cut down in battle. Death is not the end."

Crossing her arms, she stared at him a moment longer. Then she turned away. "I'm an archaeologist," she said. "Excuse me, but I'd like to take a look at the rest of this house."

"Kitt, come here!" Michael appeared in the doorway. He had on a silk top hat and a flowing black wool cape, like a phantom or a magician.

"What are you doing in that outfit?" she asked, stifling a laugh.

"Come take a look at what I've found. It's an anthropologist's dream."

He vanished with a swirl of black rustling fabric. Kitt smiled and glanced down at the photograph in her hand. It was a small picture, tinged with the sepia tones of an old daguerreotype. Kitt held it close to the lamp.

A small-framed woman with striking deep-set eyes stood beside an old man in a chair. One hand, slender and pale, rested on his shoulder. Oddly, the man and woman were smiling—almost unheard of in these old, stern photographs. It was as if they had pulled off some sort of grand joke. Kitt studied the writing at the bottom of the picture. The words had been printed in a different hand—bold and masculine.

"Wedding day," it read.

"Kitt—are you coming?" Michael poked his head into the room.

"I found a wedding picture," she said. "But it looks like a father and daughter."

"Maybe it is."

"Didn't Hod say his mother was young but his father was old when they married?"

"Yeah, so it's probably them. Hey, come on. I'm serious. This is great."

As he vanished again, Kitt set the photograph on the table. The woman might be Hod's mother. She would contact Dr. Dean about the results of his tests—he might even want to take a look at the picture.

She stepped into the hall and headed for a pool of lamplight at the far end. When she entered the room, she caught her breath. Looking like a boy who had just discovered Santa's workshop, Michael sat amid stacks of antique clothing, utensils, books, furniture, trunks.

"You won't believe this stuff," he said with a laugh. "It's enough to fill a small museum. And the quality—I mean this is fine furniture. Take a look at this dress."

He held up a gown of turquoise silk, heavily embroidered and encrusted with tiny silver beads. He shook it a little, and a fine powdery dust cloud drifted out and settled onto his lap.

"Hod must have moved most of the house's contents in here as his piles of newspapers grew in the other rooms." Kitt waded in, feeling like she was walking into someone's private treasure trove. A huge buckled trunk stood in one corner. She stepped over the stack of framed photographs that Michael was sifting through. The trunk's leather straps had deteriorated, but she gently unbuckled its heavy green lid.

"Oh, Michael," she said in a whisper. The trunk was filled with women's clothing—beautiful dresses and skirts, artfully embroidered chemises, delicate cotton petticoats. Each was tied with a blue ribbon. A scrap of paper had been pinned to the ribbon. "Mrs. Samuel Whiting," one read. "Eliza Morgan." "Nellie Wirth."

"This was her sewing trunk, Michael," she murmured. "These must have been her customers' names. Look at the different colors of threads in the bottom. And here's a pattern she made out of butcher paper. Oh, Michael—here are her scissors."

Kitt held up the tiny silver sewing scissors molded into the shape of a stork. "I don't feel right about this, Michael. These are Hod's personal things. I think we should go back to the motel."

He nodded. "I'll tell Charles Grant about it. He might want to talk to Hod. It's a shame to let everything deteriorate."

Kitt buckled the trunk and moved to kneel at Michael's side. "I wish we could do something for Hod. He seems so alone."

"We could look for his lost gold."

"He's been searching most of his life. I doubt we'd find it—even if it does exist."

"If we found the gold, he could die in peace."

"You really believe everything, don't you? The gold, the stories he tells."

Michael's blue-gray eyes focused on Kitt. "Maybe I'm just a fool for love," he said, his voice almost inaudible. "A man and a woman battling the ostracism of society to build a home of their own. A dream home, filled with nooks and crannies and the little knickknacks of their lives. Creating a child…"

They sat in the silence of the cluttered room, neither speaking. Kitt studied the folds of the black silk cape draped across Michael's thigh. She realized he was touching her, and it felt so natural she hadn't even noticed. His fingers lay on her arm, tracing a little circle around and around. It was as though the two of them had stepped into a timeless place where the past had become the present. Everything seemed certain and right. Old Hod asleep down the hall. Michael beside her. Kitt nestled against him, where she belonged.

He picked up a large-brimmed, ostrich-feather hat lying at his knee. It was fashioned of black velvet with huge white plumes circling the crown. With a smile, he settled the hat on her head.

"Feels good in here," he said quietly. "Kind of makes me forget about computers and fax machines and wars, and people running amok shooting everyone or blowing themselves up. Although I guess the old days had their own worries." He chuckled. "Look at this fellow here. I wouldn't want to run into him."

He pulled a silver-framed daguerreotype from the pile on the floor. A man with arms crossed over his chest stood in a pose of supreme confidence and defiance. Face turned slightly to one side, he stared at the world with beady-eyed malevolence.

Kitt shuddered. "Not in a dark alley, anyway. Those eyes— if looks could kill. Look, someone scratched his name down here at the bottom." She lifted the lamp from the floor and held it close to the picture.

Michael bent close, trying to make out the swirling hand. "Don Santiago Querque, it says. He doesn't look Spanish to me."

"He's not." Kitt turned to Michael. Her mouth felt dry. "Don Santiago Querque was the name his men gave James Kirker, the white scalp hunter. Black Dove's boss. The scourge of the Apaches. The king of New Mexico."

Chapter Nine

❧

"Why would Hod have a picture of James Kirker?" Michael voiced the question they were both thinking.

"There are an awful lot of pictures in this house," Kitt said. "More than you would think for the historical period."

"The Kirker photograph is piled with the rest of these frames, as though it weren't important."

"Maybe it wasn't. Maybe someone in Hod's family collected daguerreotypes—sort of a hobby." Kitt turned the frame over. "But all the pictures in the bedroom were inscribed in the same hand. It's as if the owner knew the subject in each frame."

"Suppose Hod's father was a photographer by trade. An itinerant photographer. Maybe that's why he was traveling through Muddy Flats."

"With a wound so bad he needed sewing up? Photographers don't usually get shot at or stabbed."

"Good point. Maybe Hod's mother collected the pictures. But why would she have one of James Kirker?"

"Back to square one." Kitt recalled her research on the white scalp hunter. "Kirker was famous in early New Mexico. But this is a one-of-a-kind photograph. James Kirker wasn't the sort of person who would pose for a postcard. This is a daguerreotype. Kirker must have sat for a photographer somewhere, and it ended up in this collection. But how?"

"And why?" Michael reached up and stroked one of the white plumes on her hat. "Doesn't it strike you as odd that we've been talking about Black Dove and wondering whether he's buried in Muddy Flats, and then his boss's picture turns up in this old house?"

"A little strange, yes. But there could be a simple explanation for it. We'll have to ask Hod."

"Not tonight."

"No." She shook her head. "It's going to be awkward talking to him about this, you know."

"No problem. We'll say, 'Oh, by the way, Hod, we took you home the other night and decided to go poking through all your stuff while you were asleep. We opened your trunks and put on your ancestors' clothes. That was right after we dug up your mother's grave.'"

"Michael, that's not funny."

"No, it isn't. Hod's whole situation is really pretty sad. Let's go on back to the motel. I need to get an early start for Carlsbad in the morning."

When he turned to Kitt, his eyes were shadowed, deep-set in the lamplight. She knew they were thinking the same thing. Time to part again. Time to say goodbye.

Kitt permitted herself one last moment to study him, just as he gazed back at her. Michael would have done well if he had lived in Kirker's time, she thought. His body was tough and lean, as though made for driving cattle across windswept plains. And why not? He had practically lived on a horse when he was young. The honed, taut musculature had stayed with him. Even his face, it seemed, had been carved by the wind into sharp angles and rugged planes.

Her eyes traced the contours of his features. His lips were straight and masculine, and his eyelashes were tipped with a gold that reflected the halo circling his blue-gray irises.

"Don't look at me that way, Kitt." His voice dropped to a whisper.

She glanced away, suddenly embarrassed. It had felt natural to observe Michael boldly, as she always had in the past. But this wasn't the past. It was now.

Uncomfortable, she took off the hat, set it on the floor, and got to her feet. After stepping into the hall, she leaned against the cool wall and closed her eyes. She could hear his movements as he straightened the room—trunk lids falling shut, picture frames sliding across each other, dresses rustling. And then there was another sound—slow, hollow music.

When she peered inside, Michael's back was to her as he thumbed through a pile of shiny black records stacked beside a battered upright phonograph. She didn't recognize the song, but it clearly belonged to a forgotten time when big bands played lazy, melodic music.

"It's a Victrola," he said, turning to face her. He still wore the cape and top hat. "Care to dance, Miss Kitty?"

"Oh, Michael." She smiled like a shy schoolgirl. "We've got to be going."

He stepped through the jumble of furniture toward her. Along the way, he picked up the ostrich feather hat. "One dance? For old times' sake?"

Without waiting for an answer, he settled the hat onto her head and pulled her into his arms. Unable to move easily around the trunks and scattered items, they simply turned in circles to the lilting music. Neither spoke, but their eyes met and locked as they moved through their slow-motion dance.

One part of her wanted to reject it all—the unreal aura of the room, the unexpected warmth of Michael Culhane, the strange turn her life had suddenly taken. And yet she continued to move with him, letting it happen, putting aside sane, rational arguments and welcoming the joy of the moment.

Was this a coincidence? A chance merging of two lives? Or was Michael right that God somehow had engineered everything, bringing them back together for a purpose only He knew? She wanted to reject the idea. God didn't work that way. Never in the past had He done anything positive that Kitt could put her finger on. Even if Michael's professed faith had led God to intersect their lives, Kitt knew He didn't care enough about *her* to move so unexpectedly.

She wanted to feel angry. Telling herself that God was still manipulating her, she wondered if He was enjoying making a fool of her. This had to be some kind of punishment for her lack of faith. Or worse, it was a malicious game played with the intent of throwing her life into havoc. But how could she deny the pleasure she felt in Michael's arms?

As they spun, he drew her closer. His lips touched her cheek. Her fingers found the soft curls at his collar. The frozen block inside her began to melt, and she put her cheek on his shoulder, breathing in his scent…laundered cotton, fresh air, suntanned skin, a hint of dust from the day's work, a trace of spice….

"Mama?"

At the sound, Kitt stiffened and stepped away from Michael. Hod stood in the doorway, his clothing and hair rumpled from sleep, his head tilted down in confusion.

"Mama, is that you?" he asked, his voice timid and confused like that of a child awakened from a deep sleep.

"Oh, no, Hod. It's just—"

"Papa?" Hod rubbed his eyes. "I can't find it anywhere, Papa."

"What have you lost, Hod?" Michael spoke gently.

"I've lost the gold, Papa. I've looked and looked, but I can't find it."

Michael took Kitt's hand as he stepped toward the old man. "It's okay, Hod. You don't have to find the gold anymore. You can stop looking now."

"Are you sure, Papa?"

"I'm sure, Hod."

The old man rubbed his eyes again and started to cry. "Papa, where did you bury Mama? I forgot that, too."

"Come, Hod. Let's put you to bed," Kitt said softly.

The three of them padded slowly down the hall, Michael and Kitt supporting Hod between them. He continued to sniffle, dragging his feet like a tired toddler who wasn't sure where he was. Kitt settled him onto the bed as Michael drew the quilt over his shoulders.

"We'll be going now, Hod." Michael bent and kissed him gently on the cheek. "Good night."

"Good night, Papa." Hod closed his eyes and yawned. "Good night, Mama."

An envelope was taped to Kitt's motel door. She tugged it free and flipped open the letter inside. The light above the door cast a yellow glow on the paper.

"It's from Dr. Dean," she said. Michael shoved his hands into his pockets. He stood in the darkness, just beyond the ring of yellow light.

"What does it say?"

"It's the results of his examination on that skeleton. The one with the beads. A woman, he writes. Petite—around five feet tall. Age eighteen to twenty-one. Probably very pretty with wide-spaced eyes and high cheekbones. She had a delicate nose, and a small gap between her two front teeth. Found in the grave: approximately fifteen hundred beads, high-topped patent leather shoes, small brooch at neck, eight matching buttons." Kitt glanced at Michael. "It was very rare that all the buttons matched."

He nodded.

"It says a gold and emerald ring encircled the third finger of her left hand." Kitt read the words in silence, then looked up.

"What is it, Kitt?" Michael moved into the halo of light.

"Dr. Dean writes that the woman's pelvic measurements indicate she would have been unable to bear a child successfully—and that her pelvic girdle was separated at the time of death. Probable cause of death, childbirth."

Michael leaned against the motel wall and studied his shoes. The flicker of neon from the motel sign turned them red, then yellow, then red again. He knew what he wanted to ask, but he wasn't sure Kitt was ready. She was looking fragile again, despite her boyish button-fly jeans and rugged leather work boots. It was as if the ostrich feather hat had transformed her into one of those pale, genteel Victorian women who fainted easily and needed lots of tender care.

The image wasn't accurate, of course. Kitt was still tough and rational. But since he had come back into her life, he had watched her slowly change. The hardened facade she wore at the beginning had begun to bend and lift. He wondered what the softening of Kitt Tucker would lead to—and he wasn't certain he was willing to cause the disintegration of her hard-won veneer. It could only leave her vulnerable to more hurt.

Still, if they were going to work together and solve the riddle—more important, if they were going to resolve their past—they would have to take some painful steps.

"Kitt," he ventured. She looked up from the letter, her brown eyes fathomless. "If the woman's pelvic girdle was too small, and if she did conceive and attempt to bear a child, and if she died in childbirth—wouldn't the child have died, too? Wouldn't the child have died…inside her? I mean, it doesn't make sense that Hod could be her son."

Kitt's face had gone rigid, devoid of emotion. "Unless somebody removed the baby immediately after the mother died," she said evenly. "I suppose Hod's father could have performed a sort of Caesarean section after he was certain his wife was beyond saving. It would have been a real act of courage."

"And love."

They both stood in silence, thinking about life and death. Michael watched his shoes change color. But he wasn't seeing his feet. He was seeing Kitt, sitting on that brown-and-gold checkered couch in their little trailer.

"Michael," she was saying, "I haven't been feeling the baby move lately." She was wearing that oversized white shirt of his, her stomach spread out almost to her knees and a look of panic in her eyes. "I think we should go to the doctor."

And then another picture formed. Kitt was lying on a stainless steel table, her arm over her eyes while the doctor listened to her stomach with his stethoscope. Her long brown hair had draped over the edge of the table and spilled almost to the floor. The doctor was looking at them with sad, gray eyes and saying, "I can't hear a heartbeat, Mrs. Culhane. We'll need to run some tests, but I'm afraid…"

"Good night, Michael." Kitt took hold of the doorknob. "I guess I'll see you Friday afternoon."

"Kitt—" He reached for her. She slipped past him into her room and shut the door.

No one actually lived at Santa Rita. The town itself had been razed nearly twenty years earlier to make way for the mile-wide, thousand-foot-deep, open-pit copper mine. Friday afternoon and evening Michael and Kitt drove from the southeast corner of New Mexico to the southwest corner, with plans to stay in Silver City.

Needing her vehicle so they could go their separate ways afterward, Kitt followed Michael's gray compact car in the Bureau of Reclamation pickup. The highway climbed over the Sacramento Mountains and descended to Alamogordo. Their route skirted White Sands National Monument with its vast stretch of crystalline gypsum dunes, then topped the southern end of the San Andres Mountains. They stopped for dinner in Las Cruces. Late at night they continued west, passing the town of Deming and the City of Rocks State Park before their two-car caravan finally pulled into a motel in Silver City in the Mogollon Mountains.

It had been a long drive alone, but Kitt knew a certain relief to have time to think. Her last three days in Catclaw Draw had been packed with work from sunup until late in the night. She had filled out the many necessary government forms to complete the project, checked twice on the monuments in Carlsbad and gone over all the notes with Dr. Dean before seeing him off. Finally she had worked hours writing up a preliminary report on her team's findings at the Muddy Flats cemetery.

She would have to stop back in Catclaw Draw after her vacation to oversee the placement of the monument and markers. But the project was all but complete, and she was able to leave town with a sense of satisfaction.

Kitt had seen nothing of Hod since the night at his home. Michael had not called, even though he had been only a half-hour drive to the south. She felt thankful for the respite from both of them.

One evening she had finally reached Dr. Oldham and explained the situation to him. Though skeptical, he had agreed to send the notes from his research to her address in Santa Fe. He speculated that the Muddy Flats skeleton belonged to another man entirely, and that certainly more than one person could fit the description of an Indian with two gold incisors.

Dr. Oldham's familiar voice, his stalwart logic and his reasonable doubts made Kitt wonder all over again what she was doing driving to Santa Rita with Michael Culhane. Like

Dave and Sue Logan, Dr. Oldham expressed loving concern for her well-being.

The more she thought about it, the more she felt sure she had been carried away on a wave of emotion. From the moment she had seen Michael, she had done any number of uncharacteristically flighty things—dancing in the street, trespassing on an old man's property and looking through his personal possessions, kissing her ex-husband in a piney forest. Even letting thoughts of God wander through her consciousness showed a definite alteration from her normal mindset.

She wasn't behaving at all like Dr. Kitt Tucker, head anthropologist-archaeologist for the federal Bureau of Reclamation in the tristate area. Time to get with the program, Kitt.

"Smell that fresh air." Michael stretched his arms as Kitt climbed out of her truck.

She shouldered her purse and passed him with the barest twitch of her eyebrows, unwilling to be taken in by the sight of his biceps bunching beneath a green cotton T-shirt. When she stepped onto the motel's porch, he followed, lagging behind as she entered the office.

"Two rooms," she told the sleepy-looking clerk. "Tucker and Culhane. I reserved them three days ago by phone from Catclaw Draw."

The man scratched his head and ran his finger down the list of registrations. "Who'd you talk to? Me?"

"I don't know. It was a male voice."

"Probably Gene. He's only put you down for one room. It's under the name Culhane."

Kitt felt Michael brush up behind her and lean over her shoulder. "Problems?"

"They've only reserved one room."

"Nope," Michael said firmly. "We need two."

The clerk glanced from one to the other. "Well, I think I

got some vacancies. Let me see… Okay, no problem." He wrote her name beside the number of an empty room. "That Gene. I gotta talk to that boy. He's always doing this to me."

In a few minutes they had registered and settled into separate rooms. As Kitt climbed into bed, she realized she was listening for the murmur of Michael's television, the hiss of his shower, the thump of his headboard against the wall. But Michael and his comforting presence were in a distant room, across the empty motel swimming pool.

As Michael opened his door to the knock from outside, the sun peeked over the edge of the motel roof. The scent of mountain pine, piñon and juniper hung in the crisp morning air. Kitt stood on the sidewalk, her purse clutched protectively in front of her.

"I thought this was your vacation," he said, squinting in the brightening dawn. "You used to sleep till noon on Saturdays."

She shrugged. "I guess a person can change a few habits in fifteen years. You ready?"

"Hang on a second." Leaving the door open, he padded across the floor to the bathroom. Taking a towel from the stack held by stainless steel rings, he rubbed his hair, still damp from his morning shower. In the mirror, he could see Kitt standing outside. She glanced from the rumpled bed to the single chair piled high with his bags. Gingerly, she leaned against his doorframe.

"I bet you'd sleep till noon again if you could relax," he called over his shoulder.

"I'm relaxed." Her shoulder barely met the edge of the frame. Her back was ramrod straight.

A chuckle tiptoed down his chest. "So, Kitt. How'd you sleep anyway?"

"Fine." She glanced at him and then looked away again quickly.

He didn't know why it pleased him to make her uncomfortable. Maybe because he felt a similar off-kilter dizziness in her presence. "My bed was lumpy," he informed her. "Guess I'm just like the prince who slept on a pea that nobody else could feel."

"It was a princess who slept on a pea."

He grabbed his jacket and crossed the room to where she stood. "The same princess who let her long hair down from the tower so the prince could climb up?"

When he brushed a tendril of brown hair over her shoulder, she shivered visibly. "That was a different princess. You're thinking of Rapunzel."

He looked into her eyes. "That's not who I'm thinking about, Kitt."

She met his gaze and couldn't hold back a smile.

"What's so funny?" he asked.

"Just picturing you in a pair of leotards."

"But you never wanted a prince, did you?"

"I think I might have. Someone to rescue me from my parents' suffocation and protect me from dragons and sorcerers."

Her words saddened him. How badly he had failed this woman. "I could become a prince, if that's what you want."

"No, Michael. I'm definitely past my Rapunzel stage."

"Maybe you've always dreamed of a cowboy. That's what I used to think. You wanted a cowboy, and that's why you fell in love with me."

"Michael, please."

"You did fall in love with me, you know."

"Are you ready, or are we going to talk in this doorway all day?" She shifted her purse strap to her other shoulder.

"You know what I was thinking about this morning, Kitt?"

"I don't have a clue."

"Remember how we used to pray together? Before the baby stopped moving and the trouble with our folks came crashing in? We would sit at the table in our trailer and pray before every meal. We hadn't been going to church in those days, but we did pray together. You started it. One morning at breakfast, you took my hands and asked to me bless the food. You said that was the man's job, to lead his family spiritually."

Unable to hold back, he slipped his hands down her arms and clasped her fingers.

"I do remember," she said, her voice low. "I had heard someone say it in Sunday school, and it sounded so good. But that was when you were still my prince."

"I was never good enough or strong enough for you. I didn't know how to be a husband. We were teaching each other, Kitt. We were young, but we were learning what the other needed. And then it all blew apart. How did we let that happen?"

"Michael." Kitt pressed her thumbs into the flesh of his hands. "You're breaking the rules, you know."

"What rules? I've had three days by myself to do nothing but think, and all I've been able to concentrate on is us."

Kitt shook her head. "There is no *us*. Not anymore."

"You're wrong. We were one. God united us forever."

"God abandoned us."

"No, Kitt. Life went wrong, and it does that. A lot. But God didn't turn His back on either of us. He wanted us strong. He wanted us together. He still does."

"Michael, do you really believe that?"

For the first time, he saw a flicker of hope in her eyes. Cynical disdain evaporated, and shining expectation took its place. And then, just as swiftly, she snuffed it.

"We're never going to get to Santa Rita by nine o'clock," she said, pulling her hands from his. "We need to get going, Michael."

Dazed, he watched her stride across the parking lot to the car. A blanket of chill morning air slammed into him where once her warmth had filled the empty space. For an instant, she had revealed herself, flung open the doors of her heart to him—almost as if ready once again to become a part of the man she had vowed to forget.

He rubbed his hand over his eyes, trying to pull back. Had he said too much? Did he really believe God wanted to bring them together again? In marriage?

The truth was, Michael had no idea what the Lord wanted where Kitt was concerned. So caught up in memory and emotion, he had done his best to pray about the situation. And yet he got no clear answer. Over and over, he had asked God the same question. What harm could there be in loving Kitt again? The query ran through his mind on an endless loop. What harm?

Now, just when he had almost reached her, some half-buried animal instinct for self-preservation reared its head. Or maybe, finally, he was hearing the voice of the Holy Spirit.

What harm? Take a look at the harm you reaped once before, Michael. Take a look at the consequences of your heady passions. What would you gain from pursuing Kitt? Why not touch her, hold her hands, kiss her? Because you would only want more of her—like you did before. You'd want to be with her again, to share in her life. But you're heading off to Beirut. Or Beijing. You're not going to be around long enough to learn how to be the man she needs. So let her go. Let her go now.

He licked his dry lips and pulled the motel door shut. He had left Kitt once. No matter what he had told her about his despair and the Gulf War and wanting to die without her— the truth was that he had deserted Kitt. He had abandoned her. Left her all alone in that battered trailer with an empty crib and an empty heart.

Sure, you're drawn together, the voice inside him said. There's still that old physical attraction between the two of you. But you're no longer married. Despite what you want to think, you're not one in the eyes of God. Keep apart, Michael. Keep separate, or you're going to hurt her again. And she will hurt you, too. Why put either of you through that again? Once was plenty enough for one lifetime.

He shut his eyes and gritted his teeth. Who was speaking to him? Was God sending out these warnings? Or was Satan accusing and taunting him, discouraging the notion of trying to right the old wrongs? In the darkness of his closed eyes, Michael saw neither God nor the enemy. He could see only Kitt. Not the Kitt with sparkling eyes and laughter on her lips. Not the Kitt who bounced into his waiting arms.

It was that other Kitt. Sitting in the white rocking chair in the living room of their trailer. Rocking. Rocking. Eyes straight ahead, dull brown, glazed. Rocking. Rocking. Not saying anything. Not eating or taking a bath or brushing her hair. Not even looking at him. Just rocking and rocking. Her stomach huge with their baby inside. Their little baby who had died inside her. Rocking and rocking and waiting for their dead little baby to be born.

Through the car window Kitt observed the man standing beside his hotel door. Tall, handsome, he once had been everything she wanted. And now, all these years later, he had walked into her life in those jeans and that chambray shirt, and suddenly all she could think about was how much she still wanted him. One look at Michael Culhane and she might as well be a sighing princess in a fairy tale.

Frowning, she crossed her arms. What was he thinking about as he stood there alone? Why had he held her hands and talked about their marriage as though it hadn't ended after all? And why had she so wanted that to be true?

She wasn't Michael's wife anymore. He didn't have a claim on her. If she wanted to drive away right now and go back to her house in Santa Fe, she could. If she decided to marry someone else, nothing from the past could stop her.

Of course, Kitt wasn't about to do something like that. The truth of the matter was, she hadn't changed as much as she wanted to believe. Michael had always been the only man for her. From the moment they first laid eyes on each other in the hall of Clovis High School, she had lived in a state of perpetual craziness. There had been no other young men for Kitt once Michael took her on that first date. And he hadn't shown a flicker of interest in any other girl.

Not that they had completely withdrawn from life. Both enjoyed other friends—male and female. But it had always been Michael and Kitt. Michael and Kitt. Michael and Kitt from the very beginning.

She let out a hot breath. What had happened to tear them apart? And if it had happened once, it could happen again.

When Michael climbed into the driver's seat, Kitt was reading the newspaper.

"I like the story you wrote about the project," she said softly. "You left out the part about the skull with gold teeth."

He shrugged. "That's the real story. I hope I get to write it."

Kitt observed his long brown fingers as they turned the key in the ignition. Had she ever told him how much she loved the shape of his fingers? His nails were blunt and white and strong. His hands bore a subtle power in every movement.

Michael heaved a sigh and turned toward her. "It may be out of my control. I talked to the chief last night, and he wants Burton to take over the Black Dove story."

The news felt like a punch in the stomach. She swallowed. "I see."

"Burton wants to interview you."

"What about you?"

"My territory is the north. Albuquerque. Crime. Government. Didn't you ever see my byline?"

"Sorry. I avoid stories about the government. I get my fill of it with all the forms I have to complete."

"Reporters tend to guard their turf."

"So after this trip and whatever you find out, you're going to hand the story over to Burton?"

"That's what the home office thinks." Michael studied Kitt's face.

She carefully folded the newspaper, unable to speak the words forming in her throat. Stay, Michael. We'll work together. We'll figure it all out. Not just Black Dove. Us. We'll understand what happened to us and make it all be right again.

"I guess we'd better head out to the copper mine," she said.

Chapter Ten

❧

"It reminds me of an amphitheater," Kitt said in a hushed voice. "Or the Forum in Rome."

The enormous pit carved into the earth gaped before them in shades of rust, gold and taupe. Tier upon tier of terraces marched down, narrowing into a crudely shaped bowl. Innumerable roads curved through the bottom of the pit, circling water-filled crevices. Steam shovels and huge trucks crawled along the roads, digging ore and transporting it to the reduction mill at the southwest end of the pit.

"It's like something from outer space," she commented. "It just doesn't seem to belong in the middle of these mountains."

Standing beside her, Michael nodded. "I wonder if it was as huge and unearthly in Black Dove's time."

"No. Back then, narrow shafts were dug down to the copper veins. The open pit wasn't started until around 1910."

At the sound of rocks crunching on the shelf of the observation point, Kitt turned. A middle-aged woman wearing sturdy walking shoes, a flower-printed dress and a blue scarf tied under her chin lifted a hand in greeting.

"I'm with the copper mining museum. My name is Mrs. Lujan. May I help you?"

"I'm Dr. Kitt Tucker with the Bureau of Reclamation and this is Michael Culhane with Affiliated Press. We're working on a project, and we were wondering where we might find the oldest records of the mine's operation."

Mrs. Lujan joined them at the double metal rail overlooking the mine. "You're going to have trouble there, I'm afraid. The Kneeling Nun Mine has changed hands so many times. Some of the companies took an interest in the history, and some didn't. A lot of the old records have been destroyed."

Kitt's heart sank.

"But we do have a nice recording about the mine's past," the woman offered. "You just go up to the museum and press that little red button on the panel by the door."

"Actually, we're interested in the very early history of the mine. Back when James Kirker was here."

"Oh, James Kirker!" Her dark brown eyes sparkling, Mrs. Lujan smiled at Kitt. "Now I see you do know your history, Dr. Tucker. The Kneeling Nun Mine dates back to 1800, when copper ore was first discovered here. Later the Mexican government operated a penal colony on the site. They built a triangular prison fort with round towers at the corners and thick adobe walls between. Native American slaves and Mexican convicts mined the copper. But I'm telling you, it was bad in those days."

She chuckled and shook her head. Kitt began to think perhaps Mrs. Lujan could help them. The woman had a love of history—the sense of its vitality and immediate presence—that Kitt often noticed in kindred spirits.

"The slaves worked in dark, cramped tunnels digging out the ore and pulling it up in baskets." Mrs. Lujan leaned forward against Kitt's shoulder, as if giving her a great secret. "When they were digging the big open pit almost a hundred years later, they found artifacts and skeletons down in the shafts, you know. Some of those poor slaves had been buried alive."

Kitt grimaced. "The shafts had collapsed on them?"

"*Claro*. I'm telling you, the slaves had these old leather bags to haul up the ore. And they used to climb up notched poles called chicken ladders. It was a pitiful situation."

"And the copper was carried by trains of horses to Chihuahua?"

"Burros. Burro trains carried the copper to Mexico to be minted into coins. Then in 1837 a fellow named John James Johnson did a terrible thing. We've got two or three legends about it, of course. But I'm telling you what most people think happened. John James Johnson, who was a part-time scalp hunter, got a brilliant idea of how to kill Apaches. He invited all the braves, women and children to a big feast in the fort. They filled up with food and liquor. Then Johnson told them they could go into the courtyard and take away all the ground corn they could carry off."

She paused dramatically.

"So what happened?" Michael asked.

"John James Johnson had buried a cannon in the middle of the food pile. While all the Apaches were grabbing cornmeal, somebody lit that cannon and blasted all those people with nails and bullets and metal shot. The Apaches who weren't killed tried to run away—and Johnson's men fired on them with muskets."

"A massacre."

"More than three hundred murdered. Evil and shameful, if you ask me."

"No doubt the Apaches began to attack the copper trains even more ferociously than before."

"*¡Claro que sí!* I would be angry, wouldn't you?" Mrs.

Lujan pushed a tendril of glossy salt-and-pepper hair firmly into her scarf. "So when the Apaches attacked again and again, the owners of the mine had to call James Kirker and his boys to kill and scalp them."

"Ulp." Michael felt an urge to rub the top of his head.

"That's what James Kirker and Black Dove and the others did?" Kitt asked, the reality of the situation sinking in. Black Dove—for all his bravado and mystique—wasn't much more than a mercenary murderer.

"We're talking about brutal people here," Mrs. Lujan explained. "Of course, the Apaches were brutal, too. They kept attacking those burro trains and killing everyone and stealing the copper. It's hard to say who started it first, and who was the most cruel."

"Did the mine keep records of the hiring of Johnson and Kirker, and all their activities?" Kitt asked.

"There are a few things over at the mine's main office in Hurley. But you aren't going to find anything that's not written down in the history books. They already pitched out the stuff that they decided wasn't important." She frowned at the huge mine.

"Are the records at the main office open to the public?"

"Some are, some aren't. But like I say, lots of it was thrown away." She frowned. "Come to think of it, a few years back I went through and picked up some of those old papers they were getting rid of. I thought the museum might want to have them, you know. But then I put them away somewhere and to tell you the truth, I never thought about them again until this minute. I didn't figure they could be too valuable."

Kitt's pulse sped up. "Do you suppose we could have a look at those old records?"

"Oh, my, let me think now. Where did I put the boxes?" She closed her eyes and tapped her chin. "Where, where, where?"

Kitt felt like she was at a football game, willing a touchdown with her whole body and her entire power of positive thinking. She leaned forward on the rail, as if she could push the memory of the salvaged records to the front of Mrs. Lujan's mind.

"Probably in the back room," the woman said. Her dark brown eyes flashed. "You want to go look?"

"Absolutely." Michael gave Kitt a victorious grin.

The Kneeling Nun Mine museum was little more than an outpost perched near the edge of the vast open pit. Mrs. Lujan pressed the button on the little panel she was so proud of, so her guests could listen to the already familiar recounting of the mine's history. For several minutes she rummaged around in her back room, clucking over the stacks of unmarked boxes and wondering aloud where, where, where she had put the old records.

"Got it!" She emerged at last, triumphantly carrying a torn cardboard baby-food carton full of tattered file folders. "It was beside the drinking fountain under my knitting. I bet I've looked at it every day for three years!"

Kitt and Michael descended on the box like a pair of vultures. Mrs. Lujan crossed her arms and watched in satisfaction as they sifted through file after file.

"I have a bunch of old medical records from the 1930s here," Kitt said.

"This one is full of medical records, too. Looks like it's from a few years earlier."

"Was there a hospital here, Mrs. Lujan?"

"We had a mission near Santa Rita for a while. Nuns, you know. I guess they took care of the sick. And then there was a small clinic for a few years. People came when they had breathing problems. There was a sanatorium at Fort Bayard. Lots of people stayed here for their health. Still do. Most of the mine workers went to doctors in Silver City for treatment."

Kitt shuffled disappointedly through more files. There appeared to be nothing more in the box than medical records. Michael stuffed two folders back in the carton and took out another.

"Medical records," he said, lifting his eyes. "Was this the only box, Mrs. Lujan?"

"It's the only one I saved. They had a bunch of them to destroy, you know. They didn't want me to take even one box, but I told them I was from the museum. One fellow and me, we really had a scuffle over it. This was the only one I could grab before they made me leave."

Kitt grinned, picturing the stout little Mrs. Lujan waging a tug-of-war with some burly maintenance man over her file box. It never failed to appall her how little understanding most people had of the value of historical records. Yet often there appeared someone like Mrs. Lujan, someone with a grasp on the ephemeral nature of history to act on its behalf.

"Hang on to these files, Mrs. Lujan," Kitt said. "Somebody's going to put them to good use one day. I'm sure your fight to save them was worth it."

"They don't have anything you want?" A note of disappointment hung on her words.

"I'm afraid not. We're looking for employment files. Records of James Kirker's stay at Santa Rita."

"There are some good books on him, you know," Mrs. Lujan said in a helpful tone.

"Actually, we're trying to find out about one of Kirker's men. A fellow by the name of Black Dove. He was a Shawnee warrior."

"Black Dove. I've heard of him. Two gold teeth?" Mrs. Lujan tapped her own incisors.

Kitt nodded. "Well, shall we head over to the mine office, Michael? Maybe they'll let us see what they have."

Mrs. Lujan waved goodbye, her blue scarf drifting around her face.

* * *

The town of Hurley lay fifteen miles from the Kneeling Nun Mine. The offices were scattered over several blocks, and it took a while before they were able to find the public relations department. The woman there referred them to two books on the mine and one on James Kirker—all of which Kitt and Michael already had read. The records were closed to the public, the clerk said apologetically, but all the important historical information had been culled and given to historians. The rest of the early records had been disposed of a number of years ago. She suggested they speak with the director of the Silver City Museum.

Disappointment almost palpable in her mouth, Kitt rode with Michael the fifteen miles to Silver City. They ate a quick lunch, then drove to the redbrick building with its cupola and Victorian mansard roof. The local museum was a treasure trove of nineteenth-century furnishings, as well as Southwestern artifacts.

"We're looking for early mine records." Kitt heard herself repeating the now familiar query to the museum director. "We are specifically interested in James Kirker and his scalp hunters. Black Dove in particular."

The woman shook her head. "I'm afraid the mine owners destroyed most of the records. You might try the Silver City library. It's just down the street."

There, the head librarian walked them through stacks of journals and periodicals that mentioned the mine—most of which were recent and nearly all of which Kitt had read. He offered to let them borrow the historical books on the mine, but Kitt was sure they would tell her nothing new about Black Dove.

"Well, thank you for your time," she said.

"I'm sorry I couldn't be more help. The Kneeling Nun Mine has changed hands several times. The owners destroyed many of the old records."

"So we've heard," Michael concurred.

They nodded to the librarian again and started for the door. From a small office beside the checkout desk a young woman ran toward them, a scrap of pink paper fluttering in her hand.

"Dr. Tucker?" she called in a stage whisper that drew curious glances from several patrons. "Ma'am, are you Dr. Tucker?"

Kitt swung around. "I'm Kitt Tucker."

"Thank goodness." She paused, out of breath, and unfolded the pink note. "Mrs. Lujan from the Kneeling Nun Mine museum called. She was really agitated because she'd called everywhere trying to track you down. She told me to look for a woman with long brown hair and a handsome blond man."

Michael straightened his shoulders. "Well, that must be us."

Kitt rolled her eyes. "So what did Mrs. Lujan want?"

"I'm not sure. The message got kind of garbled because she was going on and on about how long it took her to find you. But she kept repeating she had found it, she had found it. She wants you to go out to the museum."

"All the way back to the mine?"

"That's what she said."

Kitt turned to Michael. "What do you think?"

"She must have found something she thought we'd be interested in. Come on. Let's go."

The sun perched just above a mountain as they drove the winding road to the Kneeling Nun Mine. On one particularly tight curve, Michael took the opportunity to glance at Kitt's face. She had that familiar stubborn set to her jaw. Her dark eyes practically flashed as she surveyed the landscape. Again there was that fascinating incongruity about Kitt—she spoke in a clipped, professional tone; she held her body almost rigidly under control, back straight, chin high; she hardly gestured when she talked.

And yet over that thirty-two-year-old independent woman

suit of armor, Kitt wore a cloak of softness. Her long hair swung gently at her shoulders with the smooth flow of her movements. A full denim skirt fell almost to her ankles and was cinched at the waist with a heavy silver concho belt. Her almost fragile shoulders were clad in a soft blouse. Turquoise-colored flats on her feet seemed to whisper as she walked.

Michael wanted to draw her to him and hold her tightly to his chest. Yet he knew that if he pressed too far, held her too close, the sharp spikes of her protective armor would pierce him through her outer softness.

Once in the Gulf, Michael's commanding officer had found him sitting alone in his tent while the other men played cards in the main barracks. After a brief talk, the officer had instructed him to speak with the company chaplain about "that gray cloud he carried around."

The bearded chaplain had given Michael a pliant foam ball and told him to squeeze it as tightly as he could. But when Michael began to wad the ball up in his palm, an open paper clip buried deep inside the foam poked into his hand. "Be like this ball, Culhane," the chaplain had told him. "Moldable, adaptable and sensitive to others. But keep a point at which you start to push back. Wear some protection underneath, and you'll be a lot better off."

At the time, Michael had thought squeezing a foam rubber ball a sorry excuse for help to a young man who had lost his marriage, his wife and his child. It had taken a few years, but he had grown his own steely core after all—and so had Kitt.

Wondering if God intended them to stay that way, he turned the car into the parking lot in front of the museum. Mrs. Lujan burst through the front door, waving her arms with excitement. She had forgotten her blue scarf and her neat bun threatened to fall apart as she ran.

"You came! Thank goodness." Huffing, she caught Kitt's

arm, dragged her out of the car and began to haul her toward the museum.

"Mrs. Lujan, what have you discovered?"

"You wouldn't believe the trouble I had to find you. First I called the mine office in Hurley. They said they had told you to go to the museum. Then I called there and you had already left. I thought I would never track you down!"

Michael leaped to open the front door and Mrs. Lujan barreled through, Kitt in tow. "So what did you find?" he asked.

"At the museum, they told me they had sent you to the library. I called over there and all I got was this young girl who sounded like she didn't know anything. The librarian was busy guiding people around, so then I just gave up and left a message to tell you to come back here if the girl saw you. I can't believe you came!"

"Here we are, Mrs. Lujan." Kitt leaned across the neat desk with its guest register and donation jar. "What have you found?"

"I got this!" She swept open the top drawer of the desk and held up a tattered file folder just like the others they had already looked through.

"What's in it?" Kitt tried to sound excited.

"It's the medical records from those years when Kirker was guarding the Kneeling Nun Mine. The 1830s!"

"Really?" Michael glanced at Kitt, still unable to imagine there could be anything of value in the folder. "Do they mention Kirker?"

"Not him. I got your man right here. Black Dove."

Michael and Kitt lunged for the file at the same time, but Mrs. Lujan whisked it away. Setting the folder on her desk, she carefully turned through the yellowed papers.

"After you left, I got to searching through the box," she said. "I got to thinking that I should know what was in there, in case somebody else ever came looking. You said someone might, and I thought it would be a good idea to know what I had, just in case."

Michael hung over the edge of the desk, practically salivating while Mrs. Lujan primly turned page after page.

"Here." She slapped the paper. "It says right here that the Shawnee brave Black Dove was a patient of a Dr. Miller in August of 1838. He was nineteen years old, six feet four inches tall, weighed two hundred pounds. A big fellow!"

Michael put his arm around Kitt's shoulders. He could feel the sense of relief and pleasure flowing through her as Mrs. Lujan spoke.

"Black hair, it says here. Dark brown eyes. Doesn't say one thing about two gold teeth. How about that? It's all you ever hear of Black Dove. But this doctor doesn't mention the teeth."

"Why did Black Dove go to the doctor?" Michael asked.

"Dr. Miller must have written this part. It's hard to read—you know how doctors always have that terrible handwriting?"

"Yes."

"He says Black Dove was brought in on horseback after an Apache raid on the copper train. He had one spearhead and part of a shaft impaled in his thigh. The thighbone was broken, it says. The doctor wrote that he was able to get the spearhead out of the thigh and close the wound. He plastered the broken leg."

"So Black Dove wasn't invincible." Michael suddenly felt a sense of reality about the warrior. The Native American was no longer just the stuff of legend. He understood in a way the work the young man had done—the actual attacking and killing and scalping of other human beings. And he knew that at least once Black Dove had been badly wounded.

"There's one more thing here," Mrs. Lujan said, squinting at the paper. She held it up to the light. "Oh, yes. Black Dove had a knife tip broken off in his scapula. What's the scapula—some embarrassing part we shouldn't talk about?"

"It's the shoulder blade, Mrs. Lujan."

"The knife was buried two inches deep in the bone of the scapula, Dr. Miller writes. He tried, but he couldn't get the knife tip out of the bone. So he left it in. Can you imagine going around with a knife tip stuck in your shoulder?"

Mrs. Lujan lifted her head and smiled. "Does that help you?"

Michael squeezed Kitt's shoulder so tightly she let out a little yelp. "That helps, Mrs. Lujan," she said. "That helps a lot."

"I still can't get over it." Kitt strolled beside Michael down the streets of Silver City's central historic district. Sturdy brick Victorian homes stood in the lamplight, like old ladies waiting for a dance. The moon hung white and full over the cusp of the mountain range surrounding the city.

"What can't you get over—that you're walking along in the moonlight with your handsome husband?"

"You're not my husband, Michael."

"Aw, c'mon. Can a little piece of paper really sever the marital bond between two people who loved each other?"

Kitt glanced at the tall man beside her. She could hear the teasing tone in his voice, but it made her uncomfortable that he would speak of their marriage as though it were still in force.

After leaving Mrs. Lujan at the museum—and with photocopies of Black Dove's medical record in hand—they had returned to their motel to freshen up for dinner. Somehow out of the cloth sport bag he hauled around, Michael had managed to extract yet another pair of freshly pressed blue jeans and a white shirt. A pair of tan roper boots and a fancy buff-colored Stetson completed the outfit. Now more than ever, Kitt had the sense that the old Michael walked beside her—the former familiar Michael mingled with the new, intriguing man he had become.

"I suppose if a small piece of paper can link two people

in marriage," she mused, "another piece of paper can just as easily break the bond."

"But you don't really believe that."

"Why not?"

"You haven't married again, have you?"

"I haven't found the right man."

"Until now. It took a while for me to find you."

"Michael, please." Kitt shook her head. How long was he going to keep this up? "You weren't even looking for me when you found me. Now let's get back to the subject at hand."

"You and me."

"Black Dove. I can't believe he was in that grave at Muddy Flats. I mean, it just doesn't fit. And yet, all the pieces are there. The skeleton has two gold teeth. It belonged to a Native American, and it matches the height and build description in Mrs. Lujan's report. And there's that knife tip in the scapula. That cinches it. It has to be Black Dove."

"So what's the problem?"

"He's buried in Mexico, Michael."

"Did it ever occur to you that your beloved Dr. Oldham might have been wrong just once?"

"But you don't know Dr. Oldham. He wouldn't make a mistake like that. As his assistant, I helped him research the paper he wrote on white scalp hunters. Scholars consider it a definitive work on the subject. To date, no one has found a single error. That doesn't surprise me. Our investigations and studies of the subject are compiled into huge, comprehensive files. Even though Black Dove played a peripheral role in the history of white scalp hunters, Dr. Oldham and I carefully examined all primary and secondary sources about him. And I remember that Dr. Oldham made inquiries in Guadalupe Y Calvo. Someone told him that Black Dove was buried there."

"If Black Dove is buried in Mexico," Michael said slowly, "then who was buried in the Muddy Flats cemetery?"

"I don't know. I can't figure it out."

They wandered past an Italianate redbrick home and stopped at a tall archway. "Big Ditch Park," the sign read. From the arch, a long wooden bridge stretched across what looked exactly like a big ditch. Victorian-style lamps lit the expanse, casting a yellow light on large green trees and the well-groomed lawn leading down to the ditch.

"This ditch used to be the main street of Silver City," Michael said as they started across the bridge. "In the early 1900s, a series of floods washed the street away along with most of the homes."

"How did you know that?"

"I read the sign back there on the post."

Kitt had to laugh. "Here I am admiring your vast knowledge."

"Admire away. No telling what else you'll walk right past without me to guide you."

"I've gotten around fine for fifteen years."

Michael paused and leaned on the wooden rail of the footbridge. "You're walking right past all the signs about Black Dove."

"I want to be careful, Michael. Allow me that."

Kitt rested her elbows on the rail and followed the curve of the ditch with her eyes. Michael took off his hat, running the brim across his palm. The yellow lamplight coated the round muscle of his shoulders and carved deep shadows in his face. She could see his tanned fingers rotating the hat, and she could feel his mind working. Part of her wanted to know what he was thinking—and part of her already did.

It was their last night together. Somehow they had been brought together, and within a few hours they would be pulled apart again. Funny how, at first, she could hardly wait until he left. Now she wasn't ready for this moment. Things needed to be said. Ends needed to be tied up. Yet she felt afraid of all that—as if in finishing up their past she would truly lose him once and for all.

She knew she didn't want him...at least she didn't want to start something that could hurt her even worse. But she also knew she didn't want to let him go again. Not just yet.

"What are you planning to do, Kitt?" he asked. His voice had deepened, roughened.

"About what?"

"Tomorrow." He turned the hat in his hands again.

"I'm driving to Santa Fe in the morning," she told him. "I have to finish the reports for the relocation project, plus I need to start on the ditch research. My supervisor wants it in three weeks. What about you?"

"I'm due in Albuquerque early Monday. The governor's holding a press conference there. Education, teachers' salaries, all that. There's something going on about animal control, too."

"I'll have to start watching for your stories in the paper."

"Yeah."

Kitt picked at a splinter of wood. At the moment, she felt she could probably tear down the whole bridge splinter by splinter for all the tension shooting through her arms and back. Michael just kept turning his hat.

"I have a dog," she said, trying to fill in the uncomfortable silence. "He stays with my boss's family when I'm out of town."

"What's his name?"

"Apollo. He's incredibly unintelligent."

He laughed. "You got him from the pound, didn't you?"

She nodded.

"Remember that dog we used to have? You got him at the pound, too."

"Joker. He died about five years ago."

"You kept Joker?" He turned to her.

"Of course I did. He was our dog."

"Kitt."

Michael turned and gathered her gently to him. She came, still trying to remain stiff and distant. *You don't just go off and leave a dog because you're having a little trouble,* she wanted to hurl at him. *You don't just go off and leave your wife, either.*

"Thank you for taking care of Joker all those years," he murmured into her hair.

She closed her eyes and leaned her forehead on his shoulder. He was going to say sweet things—she could just feel it. And if he said tender words, she was going to melt. She was going to forget the hurt he had brought her. She felt torn in two, wanting his tender words and his loving touch, wanting to run away and hide from him.

"Michael," she began. She lifted her head and looked into his blue-gray eyes. But he didn't say the tender words she had expected.

Instead, he drew her close and kissed her. His lips moved over hers with the longing of many empty years. His hands wound through her hair, holding and caressing it as if he could not get enough.

She caught her breath. His touch bore the indelible stamp of man. Not the fumbling teenager, this was the new adult Michael.

He pushed her hair aside and bent to kiss her neck. His mouth moved down her skin, his breath warm. How could she resist him? He was the man she had always desired.

Chapter Eleven

❧

Hardly aware of the trickle of water beneath the bridge or the rustle of birds settling in the trees for the night, Michael knew only the trace of Kitt's breath in his ear. They were alone, no passersby at this late hour. She ran her fingers down the valley of his spine.

"Kitt." At the touch, her name escaped him like a low groan.

He wrapped his hands around her shoulders as he kissed her. She smelled of flowers, and he breathed deeply. Unable to think beyond the moment, he took her hand and pulled her along the bridge away from the yellow glow of the lamplight and into the deep black privacy of a giant juniper tree. She went willingly, her head tucked against his shoulder.

The summer grass felt soft and cool as Michael eased down beside Kitt. Nothing mattered but this moment, this woman. He looked into her eyes, shadowed by darkness.

"Michael," she whispered. "I missed you so much."

Feeling that he was about to come apart with emotion for the woman who had been his wife, he gazed down at her. They did belong together, as they had so many years ago. The passion between them was no different now—the same two people, the same closeness. Only the consequences had broken them apart.

Consequences.

A flood of emotion washed over him like a chilling wave. Michael stiffened. What was he doing? What was he thinking? He longed for her again, as a man should long for his wife. But did he have any right to hold her in that way? He had made vows that were more powerful even than his wedding vow. He had given his life, his heart, his very soul to Jesus Christ. Could he now discount all that in a rush of heedless yearning?

"Michael?" Kitt's voice was soft. "Michael, I'm feeling so many things right now. Being near you is amazing. Wonderful. But I'm afraid, too. Last time…last time, look what happened."

"Consequences," he mumbled. He willed control of his body as his mind reached for God. When she didn't respond, he shook his head. "Kitt, I think we're meant to be together. And I know we want each other."

She nodded, biting her lower lip. "But it has to be right."

"I know. We can't just—" He broke off and stared into the gnarled branches of the juniper tree. So much pain lay behind them. So much could lie ahead. In the past, their love had brought the baby. And anger. Fear. Sorrow. Death.

Closing his eyes and clenching his jaw, Michael prayed for the powerful drive inside him to subside. "Do you remember the day after we got married, Kitt?" he asked her.

"I try not to think about the past."

"Your parents told you they were sending you away to boarding school in Virginia."

When she hung her head, he took her in his arms and

drew her close. "We hadn't found the trailer yet, and you were still living at home. You came to me that night—you drove out to the farm—and knocked on my bedroom window," he said. "It was raining. You were wet and crying. I climbed outside and we held hands and just walked and walked through the dark mist. I didn't even know where we were. You told me about the boarding school and how angry your parents were that we had gotten married without telling them. Remember?"

"I don't want to remember."

"But you do remember. We felt like we weren't ever going to see each other again…just like tonight."

It was all true. They had held each other as if their world were coming to an end. Michael had felt there was nothing on earth more important than that moment—that beautiful girl in his arms.

"And then you found out you were going to have our baby." Michael's words brought out the finality of the situation. "We both wanted that baby more than we'd ever wanted anything, didn't we, Kitt?"

"Yes." She swallowed hard, as if to erase the quaver in her voice.

They had wanted the baby, he thought as he held her close. They had wanted each other. But the baby had died and something inside Kitt had died, too. Everything fell apart. This time, Michael vowed to himself, they would bring God into the equation.

He stood and pulled Kitt to her feet. "Let's go back to the motel, honey."

"I plan to see you again, Kitt." Michael leaned against the motel door frame looking much as he had that first night in Catclaw Draw.

"I don't think it's a good idea. We're just bad luck together."

"That isn't true." His voice held a familiar note of stubbornness. "We still need to talk. I believe we're supposed to be together, Kitt. I know we can stay strong until we work things out."

"Oh, Michael. All those silly rules. We might as well face the fact that when we're together things get out of control. We don't think."

"It was that way back then—" He drew a deep breath. "Listen, I've been praying a lot about us. I know we're legally divorced, but that's not God's best plan. He joined us, and He wants us together. Jesus said divorce was allowed in Moses' time because of the hardness of people's hearts. But my heart isn't hard, Kitt. It never was. It was crushed and torn and broken. But it was never hard. I don't believe yours was, either."

She heard what he was saying, but it made little sense. "I know we didn't have hard hearts, but we botched up our marriage. If God wanted us together, He never would have let our daughter die. If you don't believe God is cruel, you at least have to admit He's disinterested. He did nothing to save our baby. He did nothing to hold back our parents' anger. I can't understand why you give God so much power, Michael. He didn't protect our little family."

"He didn't save our baby's life, but He gave up His own life for me. I'll see our daughter again, Kitt. I'll hold her in my arms and play with her and love her. God has prepared all eternity for that baby girl and me to spend together. No, I don't have her now. But I do have Him. Don't you see why that's so much better?"

Kitt stared at Michael, wondering if she even knew him. Only minutes ago, she had been ready to believe they might have a future. But who was he? Where had this deep faith come from? More important, why did it give him such peace, such assurance, such strength? Why did his confidence in God make Michael even more appealing to her than ever?

"I need to think," she told him. "I don't want to face that

kind of pain ever again, and I don't trust God to protect me from it. I'm not sure why you do."

"God protects us, Kitt, but that's not His main goal. He wants us to grow stronger in Him. If we need to suffer in order to get where God wants us to be, then He'll allow it."

"I don't want a God like that in my life. Sorry." Though she spoke the words, she wasn't sure she really meant them. Kitt liked the ways in which Michael had changed. He *was* stronger. He was better. Had God done that? Could He do the same thing for her?

Michael settled his hat on his head and crossed his arms over his chest. "So I'm supposed to walk away and let you go again? Just like that?"

She tried to make herself nod, but she couldn't. The truth was too clear to both of them.

"I need to interview you again," he said. "For the Black Dove article."

She straightened in the open doorway. "I thought you said Burton—"

"Why do you think I came all the way to Silver City? I'm going to write up our findings."

Surprise coursed through Kitt. "Are you going to write that Black Dove is buried at Muddy Flats?"

"I plan to give all the evidence we unearthed. I'd say it makes a pretty strong case."

She wasn't comfortable with this at all. "I feel a story would be premature, Michael. We still have absolutely no motive for Black Dove being in New Mexico. And we do have a reason he was in Mexico. We also know that Dr. Old-ham's files state he died and was buried in Guadalupe Y Calvo."

"What else could you do to check that out, Kitt? Go to Guadalupe Y Calvo yourself?"

She shrugged. "I need to think it all over. That's how I work. I want to review the findings at the cemetery. Then I want to go back over original research that Dr. Oldham and I did together. I'd like to talk with him, as well. I'll probably reread the primary texts relating to the period and see what I can find. I have to be careful."

"Sometimes a person can be too careful, Kitt. So careful she might miss the opportunity of a lifetime." He touched her chin. "You know what I mean?"

She read the message behind his words. But she and Michael had separate lives now. As much as they were drawn to each other, she felt sure there could be nothing more between them.

In fact, she realized suddenly, she was afraid of Michael Culhane. He held a power over her heart that no man had ever held. She could so easily lose herself to him again. But she had worked too hard to find herself. And she had no guarantee that Michael wouldn't do the same thing to her that he had done before. When the going got rough, he might just walk out on her once more. Maybe all his talk of God's will was just hot air. Michael obviously had a talent for tracking down and getting what he wanted out of life. But he wasn't made of the stuff of commitment and marital permanence. At least—she didn't think he was.

"I think the past needs to stay where it is, Michael," she said. "In the past."

"I was seventeen years old," he reminded her. "Seventeen. I'm thirty-three now."

She glanced away, her eyes filling with tears for the first time since she'd seen him. Yes, he was thirty-three. But so little had changed between them. In a way, they were still exactly the same two kids—so ready to make the exact same mistakes.

"Michael," she said carefully. "I loved you once. And you loved me. Please let that be enough."

Without looking at him again, she turned and shut the door behind her. She stood in the darkness, fingertips pressed against her eyes, letting go. Letting go.

* * *

"You came back, Dr. Tucker!" Mrs. Lujan beamed with pleasure as Kitt entered the little museum early the following morning.

"I wanted to say goodbye and to thank you again. Your find added a lot to my study."

Kitt also wanted to walk through the museum one last time before she left for Santa Fe. It was here that Michael had held her so tightly, here that they had been united and joyful for the last time—no pain, only the pleasure of discovery and the fun of being together.

"I hope you've stored those records away safely."

"¡*Claro!* I already put them in a fireproof filing cabinet." Mrs. Lujan hurried around the desk, craning her head toward the window. "Where's your young man, Dr. Tucker?"

"Michael. Oh, he left for Albuquerque sometime this morning."

"You were not with him?" Mrs. Lujan knocked her head lightly with the heel of her palm. "Sometimes I am *loca*, you know? You made such a nice match to that young fellow, I thought you belonged together. He seemed to like you a lot."

She lifted her eyebrows hopefully. Kitt smiled and walked toward the huge picture window. "We're friends from many years ago."

"I see." Mrs. Lujan edged to Kitt's side, her sturdy leather shoes squeaking a little as she walked. She had on another flowered dress, this time pink. Her bun was knotted neatly at the nape of her neck.

"The mine looks almost pretty at this time of day," Kitt remarked. "All those shades of color."

"Did you see our kneeling nun?" Mrs. Lujan pointed to a nearby outcrop of rock. "You were so busy with Black Dove yesterday, I think I forgot to tell you the story of the kneeling nun. Do you see her there on the hill?"

Kitt focused in the direction Mrs. Lujan indicated where

a strange stone formation perched on the side of the hill. In silhouette, it resembled the figure of a robed and veiled woman, bent down on one knee. The nun gazed upward, her expression a mixture of rapture and sorrow.

"That's where the mine gets its name," Mrs. Lujan explained. "Isn't she sad?"

Kitt nodded, feeling almost as though her own face mirrored that of the nun.

"Do you know how she came to be made of stone?"

"Tell me, Mrs. Lujan."

"Legend says she was the youngest in the order of good sisters who ran a little hospital not far from here. One day a wounded soldier crawled into the adobe courtyard of the hospital. He was nearly dead and in terrible pain, so the sisters brought him inside and began to tend his wounds. The youngest of the nuns took care of the poor soldier very tenderly for many days until his wounds began to heal. That soldier began to talk with the little nun, and he told her that he had been on patrol. Apaches had ambushed the men and killed all but him. Him they left for dead in the hot sun."

"What a sad story."

"But I have not told you the ending. The little nun began to support the soldier as he walked around the courtyard to regain his strength. He told her he was from the East, a beautiful land of tall green trees and fertile farms. The sister also had grown up in the East, not far from the soldier's home. Gradually, without intending it, the soldier and the nun fell in love. The soldier begged her to go with him—back to the East where they both belonged. But she shook her head. How could she leave the work God had called her to do? The pain would be too great. She let the soldier leave and rejoin his troops, who were gathering just over the ridge.

"That evening when the moon rose, the little nun could not bear it any longer. She left the hospital and set out over the desert toward the ridge. But when she got there, the troops had gone. She could see the distant cloud of dust as they rode away. The little nun knelt to pray without the strength or the heart to return to the hospital. She knew she had broken her vows. She continued to pray through the night and into the next morning. Gradually, her shoulders, her arms and then her whole body turned to stone. And there she kneels, year after year, our little nun with the broken heart."

Kitt stared at the silhouette in the distance. "Do you think she should have gone with the soldier when he asked her, Mrs. Lujan? Even at the cost of such great pain and sacrifice and uncertainty?"

"What do you think, Dr. Tucker?" Mrs. Lujan reached out and laid her brown fingers over Kitt's hand. "It is for each of us to decide."

Her little adobe home on a Santa Fe side street beckoned Kitt more than she had ever remembered. Though it was summer, the night was chilly. One of her neighbors had lit a fire, and the musky smell of piñon smoke hung in the air. Kitt drove the Bureau truck into her driveway and began unloading her bags. She would pick up her dog, Apollo, from the Logans in the morning.

Wandering through the empty house, she felt a sense of comfort within its solid walls. She had decorated with a soft mixture of Southwestern and Victorian prints. Muted shades of terra cotta, turquoise and gray formed geometric designs on her sofa, chairs and the many wool rugs scattered throughout the rooms. Antique crocheted lace antimacassars covered tables and lampshades. The fragrance of cinnamon and cloves drifted around clay pots filled with potpourri. In a niche over the fireplace, a collection of silver bowls gleamed softly.

Kitt turned on some music and filled her kettle to make a cup of tea. Her back felt stiff from the hours of driving. Her head throbbed. She'd had too much time to think. Too much time to remember the way Michael's mouth curved higher on one side than the other when he smiled. Too much time to think of the way his strong arms had held her in the darkness beneath the juniper tree. Too much time to dwell on every single thing she once had liked about him—and to find that in spite of everything, she still liked him as much as ever. More than ever.

But that was over. It had to be. Kitt opened her leather portfolio and took out the paperwork she still had to complete. Rows and columns of words and figures swam before her eyes. She stared at them blankly. Why was it suddenly so quiet in her house?

Getting to her feet, she crossed the room and turned up the music. She pulled the teabag from her cup and stirred in milk and sugar. Stretching out on the couch, she leafed through the stack of pages. She could work on the Black Dove information if she wanted to. Dr. Oldham's notes ought to be in the pile of mail her landlord had stacked on the hall table while she was away.

She stared at her ceiling. It looked blank and empty. She felt exactly like the little, brokenhearted nun. Turned to stone for fear of taking the risk of love.

Michael's article on Black Dove didn't appear in the Santa Fe newspaper. Kitt searched for it every morning while she sat at her kitchen table in her robe. She saw his byline on a story about the governor's visit to Albuquerque. She read every word. His upbeat style of writing made politics actually interesting. He also wrote a recap of the legislature's recently enacted laws and their effects on northern New Mexico. She read all of that, too.

A week of her vacation went by, and Kitt spent every spare minute finishing the last details of her project report. The gray light of the computer in her office gleamed night and day. The printer rattled on through her scant lunches and carry-out dinners. Apollo, a large golden retriever mix, yawned as he lay at Kitt's feet. She knew he wanted to play, but she couldn't allow more than a half hour each day. Too much time to think.

Dave and Sue Logan invited her over one evening, but she declined. She had too much to do, she told them. Sue dropped by and asked her to go to the new exhibit at the folk art museum. Kitt said she was sorry, but she was really too busy. Sue left with a perplexed expression on her face.

Dr. Oldham had indeed sent copies of his pertinent research, accompanied by a scrawled message of concern. He wanted to meet for lunch one day and discuss her Black Dove findings. Kitt stuffed the files back in their envelope and left it on the hall table. Why had Black Dove seemed so important anyway? In Catclaw Draw things had gotten really confused. That was all there was to it. Things that should have been important weren't. And things that shouldn't have mattered at all suddenly had seemed crucial. She had lost her balance. But that was understandable. It wasn't every day one ran into one's ex-husband.

The more Kitt thought about Michael, the more she wanted to let him go. And couldn't. She began to fear that the depression she had experienced after their baby's death had come back to haunt her. Had saying goodbye to Michael all over again been that traumatic? She tried to think what it was about him that still clung to her heart, weighing her down and making her ache inside. There was no way to deny the physical attraction between them. The passing years hadn't diminished that one bit. During their marriage, passion had been the main glue holding them together. It certainly hadn't proved strong enough to withstand the storms that battered them.

As firmly as Kitt tried to tell herself that normal human emotion was all she had felt in Catclaw Draw and Santa Rita, she knew she was deceiving herself. There was something more about Michael. Maybe there always had been. He was strong. Intelligent. Thoughtful. Persistent.

And spiritual.

Now, that was new. Where had Michael's devotion to God come from? Confused, Kitt reflected on their conversations about God. She pondered his dedication to holy obedience. Was Michael's faith in Christ a crutch? Did it make him weak? Or was Kitt the immature one—rebelling and pouting like a child in her refusal to admit God's care for her?

As much as she hated to admit it now, Kitt couldn't deny evidence of His hand. True, her daughter had been stillborn and her marriage had dissolved. But it was also true that Kitt had known success—educationally, professionally, even socially. She had believed herself responsible for every good thing in her life, but now she wasn't so certain that God's gentle touch hadn't been there all along. Maybe He had even brought Michael back.

Distressed and confused, Kitt began to alternate work on her projects with time reading the old Bible she'd had since high school. As time passed, she slowly began to feel a little more normal. She went shopping for groceries and cooked herself a roast so she'd have food for a few days. She finally accepted a dinner invitation from the Logans and took Apollo along. She finished her report on the dig. One more trip to the new cemetery site, and that part of her life would be over. She took out her notes on the new ditch project. No matter what God had been up to in the past, she knew it was time to focus on the future.

Kitt pulled into her driveway, feeling a little too full on Sue Logan's *sopaipillas*. Though it was a Saturday night, she had turned down an offer of a late movie with one of her colleagues. She planned to take a hot shower and read for a while before going to bed.

It had been good to spend time with Dave and Sue. She

had laughed, recollecting old Hod and the trouble he had given her by persistently appearing on the site at Muddy Flats. Dave had shared some of the latest snafus with the new dam being built. Sue talked Kitt into going to the folk art museum the following afternoon. They would all attend church together—the Logans gave the worship service at their church rave reviews—and then eat a quick lunch before heading to the museum. No one had mentioned Michael, and it was just as well.

Kitt lifted her shoulders and took a deep breath as she fitted the key into her lock. Apollo, dancing with joy to be home, bounded into the foyer, pounced on the throw rug and skidded across the floor into the wall—just as he did every time they entered the house. Laughing at her goofy dog's inability to learn, Kitt noted that she had forgotten to turn off a light in the living room before leaving that evening. Unlike her. Probably a result of having her thoughts in too many places these days. She wandered into the kitchen and filled the kettle to make a cup of tea.

Pulling pins out of the topknot she had worn to dinner, she started down the hall to turn off the living room light. She realized she was humming one of the songs the choir had sung in the church she had attended as a child. When she turned the corner, she caught her breath. Around the edge of the door she saw a pair of men's leather boots and faded blue jeans stretched across an ottoman. A set of long fingers stroked through Apollo's golden fur.

"Hi, Kitt." Michael's long frame slowly unfolded from the couch. "I waited outside for about two hours, and it got a little cold. You'd left that front window open. Hope you don't mind that I came in to get warm."

Rigid with a mixture of waning fear and growing fury, Kitt stood stock-still in the hallway. She couldn't speak.

"You ought to be careful about leaving windows open, Kitt. I mean for all its Old World charm, Santa Fe is getting to be a big city. If you're going to bother locking your door, you probably ought to lock your windows, too."

"What are you doing here?"

It was all she could manage. The balance she had worked so hard to regain had suddenly slipped askew all over again. Here was Michael—in her living room. He wore a pale blue oxford shirt, open at the collar. Denim jeans and a thick cable-knit sweater gave him a soft, comfy appearance. He smiled at her, his eyes a dark blue in the lamplight.

"You had better stop climbing through my windows, Michael Culhane," she sputtered.

"How come you didn't look over Dr. Oldham's notes?"

"I mean it. If you climb through one more window of mine—"

"He's got some interesting stuff here. I can see where he got the idea that Black Dove stayed in Mexico."

Michael tossed the manila envelope onto Kitt's round oak coffee table. She wanted to be furious over his prying, but she couldn't summon anything but dismay. Why did he have to look so good on that sofa? She had bought it for herself. But with her dog panting happily at his side, he seemed very much at home.

"How did you find me, anyway?"

"I looked in the Santa Fe phone book and there you were. Kitt Tucker."

The kettle began whistling in the kitchen.

"You have no right to read my mail, Michael. Dr. Oldham's letter was addressed to me."

"Where have you been for three hours?"

"None of your business." Kitt walked past him and took a china teacup out of her corner cupboard.

"Did you go on a date?"

"Jealous?"

"Yes."

She faced him and saw the deadly serious expression on his face.

"Excuse me, I have a nightly routine." And you're not part of it, she added to herself.

Passing him again, she stepped down the hall. Her head felt light. Again she was torn in two and tripping over her emotions. Her heart pounded heavily as she poured boiling water over a bag of Darjeeling tea. He had come back. He had looked for her and found her. Michael had come back.

But she didn't want him. She'd made a second break—and even that had required some healing. If he kept coming back, she would have to keep losing him. Where did it end?

"Do I get a cup of tea, or am I being punished for climbing through your window?"

Kitt swung around. Michael Culhane was in her kitchen. He looked as though he belonged there, leaning comfortably against her refrigerator. The knitted diamonds on his cardigan complemented the geometric print in the wallpaper border. He blended.

"If you want some tea, the cups are in the corner cabinet in the living room."

She walked toward the refrigerator to get the milk. Michael leaned on it, not moving.

"You look beautiful tonight, Kitt."

"Oh, Michael," she said, letting out a deep breath. "Why are you here?"

He watched as her slender, tanned arm lifted the heavy milk jug from the refrigerator. Her silver bracelets clanked together. Kitt *was* beautiful. Too beautiful. Her hair draped across her shoulders. A colorful cotton belt cinched her dark purple dress. The full hem of her skirt swayed around her ankles.

Michael knew she hadn't been on a date. The calendar in her office was clearly marked with the dinner invitation to her boss's home. He had enjoyed walking through her house, looking at her things. She decorated the way she dressed—tastefully, but with a touch of the exotic.

Snooping was one of his best assets as a reporter. Michael could tell more about a person by studying his or her living quarters than most people could learn in a two-hour conversation. Kitt, he had confirmed, was organized, punctual and a little rigid. Her many shelves of books revealed eclectic tastes. She didn't like to cook. There was a sad-looking, half-eaten roast in the fridge, along with a couple of yogurt containers and a wilted salad.

He had noted with interest that she had only a single-sized bed in her master bedroom. She had pushed it into one corner and covered it with pillows, leaving little room for sleeping. An old Bible, open to Psalms, lay on a side table. The rest of the room had been turned into a second living room—two love seats, a potted palm and an Indian rug on the floor.

"If you're not going to get a cup, Michael, I don't see why you asked if you could have some tea." She was stirring an inordinate amount of sugar and milk into her own cup.

"I wanted to watch how you did that. It's sort of tea-flavored sweet milk now, isn't it?"

"I like it this way. You can do whatever you want."

Without casting him a backward glance, she stepped out of the kitchen into the hall. He followed her, took a cup and saucer from her collection in the corner cupboard, returned to the kitchen and filled it. Her refusal to serve him was expected. She was acting miffed—almost angry—but he knew it was a cover. Kitt had always been an open book to him. He could sense the mixture of hesitation and relief in her eyes.

"I like the way you've done your house, Kitt." He settled onto the couch with his tea. "You've been reading the Bible. I saw it on your beside table."

"My Bible…Michael, this is my home and my space. You had no right to intrude."

"But I had to come."

"Why?"

"I told you once, I'd come if you needed me."

"I don't need you."

"Yes, you do."

"I needed you when I was seventeen and you were my husband. That's when I needed you."

"I'm beginning to think what you really needed at seventeen was just what you got. Time to grow up. Time to find out who you were. I think I needed that, too, even though I didn't realize it."

"And now that I'm grown up and independent, you think I suddenly need you again?"

"Yes."

Michael stirred his tea. He knew Kitt felt awkward and maybe even a little scared finding him in her living room. Her eyes slid across to him, and then she looked away again. He decided he'd better get to the point.

"I've been doing a lot of thinking, Kitt. And the truth is, when you're as young as we were, the only kind of love you can really have is a needy love. We needed each other like two empty teacups. I needed you to fill me and you needed me to fill you. But really, in the end, we were both empty."

"I don't think we were empty. Not completely."

"We were empty of what we needed to make a marriage— maturity, goals, a sense of self. We certainly didn't give a thought to God or what He might want for us."

"What are you trying to say, Michael?"

He leaned back. "Now that I know myself and feel like I really don't need anybody, I think I'm just about grown up enough to make someone a pretty good companion for life."

Kitt stiffened. Her hand trembling slightly, she set the teacup on a side table and observed her fingers for a full minute. Michael knew he was right. And he could see that she knew it, too. She had needed to grow up. So had he. But was she ready—now—to allow him to walk beside her? Was she ready to step from the path she had believed was her own? Michael had been asking himself the same questions for a week, and by the time he had found Kitt, he knew the answers.

"Why did you come here, Michael?" she asked.

He slid a hand into his jeans pocket and took out a small envelope. "I came to bring you a present."

"What is it?"

"Open it."

She took the envelope and pulled back the loose flap. Inside lay two airline tickets. She drew them out and read the name of the destination on the typed itinerary.

Guadalupe Y Calvo, Mexico.

Chapter Twelve

❧

Guadalupe Y Calvo. Kitt knew what the tickets meant. They represented an offer from Michael. He hadn't written the story about Black Dove, as he'd told her he would. Now he was giving her one last shot at finding out the truth about the man buried in the Muddy Flats cemetery.

But there was more. Kitt lifted her head and met Michael's even gaze. These tickets would bring one more occasion for them to be together. One more opportunity to work through their past. A last chance to learn what a future might bring.

"I'm not going to walk away and leave you again, Kitt," he said. "And I'm not going to let you walk away, either. I'm going to keep finding ways to see you until we work it out."

"Until we work it out," she repeated. "And after we work it out, *then* you can walk away?"

"No."

"Then what? What's the deal, Michael? What are we

working out, anyway? We both know what happened to our marriage. I think we even understand why. So tell me what you want out of this. What do you want from me?"

"I don't know yet." He turned the teacup in its saucer. "I just know that when we're together, good things happen. I feel right. Don't you?"

"No. Yes. I feel confused. In some ways, I enjoy being around you. But on the other hand, you turn on a lot of negative tapes in my mind."

"Well, I'm glad you at least feel *something*." Smiling, he stood and patted her dog on the head. "You're going to have to erase the tapes, Kitt."

"That's not possible."

"I think it is. I'm erasing mine."

"How?"

"I'm recording over them. New stuff. Better stuff…with you." He walked past her, his leg brushing the side of her chair. "Got to run, Kitt. I need to finish up a story before we leave. I'll see you in the morning."

"Michael." She jumped up from her chair and followed him down the hall and out the door. "What are you talking about? I can't go anywhere tomorrow. I'll be at church with the Logans in the morning. And then I'm going to the museum. I'm not going to—"

"Our flight leaves at ten. It's the only one I could get that would connect with the puddle-jumper taking supplies into Guadalupe Y Calvo twice a week."

"Puddle-jumper…"

"See you at the airport at nine, Kitt." He lifted a hand as he ambled down her driveway toward his car. "On the flight, you can sing me that hymn you were humming a few minutes ago. I'd like that."

"For your information, Michael Culhane, I have a lot of work to do—"

"No, you don't. You're done with your project, and you're

not due to start on the ditches right away. I checked the calendar in your office."

He was almost shouting at her as he got farther away. She could barely see him through the darkness. His car door slammed shut.

"I am not prepared for those ditches, Michael," she shouted back. "I still have a lot of work to finish."

"Finish it tonight," he called out the window as he drove off. "See you at nine!"

Sometime in the middle of the night as she was nursing her printer, Kitt realized she did have a choice. Just because Michael was bullheaded and insistent—just because it had always felt good to do what he wanted because she knew he loved her, she suddenly saw that she still had a choice. She could go with him to Mexico or stay in Santa Fe.

She studied the tickets lying on the chair where she had dropped them. The flight was open-ended. How characteristic of Michael. She would have felt a lot more comfortable knowing how many days to expect to be there. She wanted life tidy. Finishing up the cemetery project would give closure there. The ditches promised time-consuming, interesting labor with a set deadline. For Kitt, life worked better in an orderly fashion. She had her morning run to the nearby park with Apollo, her monthly meetings of the historic art society and her quarterly newsletter to write for supporters of projects undertaken by the Bureau. Adding church to her list of weekly activities might be feasible. Maybe she would join the choir.

But Michael Culhane wasn't something she could control through careful scheduling. She did have a choice, however. She could refuse to go to Guadalupe Y Calvo. She could refuse to ever see him or speak to him again. She could go on with the life she had made for herself as if the past weeks had never happened. Erase *those* tapes, not the old ones.

The life she had made for herself. Until now, it had seemed good enough. Maybe not happy, maybe not deliriously exciting like her marriage had begun—but stable and efficient and comfortable. Risk free. That was it. She had chosen not to take risks anymore.

Michael was a risk.

The printer stopped humming. Kitt slowly set the tickets on the ottoman where his feet had been. She stood and checked her watch. Two in the morning. Walking down her long hall, she turned into the master bedroom. She sat on her narrow bed and stared at her feet. Then she knelt on the floor, reached under the bed and pulled out her suitcase.

"You'd like the view if you could look down." Michael was gazing out the window of the tiny four-seater airplane. "It's all mountains and tall green pines down there. Just beautiful."

Back rigid and fingers dug into the sides of the seat, Kitt was chewing gum like it was her last meal. She didn't look at him, she just stared at the mesh compartment divider between the pilot's chair and the two back seats. The floor between them was littered with baskets of bananas, boxes labeled with soap and cigarette brands, cartons of wool dyes. Behind them stood row upon row of full gasoline cans, sloshing their contents as the plane bumped through the clouds.

"*¡Cerca, señora!*" The sweaty, unshaven pilot leaned past the mesh divider, waving his half-smoked cigar. "*¡Muy cerca!*"

"He says we're almost there, Kitt," Michael informed her helpfully.

She turned to him, fighting nausea. "I speak Spanish."

"I'm sure Diego has flown this plane to Guadalupe Y Calvo hundreds of times, Kitt. If you could just relax, it's not such a bad flight."

Kitt studied the mesh divider, sure she would never forget its tiny knotted pattern as long as she lived. Especially if she only lived another two or three minutes—which seemed highly likely.

Risks, she fumed. Risks! What a great start she'd made at beginning to take risks again. She was riding in an unpressurized flying Molotov cocktail right over the tops of pine trees.

"The Sierra Madres are some of my favorite mountains," Michael was saying, his eyes again on the view outside.

If she'd had the strength, Kitt would have socked him.

"*¡Aquí está!*" Diego pointed to the ground below the plane. He stubbed out his cigar on the instrument panel and banked the plane into a severe turn. Kitt shut her eyes and clamped down on her chewing gum.

"It looks like we're going to slide in right between those trees up ahead." Michael's voice held a note of excitement. "Whoa, Diego. Careful now. *Cuidado, hombre.*"

"*No, señor—es como amor. ¡Entrar rapido! ¡Aiyee!*" His white teeth flashing at Kitt, Diego cut the plane through the tips of the pine trees and down toward a tiny strip of cleared meadow on the crest of a mountain.

"What did he say?" Michael called over the roar of the engines. "I couldn't quite catch it."

Kitt opened her eyes into slits. The plane was vibrating so badly she felt like her teeth were going to fall out.

"He said it's like love. You have to move quickly." A basket of bananas tipped over on Kitt's feet. "He's a man after your own heart."

As Michael chuckled, the plane bounced onto the ground with a spine-jarring thud, then rose. Seconds later it slammed down again. This time Diego let out a whoop and slowly braked the plane to a halt just at the end of the grass airstrip.

"*¡Bienvenido a Guadalupe Y Calvo!*" Jerking the safety latch, he threw the door open and kicked down the rickety steps.

Kitt gingerly lifted the bananas from her feet. "If you ever try to talk me into anything like this again, I won't speak to you for as long as I live."

"Come on, Kitt. That wasn't much worse than a roller coaster ride."

"I've always hated roller coasters. Especially ones that travel twelve thousand feet in the air." She swallowed and her ears popped. "And don't try to tell me you weren't scared, too."

"Scared silly. That's part of the fun."

She had to smile. "Come on, Marco Polo. Let's go exploring." Pulling herself up from the seat, Kitt picked her way through the boxes to where Diego, ever the gentleman, was waiting to give her a hand down.

"Le gusta el vuelo, señora?"

"Sí, Diego." Kitt stepped out into the chill evening air. "It was a lovely flight."

At the edge of the airstrip where the mountain seemed to drop off into nothingness stood a squat young man in a straw hat and a brightly colored serape. Six small horses grazed beside him. The man smiled shyly at Kitt as he rounded up his horses and began leading them toward the plane.

"Where is Guadalupe Y Calvo?" Kitt asked aloud. She turned to find Diego staring at her with a puzzled expression. *"¿Dónde está Guadalupe Y Calvo?"*

"¡Abajo!" He pointed over the ledge of mountain.

Down? Kitt waded through the stubby grass in the direction he had pointed. She glanced back. Michael was helping Diego and the young *caballero* load the ponies with provisions from the plane. He was chatting away in Spanish as though he felt right at home. In tan slacks, boots, brown sweater and an olive bush jacket, pockets heavy with film, camera, notebooks and tape recorder, Michael looked every bit the intrepid journalist.

She sucked in a deep breath of thin air. She felt dizzy and a bit queasy. Altitude, she told herself. She wasn't about to let a hair-raising plane ride and a shortage of oxygen get her down. After all, wasn't this something she'd always ached to do? Leave academia and bureaucracy behind. Venture into unknown realms. Document uncharted anthropological data. Interview people of other cultures and languages. Put all her learning into practice—not just in the classroom, or on tame domestic digs. See what the rest of the world had to offer.

She stepped forward. Grass thinned to bleak gray rock at the edge of the mountain. She grabbed the spindly trunk of a pine tree and leaned over the side to look down. Covering her eyes, she swung herself back onto firm ground and swallowed. She took another deep breath, then she opened her eyes and leaned out again.

Far below, in the tiny cup of a valley between the towering Sierra Madres, nestled a village. The descent to it consisted of a series of rocky, shale-strewn ledges. Tendrils of white smoke curled upward from the chimneys of little shingle-roofed houses. Cattle grazed at the foot of the peaks. Shaggy green gardens of corn and beans stood out on cleared patches of earth.

"Looks like about a forty-five degree angle to me," Michael guessed from behind her.

"I think I'll crawl down on my hands and knees."

"You won't need to do that. Diego arranged for horses."

Kitt lifted her eyebrows. "Horses? You think we should ride down a forty-five-degree rock slide on horses?"

"Pedro is."

She studied the stout little *caballero* perched atop a knock-kneed mount. Well, if he could do it...

Without looking back, she stepped to the horses and climbed onto the one Pedro indicated. Chill evening air nipped at her cheeks. Thank goodness she'd had the presence of mind to wear khaki slacks and desert boots, along with a turtleneck and a thick cotton sweater. The shaggy brown horse gave a sharp nod as she settled her feet into the stirrups.

"*¡Vamonos!*" Pedro gave his mount a jab with his heels. The string of ponies headed for the mountain ledge. Kitt clenched the reins in a death grip and gave Michael a wan smile.

"*¡Adios, amigos!*" Diego called from behind.

Kitt thought about looking back and waving goodbye, but at that moment her horse stepped off the meadow onto the rock ledge. With a bouncing gait that left her breathless, the bony animal began trotting along a nonexistent path of crumbling shale. She caught her breath and shut her eyes. The horse leaped to a lower ledge, landing neatly and moving straight into his comfortable gait. She glanced behind. Michael flew over the same emptiness with a wide-eyed expression.

"Yee-hah!" he cried out. "This is nearly as good as that plane ride."

"Better, I'd say." Kitt mustered a grin.

She decided the best thing was to let her horse have its own way. Relaxing her hands on the reins, she settled into the saddle.

The sun dipped behind the western peaks, leaving a gold-streaked sky behind. The little village grew nearer. The smell of freshly baked bread mingled with the acrid tang of pine smoke. Old men sat in doorways, smoking pipes and chatting. Some children chased a puppy down a street. A baby cried.

The ponies bounced down the final ledge almost into a town street. From a nearby shop, an electric light bulb went on. A hefty middle-aged man stepped out onto the porch of the shop and waved a pudgy hand.

Michael rode his horse alongside Kitt's. "I bet that's Señor Martinez, the general store owner. Diego told me he'll be able to help us find a place to stay."

The horses drew up in front of the store. Señor Martinez waddled down the steps and introduced himself with a wide, congenial smile. No, there was no hotel in the village, he told Michael and Kitt, but he had a couple of rooms they could rent for as many nights as they wished.

Michael glanced at Kitt, and she nodded. This was no time to make a big deal about sleeping arrangements. She was too sore to do anything but crawl into bed.

Señor Martinez had a short but ample wife and seven pudgy children, ranging in age from about fourteen down to a couple of months. The *señora* showed her guests to a matched pair of small, lamplit bedrooms at the rear of the wood-frame home. In each room, a bed covered in thick gray blankets stood against one wall, three iron hooks protruded by the single window and a rickety chair leaned beside the door. She told them dinner would be ready in a half hour, and left them in the semidarkness.

"I couldn't be happier to see the Ritz," Kitt said as she chose the room to the left. She slung her bag onto the cleanly swept floor and sagged into the chair.

"You were a real trouper on the plane and the horse, Kitt," Michael began. "If I'd had any idea—"

"I hope you would have asked me along all the same."

"I would have."

"I know." She studied him for a moment. "Thanks, Michael—for the tickets, the trip… It was a good idea."

He studied her face in the lamplight. Wisps of brown hair had come loose from her braid and trickled beneath her chin. Her cheeks were pink from the chilly air. A soft smile played about her lips. Her eyes looked luminous—almost black.

"You're beautiful, Kitt."

"Quit saying that." She laughed and flipped the braid over her shoulder. "I expect my face was green after that plane ride."

He sat on the bed near the chair, picked up her hand and wove her fingers between his. "It feels good to be here. Our first international trip together."

"We certainly are isolated here."

"Affiliated Press knows where we are. But I doubt if they'll come looking."

She reached up and touched the strands of hair that had fallen over his forehead. Bending toward her, he kissed her lightly on the cheek. "Breaking rules," he said. "I know."

She sighed. "Somehow…here…it feels all right."

Dinner was a hearty meal of beef, potatoes, bread, tortillas, mangos, bananas and an excellent white cheese. Señora Martinez served heaping bowls of frijoles—refried beans—along with the other food. The children ate like they hadn't had a meal in days. Kitt saw where they got their pudgy physiques and fat cheeks.

After dinner, Señor Martinez settled back in his chair with a steaming cup of black coffee. He smiled expansively. "How do you like my light?" he asked his guests in Spanish.

Kitt glanced up at the bare forty-watt bulb hanging from the ceiling by a black wire. She looked at Michael, who appeared as confused as she.

"It's very nice," she said.

"Only three electric lights in the whole village of Guadalupe Y Calvo. One is in my store in the front. One is here. And the other is in the school. The electricity comes by gasoline generator. We bring the gasoline on the airplane from Chihuahua. Very expensive."

Kitt nodded, remembering the gas cans sloshing behind her on the ride in. She decided she preferred the orange glow of the nearby fire in its beehive fireplace to the naked glare of electric light.

"So tell me why you have come to Guadalupe Y Calvo," Señor Martinez said. "We have few visitors in our little village."

Kitt briefly explained their search for information about Black Dove—*Paloma Negra*. Señor Martinez scowled and shook his head.

"I have heard of him." He took a long sip of coffee, swirled it around in his mouth and swallowed. "That man was an Indian. He was not trusted, even though he had been hired to protect our town."

"But he was a Shawnee—not an Apache."

Señor Martinez shrugged. "An Indian all the same."

"We hope to find burial records for Black Dove in the church," Michael explained.

"Then you must speak with the padre. He will show you the records. But I cannot imagine that an Indian would be buried in the church cemetery. It would not be thought proper."

"Do you know any stories about Black Dove's time in Guadalupe Y Calvo?" Kitt asked.

"For that, you must speak with old Santiago."

"Santiago? Who is he?"

"Santiago Garcia, of course. The grandson of Black Dove."

A prickle ran down Kitt's spine. "Black Dove had a family—children—in Guadalupe Y Calvo?"

"You don't think he was going to live here all those years like a monk? Of course he had a family. He took as a wife—not a proper wife, but a woman to live with—the daughter of the schoolteacher. They had a baby, a daughter named Maria. Then Black Dove's wife, she died."

"Of what?"

"Who knows? Maybe it was a woman sickness—but no one would tend her. She was not well thought of by the villagers. She lived with the Indian, you see. At the time Black Dove's wife died, their daughter, Maria, was about twelve years old. The schoolteacher, he came and took Maria away from Black Dove, her father. This man told the warrior he would not be able to care for his daughter in a good way. So she was taken from him. A short time after that, Black Dove was killed."

"Killed?"

"Killed. By Apaches. You talk to old Santiago about that

part. He knows it better. Maria grew up and got married. Santiago is her son. Black Dove's grandson. He lives just two streets over. We'll go tomorrow morning after you talk with the padre. Good?"

"Good," Kitt and Michael said in unison.

Michael sat on a bench near the beehive fireplace in the dining room. Señor Martinez had switched off the electric light, and he and his family had retired to their upstairs rooms not long before. The night air through the open window chilled Michael's fingers as he worked at the clasp on Dr. Oldham's manila envelope. Beside him, Kitt held a kerosene lamp at shoulder height.

"I don't remember reading anything in Dr. Oldham's notes to contradict what Señor Martinez just told us," he said.

"You shouldn't have been reading my private mail in the first place. And I'll take that, thank you." Kitt slipped her fingers into the envelope and pulled out the sheaf of papers. "You sneaked into my house, read my mail, studied my calendar. What else of mine did you snoop around in?"

"I'll take the fifth amendment on that."

"Take this," Kitt replied, elbowing Michael in the ribs.

"Ouch!" He couldn't help grinning. He felt relaxed at her side, his brown sweater pushed up at the sleeves. His hiking shoes lay in a tumble where he had kicked them off beside Kitt's neatly aligned desert boots. Shifting his attention from the proximity of her shoulder and the woodsy scent clinging to her denim jacket, he took the lamp as she began flipping through the notes.

"So what does Dr. Oldham have to say about Black Dove?" he asked.

"These mostly concern others who rode with James Kirker," Kitt murmured. "This part tells about Spybuck. He was Kirker's right-hand man. Part Shawnee. Quite a character. Here's something about the fellow named Andy. He fought with Kirker in an attack on Cochise.... The stuff on Black Dove must be near the end."

Kitt shuffled through a few more pages, scanning each page carefully for mention of Black Dove. Michael noted Dr. Oldham's meticulous work, and he understood why Kitt respected the scholar so highly. Each character in the cast of players had been well documented. A thorough bibliography appeared at the end of every section. The entire sheaf of photocopied documents accompanying the research data had been cross-referenced and annotated.

"Here." Kitt lifted the page labeled, in bold black type, Black Dove. Michael leaned closer, his shoulder behind hers, as they read in silence. "Shawnee Indian; tall; physically fit; two gold front teeth."

"He doesn't mention the knife tip in the scapula," Michael said.

"Dr. Oldham wouldn't have had access to the records at Kneeling Nun Mine. Look right here—he writes that he contacted the mine supervisors with no success."

"This is the part I read last night. It's about Black Dove losing his teeth in the fight with another boy. Can you believe Black Dove bit the kid's nose clean off?"

"He had no qualms about tomahawking people and cutting their scalps away. Biting off a nose would have been a piece of cake."

Michael grimaced. "Cake?"

"Hey, listen to this footnote." Kitt jabbed her finger at the page and began reading aloud. "In 1842, after guarding the gold mines in Guadalupe Y Calvo, James Kirker and his men were called to Chihuahua City by the Mexican government. This time, Kirker was promised a significantly greater amount for each scalp. During this period Kirker's men found an abandoned gold mine in the Sierra Madres.

"After routing some Apaches, the men happened upon the ruins of what once had been a lively community. They discovered the foundation of an old church, the remains of a smelting furnace, a pile of cinder slag and some copper and silver dross. One of the men found a gold nugget. But they were on their way to Chihuahua City with what they thought was even more valuable—scalp poles hung with Apache scalps. None of the histories mentions this mine again. It may be assumed Kirker and his men never revisited it."

"An abandoned gold mine in the Sierra Madres." Michael shook his head. "Old Hod should hear about this one."

He stared at the lamp, remembering the determined old man watching Kitt from his spot beneath the cottonwood tree. Poor, lonely Hod. Michael wondered if they would ever see him again.

"I bet Black Dove finally got his new gold teeth from nuggets found at that mine," he said.

"I doubt it. Dr. Oldham doesn't think anyone ever went back to the mine."

"Well, if Black Dove eventually settled in Guadalupe Y Calvo after he'd left Kirker for good, maybe he did go back to the mine. At least to get some teeth."

Kitt laughed. "Would you stop bugging me about those teeth? I'm sure Black Dove had his gold teeth made a long time before. He certainly would have had enough money."

"Porcelain teeth, maybe. But I bet he got the gold ones from that old mine they found."

"You really think Black Dove would have gone there?"

"Kitt, if you ran across a gold mine and found a nugget, wouldn't you think about going back to it one day?"

"I guess so."

The moment Michael asked, he remembered that wealth and all its trappings had never held much appeal for Kitt. She had shared in her parents' financial prosperity while growing up. Money drove people, she used to tell him. It had driven her father. Now she had seen how it tormented old

Hod all his life. Maybe it had driven Black Dove, too. Kitt had always said she could do with just enough to be comfortable, which was a good way to feel for a young man and his pregnant wife living in a trailer.

"I'd go looking for the gold," Michael spoke up.

"Why?"

"For the adventure of it."

"If you had gold, people you didn't even know would be knocking on your door for handouts. Treasure hunters would be all over the place trying to find your mine. They'd desecrate historical sites, pollute the environment—"

"Okay, okay!" He held up his hand with a laugh. "Never mind. I'll go on being a happy but impoverished journalist for the rest of my life."

"You're not impoverished, Michael."

"Not right now." He stroked down her cheek with the tip of his finger. The sides of their knees met, and he felt the warmth of that one tiny spot more intensely than he felt the worn old wood beneath him.

Distressed at the powerful reaction he experienced in touching Kitt once again, Michael fixed his focus on the plastic end of his shoelace. An almost overwhelming mixture of pleasure and sadness flooded through him. Kitt was here with him. He might lose her again. But he might not. If he lost her, he wasn't sure what he would do to keep going. If he didn't lose her, he wasn't sure how they would handle having each other in their lives.

"I've got everything I need," he said softly. "It's good to be with you now, Kitt. All those months in the desert, I thought I'd never see you again. I didn't want to see you because I knew you hated me. But the thought of never holding you or touching you…"

"I didn't hate you, Michael. I've told you that."

"Then what happened?" His eyes met hers. "Please tell me what happened to you after we found out about our baby."

"Is this why you wanted me to come here with you? To make me talk about things I can't bear to remember?"

"I want to be with you. Those days after I left you in Santa Rita were really empty, Kitt. I missed you. Did you feel some of that, too?"

Kitt knotted her fingers and shifted on the bench. "After I got to my house in Santa Fe and started back in a routine, I adjusted to my old life." She paused a moment before speaking again. "I didn't regret seeing you again, but I was all right by myself. Just me and my dog."

Michael sat silently, staring at the flame in the glass lamp. A fear had crept into his stomach to tangle with the other emotions there. Maybe Kitt was telling the truth and had been all along. Maybe she really didn't need him. Maybe she didn't want him the way he wanted her.

He weighed that thought, turning over in his mind her physical response to him as opposed to what she said. With her words, she was far away. With her body, she was near. Maybe it was only the easy familiarity of old friends. He could have been wrong about her. But if all he evoked in Kitt was a physical—and partly sentimental—reaction, that wasn't enough. He had loved more than her body. He had loved her spirit, the part deep inside her that made her unique.

But she didn't seem to love his hidden, inner self anymore. And that was what he wanted from her more than anything.

"I'd better get some sleep," he said, rising from the bench.

Kitt caught his wrist. "Michael, listen."

"No, it's okay."

"Michael." Kitt rose beside him and turned him to face her. "When I got back to Santa Fe...I missed you. I missed you so much. Will you hold me?"

Chapter Thirteen

❧

"I used to find it hard to speak my mind, Kitt." Michael towered over her in the golden light. "Now it's hard for me to stay quiet when I have something to say."

"Say what you have to say to me, Michael."

"Do you love me, Kitt?"

She tried to force herself to breathe but the air wouldn't seem to come. "I used to love you."

"That's not enough, Kitt. Do you love *me*?" He jabbed his chest with his thumb. "Not the boy I was at seventeen but this man standing here who's thirty-three? Do you love Michael Culhane?"

She jammed her hands into the pockets of her jacket and let out a cloud of white breath. "I'm cold. That's all I meant when I asked you to hold me. I just wanted to tell you that I feel okay with you. I'm not asking you to love me, Michael. I'm not asking for commitment. Could you just put your arms around me without turning it into a question of love?"

"All right."

His voice was brusque, almost angry. He bent and blew out the lamp. For a moment, neither of them moved. Then Michael slowly drew her against him, turning her and folding her into his embrace. Kitt could feel the firm mass of his frame molding to her. She relaxed a little and rested her head on his chest. This was all she had needed from him. His presence. His warmth. Was that too much to ask?

Then Michael pulled her closer. She shivered at the strength of his muscled arms as he curled them around her back. His face pushed into her hair and his breath warmed her neck.

Her own arms relaxed and slipped around him as she stared at the black wall and the star-filled window set into it. The rise and fall of Michael's chest was labored. She knew she had wounded him. But did he really want her to love him again? To love him body and soul, as she had done before. Did he love her that way? Did he truly believe God intended to put their marriage back together? To her, that was a scary, overwhelming thought. Almost unthinkable. Yet maybe he saw it that way. Why hadn't she asked him?

She didn't want to know, that's why. It was too frightening to think that somewhere deep inside herself she might love Michael just as she had—no, more deeply than she had. And he might love her the same way. It was impossible to believe that the distant, unloving, betraying God she had rejected might have been watching and caring about her all along. That He might have been working in her life, preparing her for Michael all over again.

As always, when Kitt thought of loving this man who now held her in his arms, her thoughts went to their child. In her mind's eye, she saw Michael sitting beside her on the bench only moments before and asking her once again, why? What happened, Kitt?

"The doctors called it a major clinical depression," she said softly to the black wall. "Lots of women have postpartum depression. It's hormonal. For months, the body is in high gear nurturing and growing a baby. And then that stops. There's also something called situational depression. It's caused by a traumatic event. My depression was probably some of both. It started when the baby died."

Michael had stiffened the moment she began speaking, but he said nothing.

"I kept thinking about our baby being dead inside me," she continued. "Our daughter. I wanted the baby to go away, that dead body inside me. But I also loved her. I wanted to keep her, hold on to her as long as I could, maybe even somehow bring her back to life. I felt sick inside. I tried to think where to turn, but I couldn't see any way out. My parents had disowned me. We were so young, and all you could do was stare at me with that look of panic in your eyes."

"You kept rocking in the old rocking chair, Kitt," Michael said, his mouth moving against her cheek. "I didn't understand."

"I couldn't do anything, because the doctors decided to leave the baby inside me until labor started spontaneously. I know that's normal procedure, but it paralyzed me. All that time while I was waiting for the baby to be born, I could think only the same two thoughts over and over. There's a dead thing inside me and I want it out. I love that dead thing and I don't want to let it go. I couldn't win. I felt like I was inside a black box with six blank walls. No windows. No doors."

"Why didn't you talk to me about it, honey?"

"I couldn't see outside of myself and the black box. I could only see me and the baby. You were too far away. I don't even really remember you during that time. I don't remember eating or sleeping or anything. I only remember that when I sat in the rocking chair, my thoughts seemed to have a certain rhythmic order. When I rocked, it seemed like I could wait."

"If I'd known what was happening, Kitt, I'd have made them take the baby out. I swear I would have." Michael's voice sounded choked. "Maybe I could have prevented what happened to us. But I was too blind and stupid to see what was going on."

"We didn't understand, Michael. Neither of us. We were kids. You thought I was hating you and blaming you. But really I wasn't thinking about you at all. I was just trying to survive."

"But even after…when the baby was born, Kitt—"

"The depression didn't end after I delivered the baby. I couldn't snap out of it. The obstetrician said it was postpartum depression because my hormones were all messed up. He said he thought time would take care of the problem. But I knew the hormonal issue was only a small part of what was happening inside me. Everything had been so horrible. The only way I could deal with it was to block it all out. I still don't remember much of that time."

Michael pulled Kitt closer, and she realized her arms had stiffened and her fingers were clenched into fists behind his back. She knew she should let him go now, let him sleep. But in spite of her pain, she finally had opened up to him, and she found herself praying that he would talk to her.

"How did you come out of the depression, Kitt?" he asked softly. "Tell me about that. I feel like it's the last thing I don't really understand about you."

She began to speak, living through it all over again as she said the words. "One afternoon, my dad came to the trailer and found me. My mother still didn't want anything to do with me. But my father had heard you were gone. He came over to check on me and saw the shape I was in. He said I looked half dead, but I don't remember it clearly. Then my parents just took over."

"How?"

"They got me to an internist so that I could start to rebuild my physical strength. Then they set up a series of appointments with a counselor. My mother took care of all the divorce papers while I was still so sick. She believed my depression was all your fault, even though I had tried to explain it to her. Somehow, slowly and with a lot of work, I began to get better. Then my parents enrolled me at the university in Albuquerque. I saw a therapist there for about two years." She shook her head. "Sounds like a long time, doesn't it?"

"Not at all. You had a lot to get over." He paused for a moment. "I think it took me two or three years to begin to feel normal, too."

"After I came out of the worst part of the depression, I still had to learn to handle my anger. I was very angry with our baby for dying like that. Pretty illogical, I guess, but that's how I felt. And I was angry that you had abandoned me."

Michael let out a hot breath. "I was so blind. So stupid."

"You were young."

"Do you think you finally healed, honey?" he whispered.

"Mostly. I learned to put everything away. When it all came rushing into my mind, I learned how to take control and put it on a shelf. I couldn't erase what had happened. But finally, I was able to just stop dwelling on it. I went on with my education and built my career. It's really been a pretty good life after all."

Michael kissed Kitt's cheek. At the tenderness of his expression, she sighed and felt some of the tension slide out of her shoulders. Gently, he rubbed his hands down her back. The bottom of his chin rested on her head. She wrapped her arms around his waist and held him close.

"Did your counselor say you had done everything you needed to do, Kitt?"

She took a deep breath. "I was supposed to cry. The therapist kept telling me that if I would cry about my losses, I might finally finish the grieving process. But I just couldn't cry. Everything was stopped up inside me like a big dam. I never have cried about what happened, and I don't think I ever will."

"Kitt, honey. Can you ever forgive me for leaving you when I did?"

Kitt lifted her head. She could not see Michael's face, but she heard the pain in his voice. "Forgiveness is choosing to let go. I let go a long time ago, Michael."

He stood silent in the darkness. "If forgiveness is letting go," he finally said, "then I suppose I've forgiven you, too. I forgive you for what I thought was your hatred, for your rejection of me."

"I'm glad."

"But I've come to think forgiveness is more than letting go. When I was so down during the Gulf War, I did a lot of talking with the chaplain in my unit. I was having a hard time forgiving you and your parents, Kitt, and I sure couldn't forgive myself. The chaplain told me that because Jesus paid the price for sin—past, present and future—when He died on the cross, all I had to do was confess my wrongdoings to Him. That took care of me. But how was I ever going to forgive others? The chaplain said that in the example Christ set with His life and death, He showed us how to do it."

"I don't know what you mean."

"Jesus prayed for God to forgive us. While He was hanging on the cross, nearly dead, Jesus said, 'Father, forgive these people, because they don't know what they are doing.' The chaplain explained to me that we're supposed to pray for the people who have hurt us. We have to step beyond just putting their wrongdoing on the back shelf—we have to pray for them. It took me a while to be able to do that, but I've been praying for you for a lot of years, Kitt. I've asked God to heal you and rebuild your life and make you smile again. Have you ever prayed for me?"

She took clumps of his sweater in her hands as she shook her head. "No, Michael. And I can't believe you've been praying for me."

"And for our parents, too," he said. "I never let you go.

Not the Kitt I had always loved. I held on to my memories of you, my love for you. In my mind, our marriage never really ended, even though I didn't know if I would ever see you again."

Kitt had finally warmed and relaxed. Michael's hands on her back had eased the tightness in her muscles from the long day. She knew they both needed sleep and time to think. But Michael spoke again.

"Kitt," he whispered.

She moved against him, nestling closer. "Yes?"

"When you let go of the past, do you think you let go of me?"

"I let go of the memories that hurt so much."

Michael's hands stopped moving on her back. "But do you think you let go of me, Kitt? Me. Do you think you let go of me and our love?"

She sighed and her breath on his wool sweater warmed the tip of her nose. She felt too tired to deny it. She felt too tired and too comfortable just being with him again. "No," she murmured. "I didn't let go of you."

Waking in the orange half-light of dawn, Kitt stared at the hazy window. This was her favorite time of day. The night, with its darkness and its potential for terror, was over.

The full light of day—with all its promise of fulfillment and pleasure—waited only moments away. But right now, in the twilight of the dawn, she could rest.

Michael lay in his room next door. She thought about their parting the night before, how he had cupped his hands around her face, woven his fingers through her hair and gently kissed her forehead. The memory curled through her like a blessing, and she relived it in her mind as the sunlight crept over the windowsill.

A strange sense of release had settled over her as she slept. Perhaps it had something to do with her talk with Michael the night before. Perhaps it was the way he had held her, drawing her close and keeping her warm as he had long ago.

Or maybe it was just the fact that she'd taken in a lot of excitement and fresh air. Looking at it one way, she realized, this crazy adventure was her first vacation in years. People took vacations to unwind. Maybe she was unwinding.

Kitt thought about Michael's face. How strong and masculine it had become over the years. A thick growth of light brown whiskers had shadowed his jaw by nightfall. She tried to picture him with a beard. A smile drifted across her mouth as she thought of the scattered peach fuzz he'd been so proud of at seventeen.

She was glad Michael had grown up. As much as she had loved that gangly boy, she could appreciate the fully adult man more. He talked better, he cared more deeply, he fought harder.

Forgiveness. Prayer. Christ bleeding and dying on a cross. Things she had put out of her mind for so many years. And now here they were, spread out before her by Michael, who had embraced them all. Was it true he had been praying for her all those years? If so, then maybe God—and not Kitt— was responsible for all the good that had happened in her life. All the healing. All the rebuilding. Maybe she wasn't so self-sufficient after all.

She hardly knew whether to be angry…or grateful. Michael had prayed for her, but she had never prayed for herself. And certainly not for him.

Turning on her side, Kitt studied the golden light warming the little room. It was time. Long past time.

"So," she whispered in a voice so low she couldn't even hear it. "It's me, God. Kitt. I guess Michael hasn't let You forget me, after all. I need to talk…to pray for some people… and I hope You'll listen…."

* * *

They met in the narrow hall on their way to breakfast. Michael's blue-gray eyes settled on Kitt's face. They exchanged good mornings and how-do-you-dos. Then Michael halted, pushed his hands into his pockets and nodded as if he'd finally made up his mind.

"Okay, I have something to say," he told her. "I love you, Kitt."

She leaned back against the wall and closed her eyes, all the air going out of her lungs at once. "Michael."

"You don't have to say anything, Kitt. I just wanted you to know."

"Well…thank you."

It was an inane response, but her mind had suddenly catapulted into confusion. Why did this man always have to be so blunt? Didn't he realize what such powerful words could mean? Didn't he think about the future and the past and all the tangle their lives could become again if they talked like that?

"I've never seen your hair looking so beautiful, Kitt."

She pursed her lips. "Okay, wise guy. I know my hair's a mess. There's not even a mirror in my room, so this is yesterday's braid."

"I mean it. Something about the way the light is coming in. Makes it look almost red. Auburn."

He leaned toward her shoulder and lifted the shaggy braid. Before she could react, he had kissed it. And then he was kissing her.

Kitt caught her breath at the unexpected jolt of a man's arms around her and his lips on her mouth. At this hour of the morning. In a stranger's house. And so wonderfully, powerfully delicious.

"I didn't say I loved you, Michael," she whispered in a last-ditch attempt at control.

"I can wait for the words. They're in your heart trying to get out."

"You don't know that."

"I have faith."

His lips grazed her ear as he said the words. Kitt shivered and turned to him, wrapping her arms around his chest. She lifted her mouth and their lips crushed together. Unable to resist him, she savored the familiar joy of her husband's morning kiss. Her heart hammering in her temples nearly drowned out the melodic voice in the distance.

"Desayuno, señor y señora," Señora Martinez called softly.

"Breakfast," Michael whispered.

Kitt shut her eyes against his shoulder. "I don't want you to let go, Michael."

He lifted her chin with the crook of his finger. "I've got you."

"Later, I might not want you to hug me. I might change my mind about all this."

"You won't change your mind."

"But you know how I am."

"I know everything about you." With a sly grin, he gave her one last kiss. As she reached for him, he stepped away, leaving her empty-armed and longing.

"There's the padre, over by the candles." Michael took Kitt's cool hand and walked beside her down the stone floor of the church.

Like a miniature version of the cathedrals he had seen while on leave in Europe, the Iglesia del Sangre de Cristo had an aura of holy beauty. Dimly lit, smelling of incense and candle wax, the air wore a musty cloak. The ceiling soared on stone pillars. Carved cherubim and seraphim encircled the tops of the columns. Niches in the side walls displayed peeling portraits of Christ's long journey to the cross. Rows of worn wooden pews filed down the nave facing the giant wooden crucifix that hung between two stained-glass windows.

On a back bench, a ragged young man lay asleep with his arm angled across his eyes. His snores mingled softly with the sound of footsteps as Michael and Kitt made their way through the cavernous sanctuary. Near the front, an old woman in a black mantilla rose from her knees. She genuflected in the aisle before passing the visitors without a glance.

The padre, dressed in a black robe, was small and nearly bald. His thin fingers gently straightened rows of half-burned candles. But his bright black eyes were fastened on the newcomers.

"*Bienvenidos.*" His voice was almost inaudible as he greeted them.

When Kitt explained their mission, the priest gestured toward a wooden door at the side of the apse. His feet invisible beneath his floor-length robe, he glided ahead into a small room containing a table and chairs and the rail to a descending staircase.

"Down there," he said in Spanish, "we keep the records of every baptism, marriage and death in Guadalupe Y Calvo."

Michael glanced at the wooden railing and the crumbling stone circular stair. "May we please look through the records? It shouldn't take us long."

"I have already looked for a burial notice of Black Dove. He is not mentioned."

"But we were told that Black Dove was buried in Guadalupe Y Calvo," Kitt countered.

"Not here," the priest said. "He was killed outside the town, the legends tell us. But not buried at the church. I wrote a letter to Dr. Frank Oldham, the colleague of whom you spoke. I told him the legends, including the account of the outlaw's death. He asked me to search the church records. I did search, and when I found nothing, I wrote and told him that."

"So all Dr. Oldham knew was that you had said Black Dove was killed near Guadalupe Y Calvo," Michael said. "But you actually found no documentation of his burial?"

"Not surprising. Do you think we would bury an unrepentant, non-Christian murderer in our midst? Certainly not. It would be a defilement. I believe Black Dove must be buried in the mountains where they found his body."

"So they *did* find his body." Michael sensed that the priest was being evasive.

"That, *señor*, I do not know. I am much too young. I know only some of the stories of Black Dove. For more, you will need to speak with old Santiago, the grandson of the Indian."

"Well, thank you for your time," Kitt said.

"Wait." Michael laid a hand on her arm. "May we look through the records ourselves, Padre? Perhaps we will find some mention of his wife and children."

"Maria was not a real wife. They were never married in the Church."

"We understand that," Michael said. "But please—may we look?"

The priest turned his head toward the dark staircase. "Only the oldest records are kept below. The books are very heavy. They are crumbling. It will be difficult for me to bring them up to you."

"We'll go down."

The priest shook his head. "That place is not pleasant. In the old days, before the cemetery we now have behind the church, the bodies were placed in the crypts below."

"It's all right, Padre," Kitt said. "I'm an archaeologist. I'm used to seeing skeletal remains."

"The crypts form a difficult maze. You will find the records in the first room to the right, behind a metal door.

Please do not wander around. I'm not sure I would be able to find you if you became lost."

"We'll just look at the records and come back up."

"Very well." The priest handed them a lantern and a box of matches. "Go with God."

Michael lit the lamp as the priest stepped away. "I didn't realize we were going to be walking around in a mausoleum," he whispered. It had been strange enough watching Kitt uncover the remains of the woman with the thousand beads. But a bunch of skeletons scattered around in a dark maze sounded particularly bizarre. "We could just trust the guy. He is a priest, you know—I doubt he'd lie."

"I know. I believe him. But remember Mrs. Lujan and the Kneeling Nun Mine? I'll never get over failing to look more closely at those medical records of hers. You can never be sure about something unless you check it out yourself."

Taking the lantern, she started down the steps. Michael followed. It was one thing to cover a war and quite another to meander around in a crypt. A chill colder than refrigerated air crept around his ankles and up his pantlegs. As his fingers slipped down the worn, curved railing, his eyes adjusted to the darkness and he sniffed the familiar smell of age. Old, dank stonework, dusty cobwebs, must, niter. Smoke from incense had drifted down and mingled with the other smells, leaving an almost tangible taste on Michael's tongue as he stepped onto the damp stone floor.

"First door on the right," Kitt said in a low voice. "There must be an underground stream nearby. See how I'm leaving faint wet footprints? Wow, take a look at these remains. Wouldn't Dr. Dean love this?"

Michael swallowed as they filed past rows of reclining skeletons. He could see the jaunty sway of the lantern ahead of him. Kitt was moving back and forth, holding the light up to the skulls in their niches as if greeting old friends.

"This is excellent!" she exclaimed. "Look how well preserved they are. We could learn a lot about the people of this area if we studied these remains. You'd get a real cross section of the population. Despite what the padre said, I bet some Native Americans are buried here. Most of these people have Native American blood mixed in with their Spanish heritage—whether they want to accept that or not. You know what I've always wanted to do, Michael?"

She whirled, her brown eyes glowing in the darkness. He hooked his thumbs in his pockets and grinned. "Live in a cemetery?"

"No, silly."

She looked beautiful at that moment. Her hair had fallen around her shoulders and her face was rosy, full of life. If she hadn't been standing in the middle of a crypt full of dead people, he'd have picked her up, swung her around and given her a big kiss.

"Tell me what you've always wanted to do, Kitt."

"This!"

He glanced around. "Walk around under a church and look at bones?"

"See the world! You wouldn't believe the archaeological and anthropological mysteries no one has ever even thought of exploring. I'd like to do an intensive study of some of the Latin American peoples who were wiped out by the Spaniards. And there are populations in places like Tierra del Fuego that hardly anyone has studied. And Africa! Now think about that—there are hundreds of tribes. Each has its own language. Its own culture. Some of the languages are still unwritten, Michael. You know what I'd really like to do?"

"Tell me, professor."

"I'd like to lead a project to gather all the legends and oral histories of the tribes in a certain area of Africa—or Latin America, or anywhere. And I'd like to have them translated and then compare them. I know it would be astounding!"

"Stupendous." He couldn't keep the note of teasing from his voice.

"You don't think that would be interesting?"

"I think it would be fantastic, Kitt. Do you suppose you could tell me more about it when we're standing out in the sunshine? I'm afraid Transylvania inspires my imagination differently than it does yours."

As if seeing him for the first time, Kitt studied the man who had accompanied her. Michael had been forced to dip his head because there was not enough room for him to straighten. A spider web draped off one shoulder. A yellowed femur lay near his shoes.

"Sorry." With a giggle, she headed down the corridor.

He couldn't blame Kitt for her joy. Antiquities were her love. She didn't see the past and all its mysteries the way others might—as slightly spooky. Still, he was glad he had come with her. It felt good to hear Kitt pour out her dreams.

"This must be the door." Michael turned a large, corroded iron ring that he had spotted on a side wall. At first he thought the door had rusted to the floor. Bracing one foot against the wall, he pulled hard on the ring. He heard a squeak, and finally the door swung open.

"A metal door in a damp crypt. That doesn't make sense— it was bound to get rusty." Kitt held the lantern high and walked into the small room.

Michael caught his breath. "Books—and they're not just records."

Sagging wooden shelves lined the four walls. Row upon row of books, some tattered and worn, others hardly used, filled each shelf. Two locked trunks sat on the bare stone floor. Grabbing Kitt's shoulders, Michael turned her toward a row of gold-lettered volumes. She lifted the lantern.

"These are religious books. Missals. Scriptures." He slid one out and gingerly pried open the yellowed pages. Illuminated, gold-leaf figures filled the borders. "This has to be a medieval or early renaissance text."

"See what I mean? Treasures are everywhere, Michael. But we're looking for records of Black Dove." She moved away, leaving him staring at the old text in the darkness.

"Black Dove? Kitt, these are valuable manuscripts. They're Latin. I bet they were brought over during the Spanish Conquest."

"By missionaries, I expect."

Michael closed the book and carried it across the room to where Kitt was scanning an old journal. He glanced at the door and wondered whether he should have wedged it with a stone. The place made him think of scenes in old movies when the door suddenly slams shut, trapping everyone inside.

"This is it." The excitement in Kitt's voice pulled him away from his imaginings. "Guadalupe Y Calvo burial records for the late 1800s. Look at this strange, old-fashioned penmanship."

Michael took the lantern and held it over her shoulder as they read line after line in search of Black Dove. The 1850s, 1860s, 1870s, 1880s. A lot of people had passed away in the little town. But none of them was named Black Dove.

"Maybe he went by some other name while he was here," Michael offered as Kitt set the book in its place.

"Everyone in this town who knows the legend calls him Black Dove. Or *Paloma Negra*. I looked for both."

"Then I guess the padre was right. He wasn't buried here." Michael picked up a heavy brown book and began to look through it.

Kitt flipped page after page of the old burial record a second time. "This is so frustrating. How could a town hire a man to help them and then refuse to acknowledge him? It was as if Black Dove had not even been considered a human being here. Was he unable to marry because of his race? Or his religion? Or did he choose not to marry but just to live with the schoolteacher's daughter? And what sort of woman was she? I mean, she took up with Black Dove despite the disapproval of the whole town."

"I've got something." Michael's voice held a note of controlled excitement.

"What is it?" Kitt closed the book of marriage records, marking her place with her thumb.

"A baptism. Right here." His finger pressed the page.

Kitt read aloud. "The baptism of Maria, female child of Maria Cristina Gallegos and Black Dove, the Indian. April 23, 1858."

"A birth record! So Black Dove *was* here. He did live with the schoolmaster's daughter. Her name was Maria Cristina Gallegos."

"And they had a baby girl whose name was also Maria. If Maria was born in 1858, she would have been twelve years old in 1870—the year she was taken from her father because her mother had died."

"There ought to be a burial record for Maria Cristina Gallegos in 1870." Michael spoke the words, but Kitt was already searching the volume of burial records. It took only a moment. There was the name in faded ink. *Maria Cristina Gallegos, died May 17, 1870. Buried May 18, 1870. Guadalupe Y Calvo.*

Michael straightened. "We've got a man. We've got a wife. We've got a daughter. But what happened in 1870 after Maria Cristina Gallegos died and the twelve-year-old Maria was taken away from Black Dove?"

Kitt shut the book with a smile of satisfaction. "Let's go see old Santiago. Maria's son. He'll know."

Chapter Fourteen

❧

The priest looked faintly surprised when Kitt and Michael emerged from the crypts. Perhaps he hadn't expected to see them again, Michael thought. After all, it would have been tempting to explore the underground passageways. Who could tell what might be discovered beneath the old Sangre de Cristo church? Perhaps the site dated back to the precolonial era. But Michael knew he and Kitt had more pressing matters than a long trek through a maze.

They thanked the padre and climbed the gentle hill to Señor Martinez's store.

"It's true what the brochure said about this place." Kitt studied the bustling village as they walked through it. "I don't see any wheeled vehicles at all."

"Feels like we've stepped back in time."

"The clothing is so colorful—hand-woven reds and blues. Have you noticed how bright the children's eyes are? Everyone looks well fed and content. It's not the way I imagined the Third World."

"They're self-sufficient, I expect. Agricultural, without much need for imported goods."

"Matches and soap and dye."

"And gasoline for the light bulbs."

Michael took in a deep breath of fresh mountain air. He didn't mind chasing drug smugglers through Juarez, or tracing a murder case across the back alleys of downtown Albuquerque. But strolling around in a crypt was not his idea of a good time. Kitt continued to fascinate him with her enthusiasm and store of knowledge.

"You know, Santiago has got to be pretty old," she was saying. "If his mother was born in 1858, he'd have to be in his nineties—even if she was in her forties when she gave birth to him."

"Old like Hod. I wonder how he's doing, poor old guy. Probably misses the crew at the dig. I keep thinking about that picture of James Kirker—Santiago Querque. And now we have another Santiago. Do you suppose Maria named her son for a scalp hunter?"

"Who knows? There are some things we may never figure out." Kitt waved at Señor Martinez as he ambled down the steps from his store.

"Michael! Kitt!" He pronounced her name *Keet*. "I have been waiting for you. My wife is very concerned that you were lost in the tunnels under the church. After you left, we began to worry."

"It's a fascinating place," Kitt replied. "I want to go back when I have more time."

"*¡Caramba!*" He crossed himself. Then he leaned over and whispered. "Sometimes when I am praying in the church, I think about the maze beneath the floor and all those dead people." Señor Martinez shivered. "Come, you will want to meet old Santiago. There is his house. On the left, with the blue posts. I will take you."

The door swung opened to reveal a dark-skinned, white-haired fellow who had no teeth. Dressed like the other villagers in a brightly knit sweater and dark wool trousers, he wore a pair of worn leather boots. With a wrinkled hand, he beckoned his guests to enter.

"Santiago will serve your lunch. Return to my house for dinner," Señor Martinez said on parting. "You will not see the light on the porch at that time of day, but I think you know my shop."

Kitt nodded, but Señor Martinez wasn't through. "The generator is too expensive to run before the sun has gone down, even though some days are very dark in Guadalupe Y Calvo. One evening the bulb burned out just as I lifted the switch...well, I will tell you about the light bulb while we eat our dinner."

Michael glanced at Kitt. She wore the faintest trace of a grin on her face as they stepped into the warm front room of Santiago's home. The old man gestured for his guests to be seated, then settled on a small stool beside the fire.

"I live here alone," he said in Spanish. "My children and my grandchildren all have homes in the village of Guadalupe Y Calvo, but I wish to live here in the house of my mother."

Michael nodded, trying to think how to begin an interview about the past. He wasn't sure Santiago was totally alert. The man's thin fingers traced patterns on his trousers. His head was turned to the fire, and he almost seemed to have forgotten his guests.

"I am lonely," he said. "In the old days many of us lived in the little house."

"How many children did your mother have, Santiago?" Kitt asked.

"Nine brothers and sisters. All dead now, but me. I was

the youngest. Santiago, the baby." He chuckled, keeping his eyes on the fire.

"Your mother, Maria, was the daughter of Maria Cristina Gallegos and the Shawnee, Black Dove, wasn't she?" Kitt asked gently.

"I was born when my mother was forty-seven years old. A big surprise for everyone, even for my mother when she first learned a baby would be coming."

"Did you know your mother well, Santiago?"

The old man turned and laughed. His bare gums gave him a childlike expression of innocence. "Of course I knew my mother. She lived to be almost one hundred years old. We have long lives, we who are descended from the Shawnee warrior. My father was not so lucky. Kicked in the head by a horse when I was five."

"So Black Dove was your grandfather?"

Santiago nodded, then he rubbed his hand across the air as if to erase the subject. "Let us eat now."

While Michael and Kitt sat in silence, the old man shuffled over to his stove and began preparing a meal of frijoles, fresh fruit and glasses of creamy milk. Michael slouched in his chair, one arm hooked over the back. He took the opportunity to study Kitt's face, pausing on her eyes, her lips, her neck.

Did she have any idea how he felt being so near her? Wanting her so much? He reflected on their short marriage. What would it be like now if they had stayed together, married and content and at ease with each other? During the days that had followed their trip to Santa Rita, he had realized that his love for Kitt hadn't died with their break-up. Not even close. He still loved her, desired her, wanted her as his wife.

Santiago was humming a tuneless melody as he stirred the frijoles. Michael decided to evaluate what he and Kitt had learned so far about Black Dove. That would require concentration, but he was a professional on a business trip, after all.

Then his eyes caught Kitt's and held them for a full minute. He knew she could read his mind. He gave her the same look he had sent her across a classroom full of high school seniors. It was the look that meant, I'm thinking about us. I'm thinking about your lips. I'm thinking about kissing you, holding you in my arms....

"Almuerzo." Lunch. Santiago thunked a chipped porcelain bowl on the table beside Kitt. She gave an involuntary start. Michael chuckled in a low voice. Standing, he lifted his chair to the table and placed it in front of a second bowl of mud-brown beans.

"So, Santiago," he said, forcing his attention to the matter at hand, "please tell us about Black Dove, your grandfather."

Feeling like a kid caught with her hand in the cookie jar, Kitt joined him at the table. All Michael Culhane had to do was stare at her and she began acting like some out-of-control teenager. This was not how she normally behaved. She dipped her spoon into the beans. Other men took her on dates, other men gave her longing looks. How was it that this one certain man—and only he—could transform her composure to chaos?

There he was across the table, chatting with Santiago, waving his spoon around as he spoke. Did he know how much she wanted to reach across and touch that little curl of dark gold hair that was sitting on the collar of his sweater? Then she could run her hands around his shoulders.... Get a grip, Kitt. Why would you be embracing him while he's glibly conversing over a bowl of refried beans?

"But Black Dove himself died when he was still quite young, we understand," Michael was saying. He glanced at Kitt.

She smiled with as little emotion as possible.

"My grandfather was killed on the side of the mountain,"

Santiago said. "You see, they took my mother away from him when she was twelve years old, after my grandmother died. From that time, Black Dove did not wish to live. He became careless, my mother told me. One day, he was trying to stop an Apache attack on the burro trains carrying gold to Chihuahua City. During the battle, Apaches killed my grandfather Black Dove. The murderers took away much gold that day."

"After his death, wasn't your grandfather buried in the church at Guadalupe Y Calvo?" Kitt asked, willing herself to concentrate.

"Of course not. He was an Indian. My mother told me no one knew of the massacre for many months. Not until word came from Chihuahua City that the gold train had never arrived. Then searchers went looking. There they found the dead."

"And your grandfather, Black Dove, was among those killed in the attack?"

"After so many months, it is difficult to tell about such things. One man whose body was found at the place of the ambush was wearing the cross my grandmother had given to Black Dove. My mother believed that man was her father. Black Dove always wore the cross, and so Black Dove had been killed."

Santiago held up a hand and began digging into the folds of his shirt. Kitt looked at Michael. He had set his spoon on the table. They watched as the old man fumbled with the buttons beneath his sweater.

"Here is the cross of Black Dove." Santiago slid a bright chain from his shirt and held it out. In his leathery palm lay a large but simple crucifix of yellow gold. It might have been any cross of gold. But Santiago took the end and carefully turned it over.

Kitt leaned forward. Tiny letters had been engraved in the gold. *"BD—Ma C G,"* she read. *"Mi Esposo En Dios."*

"My husband in God," Michael said to Santiago. "What did your grandmother mean by this inscription?"

"The church would not marry them. So they were married by God. It is even better, no?"

Michael focused on Kitt. "Either way is good…isn't it, Kitt?"

Kitt felt fragile suddenly—a sensation she rarely experienced before meeting Michael again after all those years. Now it kept emerging inside her, flitting through her chest so fast she was almost unaware of it. She was still herself—the tough Kitt who could look out for her own interests. But she was bending some, too. Allowing herself to feel things, and to want what she hadn't wanted for such a long time.

"Come and sit with me beside the fire," Santiago said. Kitt picked up the empty bowls and glasses and set them in a pot of soapy water by the stove. Michael wiped the table with a cloth. Then they joined the old man in a semicircle around his beehive fireplace.

"My mother told me about that day," Santiago said. His voice was barely audible. "It was the day she remembered most out of all the days of her whole life."

"Which day was that, Santiago?" Kitt asked him.

"The day her own mother died. My mother told me she crept like a little mouse into the room of her mother. From the door she watched. Her father was sitting on the bed where her mother lay. He was weeping. Can you imagine—the warrior Black Dove weeping and holding the hand of his wife? No doctors would come to the house to tend her. Black Dove did not know what was wrong with her. She had great pain. Black Dove climbed into the bed with his wife and held her very close to his chest. And then she died. He screamed and beat his chest and ran out of the house to his horse. He rode away into the mountains. My mother told me she was very afraid then—only twelve years old. She wanted to be with her father, but he had gone away in his grief."

"What happened after that?" Kitt said.

Santiago began tracing patterns on his trousers again. "The schoolteacher came to the home of Black Dove and Maria Cristina Gallegos—who had been his daughter. He took little twelve-year-old Maria—my mother—away from the house. They buried Maria Cristina Gallegos in the church the next day, but my mother was not allowed to see her."

"What about Black Dove? Did he ever come back for his daughter?"

Santiago smiled. "He came back, all painted for war— with red and black colors on his face. He rode up to the house of the schoolteacher and waved his tomahawk. He shouted that he wanted Maria and he would kill anyone who stood in his way. Then the schoolteacher, who was much afraid, forced my mother to go out onto the porch and tell Black Dove that she wanted to be safe and live in the village with the schoolteacher."

"Was that the truth?"

"Oh, no." Santiago sighed. "My mother loved her father very much. Black Dove was a gentle man. He taught her many games, and words of his language. He was quiet and good to her always. But that day the schoolteacher told her that if she did not make Black Dove leave the village, the whole town would go after him and kill him. Black Dove was a bad man, the schoolteacher told her—a hired killer."

"So Black Dove left?"

"He went into the hills, and soon he got killed by those Apaches."

"And what happened to Maria?"

"She lived with the schoolteacher for many years. But she never loved him. He had taken her away from her father. My mother always told me that Black Dove was a good man— loving, kind, generous. No matter what the others said about him, she told me she would believe only what she knew. Her father was a good man."

"So Maria grew up and got married and had nine children."

"The last one was me!" Santiago chuckled. "Now I have the cross of my grandfather Black Dove...I have something else, too."

Michael leaned forward. "What do you have, Santiago?"

The old man shook his head. "You would like to know—but I cannot tell you."

"Why can't you tell us?"

"Because it is the secret of Black Dove."

Kitt put a hand on the arm of the old man's chair. "Santiago, do you understand why we're here, asking about your grandfather?"

"Many people want to learn the story of Black Dove. I have told it often."

Kitt briefly related the discovery of the grave in New Mexico. She stressed the importance of confirming or disproving the theory that Black Dove might have left Guadalupe Y Calvo and gone to Muddy Flats.

"If you have anything at all that might lead us to the truth, Santiago, we need to know."

The old man closed his eyes and sat without speaking. Kitt waited, studying him, then decided he might have gone to sleep. She glanced at Michael. He shrugged. Remembering the way Michael had gone through her house and Hod's, she decided she'd better keep her eye on him. No doubt Michael would want to explore Santiago's home while the old man slept. She was about to suggest they leave when Santiago opened his eyes.

"This, I think, will be proof that the man killed on the mountainside was Black Dove. But if I show it to you—promise not to speak of it to anyone."

Kitt nodded. It would present some difficulties to keep such a secret, but she decided to go along. Maybe Santiago had something worthwhile, maybe not. The cross was interesting, but it didn't really prove anything. She felt her heartbeat speed up as the old man rooted around in the bottom of a large metal chest beside the fire.

"Here." Santiago turned to them, smiling his gummy grin. "I have the treasure of Black Dove."

He carried a small leather pouch tied with a thong. Settling back in his chair, he placed the pouch on his knees and carefully untied it. As he loosened the thong, Kitt tried to see inside.

"What is it? What do you have, Santiago?"

"Gold!" Santiago held up to the firelight a rough nugget the size of a walnut. Laying it carefully on one knee, he lifted another to the light, this one as large as a pecan. Then another and another.

"Where did Black Dove get this gold, Santiago?" Michael asked.

"From his mine. In the Sierra Madres, not far from Guadalupe Y Calvo." Santiago closed the pouch without offering Kitt or Michael a chance at close inspection. "There is no more gold at the mine now. Black Dove removed it all before he died."

"So how does this prove Black Dove was killed on the hillside?"

Santiago pulled at the drawstring. "This pouch was found on the body of the man who wore the cross. A sign is burned into the leather of the pouch—the sign of a black dove. See?" He showed them the tiny insignia. "So the man killed by Apaches had both Black Dove's crucifix and his pouch of gold. It could only have been Black Dove."

Kitt thought for a moment. "What about the teeth?"

"Teeth?"

"Did the man killed on the hillside have two gold front teeth, Santiago?"

"My mother never mentioned gold teeth. Why do you speak of gold teeth?"

"Black Dove was said to have two gold front teeth."

"I know nothing about this. My mother said only that Black Dove was her father—good and kind, loving and gentle. Nothing about gold teeth."

Kitt's eyes followed the old man as he replaced the pouch in the chest. Maybe Maria hadn't even noticed her father's gold teeth. Children rarely noted their parents' characteristics. To Maria, Black Dove clearly had been perfect in every way. Inside and out.

She let out her breath. As hard as it might be to accept, in light of the Muddy Flats excavation, Black Dove apparently had been killed and later buried in the mountains just outside Guadalupe Y Calvo. The evidence was simply too convincing: the remains of a man wearing Black Dove's crucifix and carrying a pouch inscribed with his insignia and filled with nuggets from his gold mine. Maria certainly believed her father had been killed. All signs indicated the warrior had been distraught—his wife had died and his daughter was taken from him.

So the mighty Black Dove had been murdered by the Apaches.

And the Muddy Flats man was another person entirely, even though he bore a striking resemblance to the description of Black Dove.

"Thank you, Santiago," Kitt said gently. She reached out to take his hand, but he sat gazing at the fire, his face slack.

"I am a lonely man," he remarked. "Will you stay with me here?"

Michael placed another log on the fire and prodded the flames. "Santiago, we already have rooms at Señor Martinez's store. Would you like for us to find your family—one of your children would come and sit with you, I'm sure."

"So busy, they are. Plowing and harvesting. Not much time for an old man. But you have nothing to do. You like to sit and talk. You like the stories of old Santiago. Stay and I will tell you more stories."

Michael hesitated only a moment before he reached into his pocket and pulled out his little recorder. "Here, Kitt. It's what you said you always wanted to do. Listen to his stories and spend as much time as you want. I have something to do. I'll come back for you before dinner."

Kitt looked down at the little machine on her knee. "Thanks," she said. "I'm sure I can find my way to the store."

"I'll come get you."

Giving Santiago a firm handshake, Michael headed out the door into the afternoon. Through the window, Kitt watched him disappear down an alley. Where was he going? Or did he really just want her to have this time alone to collect an old man's tales?

"Santiago," she said, pressing the little red button on the recorder. "Tell me your stories."

"Did anything come of that?" Michael asked. "You were there three hours."

"I'd have stayed longer but I ran out of tape."

"Must have been some good information. Anything about Black Dove?"

"Wouldn't you like to know." She felt his hand brush against hers as they descended the hill to the store. It had grown dark, and Señor Martinez's two light bulbs were burning.

"I couldn't stay with you, Kitt. I had other things to do."

"Like what?"

"Things."

"Things to do with what? Black Dove?"

"Wouldn't you like to know." Michael led Kitt through a side gate and headed her toward the Martinez dining room. "By the way, we're too late to join the family. They've already eaten."

"What are we going to do for dinner?"

"Just close your eyes and walk into the room. Close your eyes, Kitt."

"You're treating me like a kid."

"Sixteen years old. Right where we left off. Now close your eyes."

Making a face at him but obeying, Kitt stepped into the warmth of the small room. She could hear Michael moving around, striking matches, clinking dishes. The scent of smoke and candle wax drifted around her.

"Smells like you're lighting a pyre in here. What are you going to do, set me on fire?" she asked.

"Something like that."

"So when do I get to open my eyes?"

"You really have gotten a lot wordier in fifteen years, Kitt. You're impatient, too." His hand touched the side of her neck. "I like that about you. And I like *this* about you."

She took a deep breath as his fingers traced the curve of her jaw. Though her eyes were closed, she could sense his nearness. He had moved behind her. His breath warmed her hair. The presence of his chest not an inch from her back was as palpable as a magnetic field.

"Open your eyes, Kitt."

For a moment, she couldn't. Waiting for him to touch her somewhere, she tensed and held her breath. But he didn't move.

She opened her eyes.

The dining room sparkled with the lights of a hundred tiny candles that perched on windowsills, tabletop, chairs and floor. Shadows danced across the ceiling. The small table was draped with a white cloth. It held a platter of fresh fruit, a plate of steaming tortillas and two covered bowls.

"It's beautiful," Kitt whispered.

The next hour was magical. A simple meal of *arroz con pollo*, rice with chicken, became a feast. Kitt could never recall such an exhilarating day. It had begun with Michael's declaration of love and their passionate kiss. Then their fascinating visit to the catacombs of the church and the discovery of Black Dove's name in the records. After that, the enchanting hours hearing history come to life through Santiago's stories. And now, this candlelight dinner with an incredibly handsome man.

As she set her napkin on the table after the meal, Kitt turned to Michael. His eyes reflected the golden light of the candles. "It's all been so amazing," she said. "Seeing you outside my motel door that night…and finding out we still enjoyed each other. It's all been unexpected…like someone used a magic wand to cast a spell over us."

"This is not magic, Kitt. It's God."

"Oh, Michael, do you really believe that?"

"Yes, I do."

"You're supposed to be one of those cynical reporters I'm always butting heads with. Reporters don't believe God moves in mysterious, wonderful ways. They only buy hard, cold facts."

"Archaeologists aren't supposed to believe in magic. Only in things you can touch." He ran his fingers down her shoulders and took her hands. Lifting them, he pressed his thumbs deeply into her palms. His eyes held her, pinning her with a fierce intensity.

"Thank you for this great dinner," she whispered, making a stab at normalcy.

"Kitt." He pulled her roughly against him. His fingers tangled in her hair, and his mouth covered hers.

"I need you, Michael," she said, her arms wrapped tightly around his chest. "I need you the way I used to."

He cradled her head in his palms and met her eyes. "I love you, Kitt. It's more than need. It's commitment."

"Michael—oh, I can't stand this uncertainty between us. It feels so wrong. Please, be a husband to me again."

"Do you mean that, Kitt?" he asked as he held her close. "Do you believe God was preparing us for this moment when He brought us back into each other's lives? Do you think He wants us together again, forever?"

She closed her eyes, reflecting on Michael Culhane and how many years she had loved him. Thinking about how he fit with her. Thinking about the way they could talk and laugh together. Yes, maybe it had been planned. All of it.

"I believe in God," she said softly. "And I believe in this moment. But I'm not at all sure about tomorrow."

"Tomorrow?" he said, brushing a strand of hair from her cheek. "If we'll let it, tomorrow will bring us everything."

Chapter Fifteen

✤

"Any idea what day this is?" Seated on a low bench, Michael leaned his head back against the sun-warmed wall outside the Martinez house.

"Thursday, I think."

"I bet it's Friday."

"Doesn't our plane come in on Friday?"

"Right after lunch. We might want to think about packing."

Kitt closed her eyes and laughed. The passage of night and day had somehow all run together in the little town. Inside the Martinez dining room, the hundred candles burned only in memory. The fruit bowl had been washed and dried days ago.

"What have we been doing since Monday?" she asked.

"Don't you remember? We went for a walk. We shopped. We talked to people."

Kitt thought for a moment. "We took a look at the old

gold mine in town, too. And we had a picnic on the mountainside."

"I do believe I remember that."

Kitt leaned toward Michael and kissed the hard muscle of his shoulder. "You know what I liked best about these past few days?" she asked.

"Kissing."

"Nope. What I liked best is the talking we've done."

"It's been good," he said. "Talking to you and kissing you. Both."

Kitt nodded. At some point during the blur of days, everything inside Michael had come pouring out. One afternoon as they sat under a pine tree, he had talked for hours, telling her about the years he'd been without her.

While she cradled him, he told her of the lonely months in the barren sand. And she finally understood that the Gulf War had been more to him than a time of coming to terms with the end of his marriage. It had been a horrifying, almost unbelievable journey of growing up. Somewhere amid the scud missiles, mortars and small arms fire, Michael had found God. And then he had found himself. Through Christ, he had risen above the pain, torment and self-blame, and he had emerged whole. College and his job as a journalist had further matured him. He had learned what it meant to live with loss—and keep going.

Kitt, too, had talked. Not about the past, but about the future. Michael had encouraged her to expand on her vision. She outlined the dream she had mentioned in the crypt beneath the old church. It had been fun, heartening, to talk about things outside the realm of probability. But now they faced the reality of leaving Guadalupe Y Calvo. And Kitt realized she wasn't any clearer about the rest of her life than she had been the first night Michael walked up to her door and turned her world upside down.

"Kitt." The word held that quiet tone she had come to

love. His deep, adult male's voice seeped down into her bones. "Where have you gone?"

"I'm right here."

"You're somewhere else. Thinking about something. Tell me."

She stared at the red-tiled roof of the house across the street. "I'm having a hard time understanding myself right now, that's all. I don't usually do brainless things like this. I'm always thinking ahead, making plans, putting my life in order."

"Brainless?"

She grinned. "You have to admit, coming to this town on a wild-goose chase wasn't exactly rational."

"So what is it you want, Kitt?"

She met his steady blue-gray gaze. He was holding her a little apart, studying her with more solemnity than she wanted. She hedged. "Well, I probably ought to rent a car in El Paso and make a quick trip to Catclaw Draw. I have to take a last look at the new site—"

"Kitt—what do you want from me? From us?"

"I don't know, Michael. I enjoy being with you. It feels right. It's wonderful to be in your arms. Here, in this little isolated town, I'm glad we broke the rules. But..."

"But you still don't trust me. You think I'm going to run off and leave you like I did before."

"I don't know. I don't know whether it even matters. I mean—people do this sort of thing, don't they? They meet someone they knew before. They say and do things they didn't expect. And then they go back to their separate homes and their separate lives...and that's really all there is to it. You know what I mean?"

"Is that what you want this to be?"

"Well, what do *you* want, Michael?"

"I don't know." He stood suddenly. Kitt watched his muscles flex as he paced the cobbled street. He was a beautiful man—animal sleek, almost wickedly smooth. Dark blond curls tangled at the nape of his neck. His back was well defined and his shoulders broad.

As he stared almost angrily up at the sky, it occurred to Kitt that she really could not imagine ever being without Michael again. She wanted to see his face every morning for years to come. She wanted his kiss on her lips and the pressure of his arms around her. She wanted the chance to grow with him, fight with him, learn with him. She wanted to bear him children....

"Kitt, there's something I need to tell you." He stood outlined in the sunlight. "It's about the future. About us."

"Please, Michael. I don't want to hear anything about the future right now. Let's discuss it when we get back." She rose and stepped to his side. He would either want to make commitments—or bring about a painless but definite ending to their time together. She wasn't ready for either. And the fact that she didn't know which direction he would choose was enough proof that she really didn't know Michael as well as she imagined.

"I need to say something to you, Kitt." He covered her shoulders with his big hands. "I don't want to leave this place without working things out. There's a lot we still need to tell each other. When I was back in Albuquerque—"

"Michael, could you just pretend you're seventeen again and you aren't really into talking?" She took his hands from her shoulders and held them between her own. "Could you let it go just this once?"

"Kitt—"

"No talking, Michael."

"But—"

She shook her head. "If we're leaving this afternoon, I have another idea of how we might want to end this time together." She slipped her arms around him, her mouth found his and words were forgotten.

* * *

"Catclaw Draw hasn't changed."

Michael swung the rented compact into the motel parking lot. "The Thunderbird Motel hasn't changed, either. Same turquoise doors."

He caught Kitt's wrist as she leaned to open her door. "I'm not running away, Michael," she said, turning to face him. "I'm still just searching."

"I love you, Kitt."

How many times had he said those words? And she still had not responded. She knew Michael could see the fear in her eyes. Kitt was scared to death of him. But he wouldn't take the pressure off. He had lost her once, he told her. He wasn't about to lose her again.

When she said nothing, Michael stepped out of the car and began unloading their bags beside the motel doors. Kitt joined him, silently putting her key into the lock and turning it. She was formulating her next words to him when his cell phone rang. He looked to see who was calling.

"My managing editor," he told her. "I have to take this."

"I'm going out to the site," Kitt mouthed as she took the car keys from his hand.

"Wait a second, Steve," he said into the phone. "When? Just give me a date on that."

Kitt slipped her hands into her pockets as the man on the line continued talking. She considered waiting until Michael had finished, but the truth was she wanted nothing more than to escape him and all the emotion he evoked inside her.

Michael shook his head. "No," he said firmly. "I told you, Steve, I can't do it until next month. I'm not ready. I've got things—" He glanced up and caught Kitt watching him. He spoke softly. "Go on, honey. It's all right."

She stood for a moment, wondering what was happening with his job. His eyes had gone cold and gray.

"Absolutely not, Steve. Yes, I told you I'd accept. But I can't be ready that fast. There are more important things going on right now. I'm working through a situation."

Kitt jangled the keys to indicate she was taking the car. Then she climbed back inside it and headed out.

The new cemetery was an almost exact replica of the old Muddy Flats site. Kitt trudged through the tall, dry grass and ran through a mental checklist. Restored headstones stood in a symmetric pattern facing west. New granite stones labeled *Unknown* marked the graves uncovered in the second phase of the project. The large monument listing every name and grave location was not yet in place. It had only to be filled with the tiny scraps of coffin wood that were being examined in Santa Fe, then it would be settled at the front of the site.

Satisfied that all was as it should be, Kitt climbed into the car. She debated whether to return to the motel right away. Michael's conversation had disturbed her. What was his boss asking him to do? In all the weeks she had been with him again, she had never seen him so adamant. But, she decided, it was Michael's private business. Besides, Kitt had one more stop to make. She pulled the car onto the highway and started for Muddy Flats.

The familiar road lay bathed in a pink light. She watched the sun sink lower and lower over the horizon. As she drove down the dusty tracks toward the project site, she could see how changed it was. The contractor's trailer had been towed out. All the stakes and string were gone. Even the ground was bare of stone and grass. It looked flat and empty.

When she pulled to a stop, a glint of reflected sunlight caught her eye and she swung around. Old Hod's battered pickup sat beneath the cottonwood tree. Squinting against the sunset, Kitt climbed down and walked over to the truck.

"Hod," she called. "Hod, are you here?"

No answer. Kitt circled the pickup. Nothing. She scanned

the area around the site but saw no sign of him. Standing on tiptoe, she looked into the cab. The old man lay crumpled on the seat like a discarded candy bar wrapper.

"Hod?" Kitt flung open the door and leaned in. "Hey, Hod, are you all right?"

The old man looked at her in silence, his eyes bright. Trying to remember her first aid training, Kitt felt for a pulse and listened for breath. He smelled of beer.

"Hod—how much have you had to drink today?" Then she noticed the florid blotches that covered his neck and cheeks. "Talk to me, Hod. How long have you had this rash?"

"Rash?" His voice was barely audible.

"You're covered in spots. Look at your arms." Breathing heavily, Kitt combed her mind for a possible cause. Heat rash? Allergies? Chicken pox?

"You can't move, can you?" she asked. When he shook his head, she reached into her purse. "Okay, then I'm going to call the hospital for an ambulance."

"Hospital? No—" Hod coughed out the words. "No, Dr. Tucker. Not the hospital."

"Hod, you're a sick man. You need to see a doctor."

"Not the hospital. It's just beer." He closed his eyes for a moment, then dragged them open. "Take me home."

"We'll go get Michael." Kitt slid into the seat of the old pickup and propped Hod's burning head on her lap. How long had he been lying out here in the desert? And what was wrong with him? He couldn't die. Not yet. She had to get help, but she didn't know the motel's phone number.

Wind and dust blew into Kitt's face through the empty windshield as she sped down the highway. Hod's eyes were shut and his head lolled back and forth as she worked the clutch. *Don't die. Don't die,* she chanted inside her head as she drove.

Slamming the truck to a halt in front of the motel, Kitt

leaned on the horn. Michael ran outside, his shirttail hanging loose.

"It's Hod, Michael. Something's wrong with him."

"Where's the car? We'll take him to the hospital."

"I left it at the site. I couldn't move him, and he won't let me call an ambulance. He wants to go home."

Michael leaned through the window and looked at the old man. "What's this rash? We've got to get him to a doctor."

"No!" Hod's head lifted off Kitt's lap. "Home."

Michael gave a growl of frustration. "Okay, you drive him to his house, Kitt. I'll call an ambulance and guide them out there. The paramedics can make the decision."

"Right." Kitt threw the truck into Reverse and barreled onto the highway. After minutes that seemed like hours, the pickup skidded to a halt in front of the rambling adobe home. She sat gripping the wheel and breathing in deep gasps of honeysuckle-scented air.

"Hod?" She touched his cheek. "Hod, we're home."

"I want to go to bed, Mother."

Kitt closed her eyes. "Can you walk, Hod? I'll help you inside, but you have to do your part."

She lifted the frail shoulders. Hod leaned against her as she slid him off the seat. For a moment she thought he would topple onto the grass, but his knees somehow held. Hanging heavily on her shoulder, he stumbled up the path and into the house. With effort, she managed to steer him down the hall to his room.

"There now. Your bed, Hod. Doesn't that feel good?"

Kitt pulled off his old shoes and set them on the floor. Gingerly, she eased him out of his jacket. Red spots covered his face, neck and limbs.

"Hod, this is more than too many beers. Can you tell me how you're feeling? When did the rash start?"

The old man smiled and took her hand.

"Have you had a fever?" she asked.

"Pretty hot…I wanted to visit my mother's grave. She wasn't there anymore."

"Hod, the graves have been moved to Catclaw Draw. Remember?"

Hod's laugh was dry. "I forgot about that. You moved 'em, didn't you? Then you went away, and I thought you weren't coming back to see me. But here you are."

Kitt squeezed the paper-thin fingers. "Here I am, Hod."

"I want the picture. The one of my mother." He swung one red-spotted hand toward the table where a group of daguerreotypes sat. "Her getting married to my father."

Kitt leaned over and studied the silvery photographs on the bedside table. The only one with two people in it was the one she had decided earlier must be a father and daughter. Blowing dust from the frame, she handed Hod the picture.

He stared at it in silence, a little smile playing at his lips. "My mother," he whispered. "Elizabeth Hodding. You put her into that box, Dr. Tucker. Number fifty-one."

He seemed to slip away suddenly, and Kitt grabbed for his hand. "Hod, stay with me," she pleaded. "Tell me about your mother."

The thin eyelids fluttered open. "Elizabeth Hodding with the dress she sewed all them beads on that my Papa gave her. She was a seamstress, you know. She sewed him up when he first came to town that day. Papa said she was such a pretty little thing."

"I'm sure she was."

"She took him in and nursed him back to health. Never mind that he was an Indian and tough as an ol' boot. She loved him. Married him."

"An Indian?"

"Sure enough. With a name like Black Dove, what else could he be? Me, I'm Hodding Black Dove—not just plain old Hod like everyone thinks."

"Black Dove." The words hung at the end of her tongue.

"I remember my papa pretty good. Old fellow with a couple of bad teeth, lots of scars and the end of a knife stuck in his shoulder. But my mama loved him. No matter what all the town thought, she married him."

"You're Black Dove's son. Your mother married Black Dove in Muddy Flats."

"Ain't that what I said?"

Kitt felt numb as she studied the old man. "So Black Dove is buried in the Muddy Flats cemetery."

"I don't know where they buried Papa. They sent me off to Carlsbad to live with another family after he died. I never did know where they put him."

"Your father was buried in the Muddy Flats cemetery. I found his grave."

Hod nodded, his eyes closed. "Him and my mama together. That's good. They belong together."

Kitt looked at the old daguerreotype on Hod's chest. Elizabeth Hodding—young, beautiful. Wearing a beaded dress. Standing beside her was the old man. Strong, his head held high and proud.

And now she saw what she had missed before. In the midst of the man's brilliant smile were two slightly darker front teeth. They shone.

"I don't feel so good, Dr. Tucker."

"Michael's bringing help, Hod. Just hold on. Hold on to me."

The sparrow-bone hand gripped hers. "I'm awful hot."

"I'll get you a cool washcloth."

"Stay with me."

"I'm here, Hod."

He opened his eyes. "The day I was born, my mama died. I never knew her."

Kitt nodded, thinking of her lost baby. "I understand that. I do."

"I loved her, but I never met her when she was alive. She

was my mama. I was a part of her. I grew inside her. But she died."

Kitt sniffled. "I know."

"I think I made her die."

"No, Hod. No, you didn't. It wasn't your fault she died."

They sat quietly. Kitt thought of the emptiness inside her heart. The part of her that had died too soon. The tiny girl buried in the cemetery.

She heard the front door open, but she hardly registered Michael's shadow behind her as he stood in the hall.

"I loved my daughter," she whispered. "She died."

Hod patted his stomach, and Kitt put her head down. He weakly stroked her hair.

"Babies and mothers," he said. "You lost your daughter. I lost my mama."

Kitt turned her face into the coverlet. Everything she had hidden away rose to form a hard knot in her throat.

"Tell me about your girl, Dr. Tucker."

"I…I can't."

"Tell me."

Her eyes stung. Hod kept stroking her hair.

"She was almost ready to be born. Three weeks away," Kitt whispered into the quilt. "She stopped moving. The doctor…doctor couldn't hear her heart beating anymore. I had to wait for the labor to start. I sat in a chair and rocked."

"You were waiting."

"I wanted my daughter so much. She was everything I'd hoped for. She was Michael and me."

Now the hand stroking her hair was Michael's. But the voice in the little bedroom was Hod's.

"You loved your baby, even though you never knew her."

"She was part of me. And then she was born. She was…she was dead. Her cord was around her neck. That's what made her die. The delivery room was so quiet."

"It's always quiet when the good go."

The quilt was soaking up her tears. Michael ran his fingers through her hair as he knelt by her side. Some part of her knew he was there. He was crying in silence, but she could feel him mourning with her.

"I went home," she whispered. "I just kept rocking, thinking about nothing."

"You felt empty inside," Hod said.

"I felt like I had died, too."

Hod made little clucking sounds. Kitt cried. She cried for the life that had been inside her. The hope of birth. The love she had shared with Michael. All the dead, lost years. Her shoulders shook and Michael leaned against her, holding her.

"Mr. Culhane—we're ready now."

Two paramedics moved into the room with tubes and a stretcher. They hovered over Hod, examining. "How are you feeling, sir? What can you tell us about this rash?"

Kitt brushed her cheek and put on her professional face. Hod was submissive as they worked over him. After inserting an IV and lifting him onto the stretcher, they hurried him out the door. Within minutes the ambulance drove off, siren wailing and lights flashing.

As a cloud of dust settled on the honeysuckle vine, Kitt leaned against the porch post hugging herself.

"Talk to me, Kitt."

She glanced over her shoulder to find Michael just behind her. "What is there to say? He's so sick."

"What about you? You look different."

She shrugged. "With me, everything feels…better."

"About our baby."

"About everything."

His face was solemn for a moment. Then his mouth tipped up. "You cried. I'm glad, Kitt."

She gave a little laugh as she nodded. "Me, too."

He walked to her and caught her in his arms. She clutched his shirttail as she hugged him with all her might. Relief flowed through the embrace. She felt alive, glowing in his arms. Relief turned to elation.

"Kitt, honey," Michael said, holding her at arm's length. "Kitt, can we let our baby go? Can we give her to God?"

"I'll never completely accept what happened, Michael. You know that."

"I do know it. But I also know it's possible to heal."

She looked into the gray-blue eyes she loved. "I think it's time for me to heal."

A short while later they stood in the emergency waiting room at Catclaw Draw General Hospital. Charles Grant from the town's museum hurried down the hall just as a doctor swung open the door.

"I need to talk with you folks," the doctor said. "Let's step over to the side here."

"Thanks for calling, Michael," Charles whispered, following them to an unoccupied corner of the waiting room. "I've notified a few others Hod would consider his friends."

The doctor met each person's eyes. "I understand the patient has no living relatives."

"That's right," Kitt said. "But we care about him. Tell us what you know."

"We're having trouble getting a grip on the nature of the illness," the doctor explained. "You seem to know him better than anyone else. What can you tell me about his activities? Anything he may have been exposed to?"

"We've been away from him for a couple of weeks now," Kitt said. "We just got back to Catclaw Draw."

Charles shook his head. "I hadn't seen him for days, either. He frequents a bar in town. I've called some of the people who work there. Maybe they know what he's been up to."

"Get them on the phone again please, Charles. I need to know anything they can tell me."

As the museum director turned and pressed numbers on

his cell phone, Michael laced his fingers through Kitt's. "What's going on here, Doc?" he asked.

"I've rarely seen anything like this. Hod has apparently had a high fever for several days. He has indicated signs of dehydration and a troublesome cough. As you can see, he's developed a macular rash on his face and extremities."

"Macular?" Kitt asked.

"Spots. His face and neck are covered with them. The rash has generalized into the trunk area and legs. He's weathering the situation pretty well, but I'm afraid this rash could develop into something worse."

"Worse, like what?"

The doctor fiddled with his stethoscope. "I believe the current condition is viral, but I'm concerned about a possible secondary bacterial infection. If the lungs or brain become involved, he'll be in serious trouble."

"What do you think he's got?"

He shook his head. "I can only say it appears to be some rare virus."

"Measles." Kitt said the word without hesitation.

"Measles? Immunization has all but eradicated the disease. I've never seen a case in my career."

"It's measles. The virus can survive in skeletal remains for years. That's why archaeologists working on cemetery sites have to keep their immunizations up to date. Check with the Centers for Disease Control in Atlanta."

The doctor's face took on an uh-oh look. "Has Hod been at the Muddy Flats site where you were working, Dr. Tucker?"

She nodded. "We did our best to keep him away, but he was persistent. At one point, I caught him examining the boxes of remains. His parents were buried there."

"So Hod may have been exposed to a living measles virus." The doctor heaved a sigh. "Well, looks like we may have a diagnosis. I'm assuming your vaccinations are current, Dr. Tucker?"

"Absolutely."

"Mine, too," Michael said. "I travel overseas."

"Good. As I recall, measles is highly contagious during the prodrome period until four days after the appearance of the rash. I need to confirm the diagnosis and find out who else he's been in contact with throughout that time. And I'm going to have to check with the CDC on the best way to control this situation."

Michael wrapped an arm around Kitt. "What about Hod? Can we see him?"

"I'm afraid not. I saw the rash and put him in isolation immediately. Excuse me." The doctor hurried down the hall, his white coattails swinging behind him.

Kitt opened her mouth, but Michael laid his finger on her lips. "I know what you're thinking, honey. Don't even start to say it."

"But it *is* my fault."

"You tried to run him off the site. Dr. Dean and your summer workers are witnesses to that. You told your boss you were having trouble. Hod insisted on being there."

"But if he dies—"

"He's not going to die."

"He's *old,* Michael."

"And tough as a turkey buzzard. Besides, he can't die yet."

"Why not? He's got measles. People die of measles."

"He hasn't found his gold mine."

"Oh, Michael!" Kitt felt like kicking something.

Instead, she rode out to Muddy Flats with Michael to pick up the rented car, and then drove it to the motel. Charles Grant called Kitt from the hospital to say that Hod already was beginning to respond to treatment. He also reported that half the tavern regulars and all the employees had gathered in the waiting room.

"We never got Hod properly admitted at the hospital, Kitt," Charles said on the phone. "Any idea of his age?"

"He's over a hundred, that's for sure."

Michael was outside his room fiddling with the key to his door. "Tell Charles to talk to the waitress who knows Hod so well."

Kitt started to relay the suggestion, but Charles interrupted her. "Any idea of Hod's full name? I know he won't have insurance, but they need his full name to admit him. None of his friends has any idea."

"Black Dove," Kitt said evenly. "His name is Hodding Black Dove."

"What?" Michael and Charles said it at the same time.

"Hodding Black Dove," Kitt repeated. "His mother was Elizabeth Hodding. His father was Black Dove—"

Michael snapped the phone from Kitt's hand "We'll call you back, Charles."

"Michael, that was rude! Charles was trying to help—"

"What were you telling him?"

"Black Dove is Hod's father. While you were getting the ambulance, he told me about it. There's even a photo. You can see the gold teeth."

"Is this for real? Black Dove actually was buried in Muddy Flats?"

"Yes."

"Unbelievable."

Kitt's cell phone warbled again, but Michael turned it off before she could take it from him. "This is a story, Kitt. My story. I don't want it to get out."

"I don't see the big deal."

"If Black Dove did come to New Mexico—and if Hod is Black Dove's son—and if Black Dove did take Hod to a mine when he was a boy, then that gold is probably what he dug out of the mine near Guadalupe Y Calvo. Hod really did see gold, Kitt."

"So?"

"So, that gold is somewhere near here."

"And?"

"I'm going to find it."

Chapter Sixteen

"Hod has been hunting for that gold mine for almost a hundred years, Michael. What makes you think you can find it?"

He fought the urge to raise his voice. After all this time, how could she fail to understand him? "It's what I do," he said. "I investigate. People. Events. Stories. I follow the trail of nuggets to the buried gold."

"You're nuts." Kitt snatched her cell phone from Michael and began pressing keys. "I'm calling Charles Grant, and you're going to apologize for cutting him off."

"Let's look for that gold, Kitt," Michael said. "You and me, together. It would be a great ending to the article."

"If Hod couldn't find it, how could we?"

"Surely there's something he overlooked. Something he didn't know about."

"Michael, the story is just fine the way it is. Hod turned out to be Black Dove's son. That'll make for great copy. But you have to leave out any mention of the gold. Promise me."

"Why would I do that?"

"Because people will start combing the area looking for Black Dove's gold. You don't know treasure hunters the way I do. They'll tear up everything in sight."

"How can I write the article and leave out the gold?"

"These people destroy valuable historical sites. They're crazy, Michael."

"Kitt, come on now—" He stopped when he saw Kitt's face go still. All the breath went out of her. She was holding a slip of paper that had slid out of the phone book. Michael recognized it. He grabbed for it, but she jerked it away.

"Nairobi." She said the word as though it was something alien. Then she looked at him, her brown eyes darkening to black. "This is an itinerary from Albuquerque to Nairobi, Kenya, Michael. This is a plane ticket."

"Give me that thing."

"You're leaving New Mexico."

"I wanted to tell you in Guadalupe Y Calvo, Kitt. I need to explain."

"This is what you were talking to your boss about, isn't it?"

"I got the overseas bureau job."

"Nairobi."

"It's in East Africa."

"I know where it is," she snapped.

"I found out when I was in Albuquerque. That's part of the reason I came to see you. Why I wanted to go to Mexico with you."

"One last fling?"

"Of course not."

"When are you leaving?"

"Next week."

Kitt carefully placed the slip of paper in the phone book. He could almost hear her thoughts. Michael was going away. Leaving. Just like he'd left before. Only this time he'd be in Africa.

She gave a little laugh. "Well, I guess that settles that."

"What settles what?"

"I need to check on Hod. Excuse me."

She slid her phone into her purse and made for the car. Michael reached out and caught her arm. She tried to pull free but he swung her around.

"What kind of man do you think I am, Kitt?" he demanded.

"You're separate from me, that's all I know. A completely separate person."

"After what happened between us in Mexico?"

"I'm not going to go through this all over again with you. I have to leave."

"You'll stay right here."

"No, Michael. Let me go. Don't drag this out."

"Kitt, will you listen to me?"

"I've been through this before with you, Michael. Remember? You told me you loved me. You told me if I ever needed you, you'd be there. But then you just walked out." She squared her shoulders. "Well, this time I'm the one who's walking out. Go to Africa. Print your gold story. Just leave me alone."

Michael watched in stunned silence as she got into Hod's old truck and drove away.

Kitt didn't know it was possible to cry for five hours straight. It was. She sat in Hod's adobe house, playing the Victrola, thinking about Michael Culhane and crying.

Hod was going to be all right. He had a mild case of measles. His friends had set up a vigil. She had stayed a while at the hospital, but Michael never came.

Hod needed clothes, so she volunteered to go out to his place. She swung past the motel. The compact rental was gone.

So that was it. Over and finished. Just like before.

She forgot about getting Hod some pajamas. Instead, she

sat in the Victorian chair playing old records and crying. Of course, it didn't make the pain go away. She remembered that Michael had danced her around this very room. His arms so strong. His face so close.

Maybe she had overreacted when she found the itinerary. But Africa?

Michael would be ten thousand miles away. She had no doubt he was going. He had accepted the bureau job. He had a plane ticket. It was a done deal.

Why had she thought things would be any different this time?

"Dr. Tucker, am I glad to see you." Hod stretched out his hand.

He looked out of place in the crisp, clean hospital bed. His face had been newly shaved. The pale green gown revealed his long, sinewy arms. He patted her hand as she sat on the end of his bed.

"They tell me I been in here almost a week now."

"How's it going?"

"I want out. You gonna help me, Dr. Tucker?"

"When you're well enough."

"Aw, come on now. I want to go home."

Kitt reached out and smoothed the thin wisps of white hair on his forehead. His spots had dried and were clearing up. He gave her a little grin.

"You look worse'n me, Doc. What you been up to?"

"I've been staying out at your house, Hod. I hope you don't mind. I did a little straightening and cleaning."

"Them newspapers. Kinda got the better of me, didn't they?" He looked sheepish.

"You have some valuable material there, Hod. You ought to think about letting Charles Grant put some of it in the museum."

"He can have whatever he wants. I don't need the stuff. Just the pictures—he can't have my pictures."

"I brought the one of your mother and father the other day. You were sleeping."

"I got it there on my table. Thanks."

"Hod…you told me your father was named Black Dove. Is that right?"

The old man closed his eyes. "You ain't gonna turn against me 'cause I'm part Indian, are you, Doc?"

"Of course not, Hod. But there's something you should know."

"What's that?"

"Your father was quite a famous man. No one knew what became of him after his days with James Kirker."

"The scalper? Oh, Papa went down to Mexico after he quit ridin' with Kirker. Lived there a few years. Had a rough time of it, he told me."

"Most scholars believe Black Dove died in Mexico."

"Died there!" Hod cackled. "Why didn't they ask me? I'da told 'em he come on up here to Muddy Flats and married my mama. 'Course he had a little trouble along the way. Got ambushed. He was near dead when he rode into town. My Mama sewed him up, see. She was a seamstress."

"Yes."

"They fell in love and got married. Papa didn't die till I was around five or six. He was old as the hills by then. He told me folk with his Indian blood live a long, long time."

Kitt pondered what she had been turning over in her mind. "Hod, there's something else you should know."

"What's that, Doc?"

"Your father had a daughter in Mexico. Her son and his children still live there."

"I'll be." Hod gripped Kitt's hand. "You mean to tell me I got a sister? I got *family?*"

"Your half sister passed away some time ago. But her son is still living. He has several children and grandchildren."

"Well, what do you know? I got a family! A family!"

"Take it easy, Hod."

He had raised up on the bed and was gazing at her with bright, shining eyes. "Tell me about my nephew, Doc. Tell me everything."

Kitt settled him onto his pillow and related her long chat with old Santiago in Guadalupe Y Calvo. Hod's expression went from one of elation to pure ecstasy. Every few sentences, he would interrupt.

"I got me a family!"

"You'd love them, Hod. I'm sure of that."

"I'm going to see them. You get me out of this bed, and I'm going down to meet my nephew."

Kitt considered pressing the nurse contact button. Hod was almost beside himself with happiness. "It's not that simple, Hod," she explained, trying to press him back onto the bed. "They live in Mexico. It's a long way, and you're a sick man. Besides, they all speak Spanish."

"You don't think I've lived this many years in New Mexico and ain't learned to talk Spanish, do ya? Now you just get me a plane ticket and I'm going down there. I'll move in with my nephew—"

"Hod, please. You have to settle down."

"You said he was lonely. You told me that, didn't you? Well, I'm lonely, too. Let me tell you something, Dr. Tucker." With surprising strength, Hod pulled her close. "I always told myself if I ever got a chance to be part of a family, I'd grab it." He squinted at her appraisingly. "And so should you."

Kitt's eyes clouded with tears for the hundredth time. "Hod—"

"I ain't finished talkin', young 'un. Now my papa and my mama had a lot of things goin' against 'em. But they stuck it out, 'cause they loved each other. Me—I spent my whole life lookin' for that ol' gold mine. I kept on puttin' other things ahead of love. Don't you do that, girl. You go find love and hang on for dear life no matter what."

Kitt reached for a tissue and blew her nose. "I've just had a lot of difficult things to deal with."

"Difficult things? Who hasn't? Life is hard. Believe me, I ain't lived this long 'cause it was easy."

"But, Hod, the way things are today—"

"Ain't no different than the way they used to be. Don't think I haven't read them newspapers I been stackin' up in my kitchen. Folks want marriage handed to 'em like they get everything else—all wrapped up in pretty packages. If it ain't workin' just right, they toss it out like some fast food hamburger in a plastic carton. Nope, girl. You don't do that way with family. Listen to old Hod."

Kit nodded, blotting at her cheeks.

"What about your young fella? That newspaper reporter. I seen the way you two was lookin' at each other."

"He's gone. He's…well, we just couldn't make it work. I lost my baby, you know. And our marriage was over a long time ago."

"Aw, there you go again. Ain't you strong enough to get past them humps, Dr. Tucker?"

"I don't think so. I'm—"

"You're tough as an old turkey buzzard, just like me. Wipe your eyes, now. Go find happiness."

"I love you, Hod."

"I love you, too, sweetheart." He brushed a tear from his cheek. "Now when you gonna get me my ticket? I'm headin' for Mexico!"

Chapter Seventeen

❦

The old adobe house held a healing power. Maybe it was the power of the love that had lived there so long ago, Kitt thought. Maybe it was the silence. Time to think, pray, reflect on choices and losses and new life ahead.

She stayed all week, cleaning and arranging rooms. It felt like she was putting herself back in order. She did the things she truly enjoyed—weed the flowerbeds, read old books, wash windows. And she tried new things. She talked to God, sometimes for hours on end, getting to know Him again. She repented the years she had rejected Christ, and she soaked up the peace she felt now as His Spirit filled her.

In those quiet days, the baby Kitt had lost somehow was found. The tiny child without breath or heartbeat now played at the feet of God and nestled in His arms to rest. Kitt left her daughter there, safe and secure.

And Michael…Michael had gone to Africa in the middle of the week. Kitt imagined his plane flying overhead, taking him away forever. Faced with the painful absence of the man she loved but couldn't permit herself to accept, she went back to her cleaning. She scrubbed the floors until the Saltillo tiles shone and the grout gleamed white and even Michael Culhane's absence didn't hurt quite so much.

She made one trip to the post office with a letter for her supervisor. Dave and Sue Logan would be wondering what had happened to her. She was supposed to start the ditch project. She told Dave she was taking an extra week of vacation. Apollo would be in good hands, and her boss wouldn't object to giving her the leave time. She had hardly asked for a day off in years.

Hod got feistier by the day. The nurses could barely hold him down for his medication. And every day it was the same question. "You got my plane ticket for Mexico yet, Dr. Tucker? You written my nephew to tell him I'm comin' to see him? Tell him to get the grandkids ready. Old Uncle Hod is movin' in!"

Kitt rose early and was dusting the glass-fronted rosewood sideboard in the parlor one morning when she heard a car pull up to the front of the house. For a moment, she was afraid it might be bad news about Hod. Then she remembered Charles Grant had promised to come and haul away the last stack of old newspapers.

Still in her robe, Kitt padded across the warm tile floor. The smell of honeysuckle enveloped her as she opened the door.

"Morning, ma'am." A thin young man stood framed in sunlight. "I've come to put up your sign."

Kitt glanced at the dusty brown car behind him. "Are you from the museum?"

"I'm with Miriam Morgan Realty." He held a big green metal For Sale notice. "Didn't Mr. Black Dove tell you we were coming?"

"Come in. Please." She stepped back from the door, but he didn't move.

"He's selling the house. I thought he would have told you."

"I hadn't heard," she said, her heart suddenly heavy. "Hod never mentioned it."

"He called my boss and said he wanted to list the house. She told him he probably wouldn't get much for it, way out here like it is—and with no plumbing or electricity. But he's persistent, you know." The young man shifted from one foot to the other. "I...um...need to take a look around so we can set an asking price, and then I'll just put the sign over there."

He turned toward the yard as a sleek gray compact car pulled up. Kitt's heart did a double flip-flop and nearly stopped.

"You can put your sign away," Michael Culhane said, stepping out of the car. He slipped his sunglasses into the front pocket of his blue oxford shirt.

"But I was sent out here to—"

"I bought the house. You can head on back to town."

The young man stared as Michael strode onto the porch. Kitt couldn't move.

"I'm with Miriam Morgan Realty—"

"I know who you work for. I just talked to Mrs. Morgan. Hod and I worked out a deal on the house. Your boss knows all about it."

"You mean I don't need to do the appraisal?"

"Nope."

Turning to Kitt, the young man gave a little shrug and carried his sign off the porch.

As the brown car pulled away, Michael stuck his hands in his pockets and leaned against a wooden post.

"You're supposed to be in Africa," Kitt said.

"You're supposed to be lining ditches with colored cement."

He had never looked so good. His blue shirt made his eyes lose their gray and take on an almost clear-sky quality. His face, tanned and smooth this early in the morning, held the faint trace of a grin.

Kitt glanced at the shaggy robe and worn slippers she had found in Hod's wardrobe. Her braid, with sprigs of loose hair hanging out, had slipped over her shoulder.

"You bought Hod's house?" she asked.

"He wants to live with his nephew in Mexico."

"I know, but—"

"He needed money, so I bought the house. Furniture and all. How do you like it?"

"I...well, I love it."

"Aren't you going to invite me in for a cup of coffee?" He strolled past her into the cool depths of the hall.

"What are you doing here, Michael?" She hurried after him, trying to smooth out the sprigs.

"I came to find you."

"But you were going to Africa."

"That's right," he said. He swung around as he passed the parlor. "What have you done with the place? It looks great."

"I've been cleaning."

"You didn't throw out all the newspapers, did you?"

"Charles Grant took them to the museum."

"Good. I intend to do some reading. Where do you keep the coffee? I've been up almost all night. That Hod is a can-tankerous old coot. He tried to give me the house for the cost of his plane ticket. It was all I could do to talk him into a fair price."

"It's up here."

"What?"

"The coffee. I keep it up here." She took a can from one of the shelves she had painted in white enamel. Mechanically, she filled the old speckled tin coffeepot. What was Michael doing here? This wasn't making any sense.

"Dave Logan called me two days ago, Kitt." Michael settled into one of the oak pressed-back chairs at the kitchen table. "He was hoping I might know where you were."

She fiddled with the cups on the shelf, then took one

down and stared at it. "If you thought I was going to come apart again, Michael, you were wrong. If you thought you'd find me sitting here in a rocking chair—"

"I didn't think that at all."

"I just needed some time to readjust."

"To what?"

"To everything. To getting my old life back."

"Don't tell me you wanted your old life back. Did you think I would go off and leave you again, Kitt?"

She looked at him. He had propped the heel of one boot on the toe of the other. His eyes held a curious light.

"You're going to Africa, Michael," she said. "You just told me that."

"True."

"Then what are you doing here?"

"We've already been over this. I came to find you."

"What for?"

"Several things. The gold, for one."

"Oh, Michael, you're not still on that kick, are you?"

He stood and took the mug of steaming coffee she offered. "I like this—taking a cup of hot coffee from you in the morning. Being together in our kitchen."

Kitt swallowed. "It's your house. You bought it."

"Hod told me it would be a good house for a family. For the sort of love that lasts a lifetime."

Unable to look at Michael, Kitt began unbraiding her messy hair. "He's excited about his nephew. That's the family he's talking about."

"Right." Michael set his cup down on the kitchen counter. "Listen, I've got a bunch of stuff out in the car, Kitt. Your files on the Muddy Flats cemetery. Dr. Oldham's notes. You want to see if we can find that mine?"

She considered for a moment. Whatever the man was doing here, she was glad to see him. In fact, the more she looked at him standing in the big bright kitchen, the more she wanted him to take her in his arms and kiss her. Wait a minute. Was he really even here? Was this a dream?

"You told me you were leaving for Nairobi last week."

"Affiliated Press owed me a couple of weeks of vacation. I changed my departure date."

She studied her slippers for a moment, pondering. "I think I know where the mine is."

He took a step closer. "I thought you might."

"Is that why you came back?"

"I came to find you, Kitt."

She fumbled the lid onto the coffee can. "I need to change clothes."

"You look beautiful this morning."

She laughed. "This is Hod's old—"

"I love you, Kitt."

"I was trying to give you up again."

"Don't give me up."

She gazed out at the honeysuckle. A ruby-throated hummingbird darted from blossom to blossom. Its emerald feathers shimmered in the early sunlight.

"There's a photograph in my files," she said softly. "It's a picture of a scrap of newspaper I found in Black Dove's grave. Do you have it?"

"Marry me, Kitt."

The hummingbird dipped its long beak into a yellow flower. She couldn't see its wings, they were moving so fast. Behind her, Michael walked down the long hallway and out the front door. His front door. She could see him rooting around in the backseat of his car. His lean legs, his leather loafers. The back of his head with its sunlightened gold curls. His blue shirt molding to his shoulders.

She would love him even if he got old and skinny and stubborn, like Hod. She imagined the two of them in rocking chairs rocking slowly on the porch of the old adobe. The honeysuckle vine scented the air. She was wearing glasses, and one of those old-lady checkered dresses. Her hair was white and cottony. His knees creaked as he shuffled her around. She could hear his heartbeat beneath his old red wool cardigan.

She knew she could sit on the porch with him all night.

Michael had waited while she changed out of Hod's old robe and into her clothes. She padded into the living room in her stocking feet. Carrying her boots, she sat down in a chair near his.

"I brought in your file," he said. "What makes you think you know the gold's location?"

"It doesn't take all that much figuring. As I cleaned out the house, I had a lot of time to think, to put together the pieces of the past. Black Dove and Kirker. Guadalupe Y Calvo. The gold mine and the Apache massacre. Black Dove took the gold, you know. He set up the massacre so he could get away with the gold train."

"I figure he planted that cross and the pouch of nuggets on someone else's body," Michael said as he flipped through her research.

"Of course. He was no fool." Kitt shoved her foot into her boot and smoothed down her jeans. "The citizens of Guadalupe Y Calvo were heartless enough to refuse to let him marry in the Church, and they took his daughter away when her mother died after the doctor wouldn't treat her. So Black Dove had no compunctions about stealing their gold."

"No wonder Hod remembers seeing both nuggets and bars in Black Dove's hideout. The bars were Chihuahua government gold. The nuggets were from Black Dove's little mine in the mountains."

She took the thick file folder and spread it out on her lap. "Are you still planning to mention the gold in your article, Michael?"

"It won't be complete without that. But if we can find the

gold ourselves, then nobody will be tempted to tear up the countryside looking for it."

"Here." She leafed through the pile of photographs. One showed a glass bottle they had found in the crook of one woman's elbow. Another was of the head of a ceramic doll.

"These are Elizabeth Hodding's beads," she said, handing him a photo. "She's Hod's mother."

"The seamstress."

"Amazing what brings people together, isn't it?" Kitt finally located the photograph she had been seeking. "Here's the scrap of paper I found in Black Dove's grave."

"Looks like cattle market prices to me."

"That's what Dr. Dean and I concluded. But here's what was on the other side."

"An advertisement for maps."

Kitt held the photograph in a beam of yellow sunlight. "This is the part I had forgotten. See this writing scribbled on the side of the newspaper scrap? I thought it was an address—the place to write for the maps."

Michael studied the photo. "It's not an address, Kitt. It's the coordinates for the location of the gold mine."

He thought about grabbing her and giving her a great big kiss. But the hurt between them was still too near the surface. Michael knew Kitt thought he had run off and left her again. He had forced himself to stay away just long enough to give her time to think over her feelings. Just long enough to prove to her that he wasn't leaving her again. Ever.

He recalled her tears as Hod held her, and he realized the old man had played a part more important in their lives than either of them probably understood. Now it was time to do something for him.

"Hod told us his father had promised to write the gold's location so he would always have it," Michael said. "But the directions were buried with him. Poor Hod didn't have a chance of finding it. Any idea where this is?"

Kitt stood. "Not positive. But if we can find the map listed in this ad, we'll probably find the location of the gold."

She stepped to an oversize antique walnut desk and lifted the lid. Rolls of maps lay neatly arranged at the back. She sorted through them, studying the inscriptions on each one. "Here it is."

Kneeling to the floor, Kitt began to unroll an old yellowed map. Michael stared at the way her hair draped over her arms and spilled onto the document. One long finger traced the directions as she looked from the photograph to the map. Her boots were curled up beneath her, and it was all he could do to keep from going to her.

If he touched her shoulder, would she abandon the map? Would she curl into his arms? Would she lift her lips to his?

"Here it is!" She swung around, her face alight. "Look at these coordinates. Black Dove hid the gold in the Guadalupe Mountains—right here at a spot called Baldy Peak. Can you imagine that? The gold is from Guadalupe Y Calvo and he put it in the Guadalupes. And Calvo means bald in Spanish!"

Kitt leapt to her feet—a young girl again. All the sadness had gone out of her face. She was rolling up the map, grabbing her jacket from the coatrack.

"Wasn't that clever of him?" she asked, shrugging on the jacket. She caught up the length of her hair and pulled it out of her collar. "Guadalupe Y Calvo. Baldy Peak in the Guadalupe Mountains. You'd think Hod might have figured that out. But without the scrap of newspaper, he didn't have any idea. That's what first tipped me off—"

In two strides Michael had caught her in his arms. Her mouth instantly pressed to his, warm and just as willing as he had hoped. She didn't resist for one instant. The map fell to the floor.

"Oh, Michael. I thought you'd gone."

"I told you I wasn't leaving you again, Kitt. When are you going to start believing me?"

"I believe you. I believe everything you tell me. Just…just don't stop kissing me. Right there—kiss me right there. Oh, Michael, I missed you."

"You won't miss me ever again," he murmured. "It's you and me together, Kitt. So let's go find that gold."

Before her sweet kisses could distract him too much, he grabbed her around the waist and pulled her out to the car.

The Guadalupes lay more than an hour southwest of Cat-claw Draw. Kitt and Michael drove mostly in silence, occupied with private thoughts and reflections. She still couldn't believe he was really in New Mexico and not in Africa. And he owned Hod's old house. And he loved her.

As they drove into the shadow of the chain of giant, flat-topped mountains, Michael slipped his arm around Kitt's shoulders. "Baldy Peak," he announced. "Here we are."

She couldn't have cared less. The car swung in to a scenic vista parking lot, and Michael tried to get out. Kitt grabbed his shirt and dragged him back.

"Nope, not this time," she said. "You're not changing the topic till I'm ready. And I don't intend to discuss Black Dove."

He smiled slyly. "You mean you don't want to look for gold right this minute?"

"Never have. I have all the treasure my heart could ever need…right here in this car."

"I want you in my life so badly, Kitt." He gazed into her eyes, his own depthless. "Marry me. Just say you will."

"Michael, these last few days taught me something I had never understood before. God didn't abandon me. He loves me. He brought us together when we were kids. He's holding our daughter in His arms. He wants the best for us, no matter what mistakes we've made or hurt we've caused each other." She brushed a tear from her cheek. "Michael, I never stopped being your wife."

With a laugh of joy, he caught her in his arms. "I love you, honey."

"I love you, too."

Speaking the words at last, Kitt knew a surge of inexpressible joy. She was ready for Michael now. Ready for life and everything it had to bring. She held him, absorbing the vibrant presence of this man she loved so dearly. Then she shuddered with ecstasy as once again, she felt her heart become one with his.

They hiked up a rocky trail, Michael looking at his compass and spouting fragments of information he remembered from his Boy Scout training. Kitt paid more attention to the terrain than the map. She had never cared much for the idea of a hoard of gold—and the desire for it that drove men mad. Michael was all business again, but she felt reborn. A warm glow spread through her body and settled on her face in a soft smile.

It was nearly sunset when Michael finally found the old pine tree bent into the shape of an upside-down *L*. The tree was exactly where it ought to be, just as the coordinates had been written. Somewhere near them lay Black Dove's fortune. They scouted around, searching for anything that might look like the entrance to a cave.

"Didn't Hod refer to the cave entrance as a sort of chasm?" Michael called from the top of a boulder.

Kitt nodded. "I don't see any chasms around here. Do you suppose it could be under a pile of these rocks?"

"If it is, it's going to take a bulldozer to find the opening."

Kitt flicked a pebble and watched it roll down the mountain. She imagined Hod rolling stones there almost a hundred years earlier. The old pine tree bent in the shape of an *L* certainly was the right landmark, but nothing seemed to suggest a cave of any sort.

Michael scrambled behind the boulder. Kitt could tell he

was getting frustrated. She studied the old pine tree. The wind must have twisted it into such an odd shape. At the crook of the tree, two main branches forked. There, a strange-looking branch stuck out like some sort of odd appendage.

Wandering closer, Kitt set one foot on a small rock and lifted herself to eye level with the crook. "Michael—hey, get over here!"

He scrambled around the boulder and joined her at the base of the pine tree. "What have you…what is that thing?"

"It's some kind of metal tube. Definitely man-made." She stood on tiptoe and grabbed the end of it. The tube wouldn't budge.

"The tree has grown up around it," Michael said. "It must have been there a long time. Here—let me take a look."

They traded places.

"It's the barrel of a gun," he said. "A muzzle loader."

"What's it doing stuck way up there?"

"I don't know. It's just the barrel. There's no stock, and the breech plug has been taken out." He caught a large branch in each hand. "I'll climb up there and see if anything's written on the barrel. Or maybe there's something with it."

Kitt shaded her eyes while Michael pulled himself into the tree. He tried to wiggle the gun barrel but it was wedged firmly in place. "Nothing here."

"Look inside. Maybe Black Dove put directions in the tube."

"You suppose Black Dove put this up here?"

"Who else?"

He fitted one eye to the barrel and squinted. The setting sun had nearly obliterated the light. "Nothing in there, because you can see all the way through it. The sides are a little rusty and corroded."

"What can you make out when you focus beyond it?"

"Just that limestone face on the cliff in the distance."

"What's on the cliff? Any markings?"

He looked again. "Nothing but a blank wall. I guess some one must have just stuck the gun up there, and the pine tree grew around it over the years."

As Michael climbed down, Kitt again imagined the young Hod. That many years ago, the pine tree would have been a sapling. If someone had placed the barrel of a gun in the crook, in time the tree would have wedged it tight. Perhaps even twisted it out of place.

"Give me a boost," Kitt whispered. For all her certainty that the treasure meant nothing to her, the realization that she might have found it had made her mouth go dry. As she climbed, she spoke softly. "Black Dove wrote down the co-ordinates for the muzzle loader barrel. He positioned the muzzle loader in the pine tree so that if you look down it, you see the entrance to the cave."

Michael frowned. "I saw nothing but limestone."

"A hundred years ago the tree was shorter, thinner. Time has grown and twisted it." She looked through the muzzle barrel, then through a small pair of binoculars that hung from her neck. "If you look a few feet down the limestone face and to the left, you'll see the crevice."

The gold was just as Hod had described it. Bars on one side, nuggets in saddlebags on the other. The slender scar at the base of the limestone cliff face had been so covered with dirt and pebbles it was no wonder the place had stayed hidden for over a hundred years. Another half-hour hike through the warm afternoon sunshine had taken Michael and Kitt to the spot, and a serious shoveling effort had re-vealed the narrow opening to the cave.

"Looks like we're set for life," Michael remarked as he shone a flashlight over the stacked bars. "We can buy a penthouse in New York and a cabin in Aspen."

Kitt straightened. "This isn't our gold, Michael. Ownership will have to be worked out between Hod and the Mexican and United States governments."

He smiled. "So how does an old adobe house in New Mexico sound instead?"

"It sounds perfect." She hefted a gold bar, then replaced it on its stack. "But what about Africa? You told me you're still going."

"I thought you might like to see Kenya. You said you wanted to record tribal folklore. I know of a fellow doing just that, an anthropologist by the name of Dr. Grant Thornton. I sent him a message, and he said he could definitely use some help."

"I'll have to tell Dave Logan."

"I already told him. Sue's planning the wedding. There's this old chapel in Santa Fe…."

Kitt stared at the shaft of light filtering into the narrow cave. Life with Michael was worth more than all the gold of Guadalupe Y Calvo. Hod had been right. This time they wouldn't give up—no matter what.

What had passed before was only the twilight of the dawn. The day of their love had come at last.

* * * * *

Turn the page for a sneak peek at
THE BRITON
by Catherine Palmer,
the first book in the exciting new
Love Inspired Historical series,
available in early 2008.

England, 1152

"Fellow Britons," Bronwen's father said loudly. "At the start of the feast, I spoke to you of a great announcement. As you know, I am possessed of two fine treasures. Stand, Bronwen! Stand, Gildan!"

Bronwen rose shakily to her feet, and the men began cheering loudly. Gildan had turned pale and appeared to be short of breath.

"Though I have no sons to continue the line of Rhodri, I have two daughters, both now of marriageable age. Each brings much with her to such a union. My daughters are fine women, and through many long negotiations, I have found worthy husbands for both of them."

So it was to be Gildan, too, Bronwen realized. Poor Gildan! For so long she had dreamed of a husband, and now that her betrothal was to be announced, she stood white and shivering. Bronwen longed to go and take her hand as she had done when they were children.

"My elder daughter, Bronwen," Edgard continued, "the child who seems almost the spirit of her mother—so nearly do they look alike—I now betroth to Olaf Lothbrok."

At the name Bronwen gasped aloud, incredulous at her father's words. Gildan cried out, and all the company of men began to talk loudly at once.

"Silence please," Edgard spoke up. "Allow me to continue. My daughter Gildan I now betroth to Aeschby Godwinson. Now you must listen carefully, Britons. Hear my will to my daughter Bronwen upon my death."

The men in the room fell silent, and even the servitors stopped to listen. Bronwen held her breath as her father continued to speak.

"When I die, Bronwen will receive all my lands and Rossall Hall into her own hands. They will not pass under the government of her husband, Olaf Lothbrok, as is the Briton custom. I shall not permit my possessions to slip from the hands of my tribe. If my daughter Bronwen gives birth to a son by this Viking, then the inheritance will fall to the son upon his coming of age. If she has a daughter or no child at her death, then these lands will pass to Lord Aeschby and his lineage through my daughter Gildan."

Edgard stopped speaking for a moment and looked long at his stunned guests. Then he began to recite the many brave deeds of his Briton forefathers, those beloved tales Bronwen knew so well. As he talked, Olaf Lothbrok moved from his bench and came to stand beside her. Bronwen drew back from the touch of his woolen tunic as it grazed her hand. She could not bear to look at this man or meet the hard gaze of the silent Briton company.

Instead, she found herself staring down at her own small slippers, intricately crafted of gold threads and purple embroidery. Edgard had brought them for her from the market fair in Preston, and she had saved them for this special feast. Her eyes wandered to the large leather boots of the Viking. They were caked with mud and sand, and small bits of seaweed clung to their thick crossed bindings.

Could she ever learn to care for the man who wore those boots? Would she one day look forward to the heavy sound of their entrance into her chamber? Would there be a time when her eyes grew accustomed to their presence beside her own thin slippers?

Bronwen shook her head, then shuddered as she felt the huge hand of the barbarian close upon her own. Why had her father done this to her? She could not see the sense in his plans. At last she lifted her chin as the Viking beside her raised their hands high above their heads.

"And so the continuation of the great line of Briton nobles is assured," her father was saying. "I have accomplished this by the favorable marriages of my two daughters to these worthy men."

Without another look around the hall she had worked so hard to prepare, Bronwen pulled her hand from the grip of the Viking and stepped down from the dais. As she hurried toward the door, she passed the nearest table and felt herself caught suddenly by her skirt.

"Welcome to the family, Briton," said one of Olaf's men in a mocking voice. "We look forward to the presence of a woman at our hall."

Bronwen grasped her tunic and yanked it from the Viking's thick fingers. As she stepped away from the table, she heard the drunken laughter of the barbarians behind her.

Running down the stone steps toward the heavy oak door that led outside the keep, Bronwen gathered her mantle about her. She ordered the doorman to open it, and he did so reluctantly, pressing her to carry a torch. But Bronwen pushed past him and fled into the darkness.

Dashing down the steep, pebbled hill toward the beach,

she felt the frozen ground give way to sand. She threw off her veil and circlet and kicked away her shoes.

Racing alongside the pounding surf, she felt hot tears of anger and shame well up and stream down her cheeks. With no concern for her safety, Bronwen ran and ran, her long braids streaming behind her, falling loose, drifting like a tattered black flag.

Blinded with weeping, she did not see the dark form that loomed suddenly in her path and stopped dead her headlong sprint. Bronwen shrieked in surprise and fear as iron arms pinned her, and a heavy cloak threatened to suffocate her.

"Release me!" she cried. "Guard! Guard, help me!"

"Hush, my lady." A deep voice emanated from the darkness. "I mean you no harm. What demon drives you to run so madly in the night without fear for your safety?"

"Release me, villain! I am the daughter—"

"I shall hold you until you calm yourself. We had heard there were witches in Amounderness, but I had not thought to meet one so openly."

Still held tight in the man's arms, Bronwen drew back and peered up at the hooded figure. "You! You are the man who spied on our feast. Release me at once, or I shall call the guard upon you."

The man chuckled at this and turned toward his companions, who stood in a group nearby. Bronwen caught hold of the back of his hood and jerked it down to reveal a head of glossy raven curls. But the man's face was shrouded in darkness yet, and as he looked at her, she could not read his expression.

"So you are the blessed bride-to-be." He pulled the hood back over his head. "Your father has paired you with an interesting choice."

Relieved that her captor did not appear to be a highwayman, she sagged from his warm hands onto the wet sand.

"Please leave me here alone. I need peace to think. Go on your way."

The tall stranger shrugged off his outer mantle and wrapped it around her shoulders. "Why did your father betroth you thus to the aged Viking?" he asked.

"For one purported to be a spy, you know precious little about Amounderness. But I shall tell you, as it is all common knowledge."

She pulled the cloak tightly about her, reveling in its warmth. "Our land, Amounderness, once was Briton territory. Olaf Lothbrok, my betrothed, came here as a youth when the Viking invasions had nearly subsided. He took the lands directly to the south of Rossall Hall from their Briton lord. Then, of course, the Normans came, and Amounderness was pillaged by William the Conqueror's army."

The man squatted on the sand beside Bronwen. He listened with obvious interest as she continued the familiar tale. "When William took an account of Amounderness in his Domesday Book, he recorded no remaining lords and few people at all. But he did not know the Britons. Slowly, we crept out of hiding and returned to our halls. My father's family reoccupied Rossall Hall. And there we live, as we should, watching over our serfs as they fish and grow their meager crops. Indeed, there is not much here for the greedy Normans to want, if they are the ones for whom you spy."

Unwilling to continue speaking when her heart was so heavy, Bronwen stood and turned toward the sea. Rising beside her, the traveler touched her arm. "Olaf Lothbrok's lands—together with your father's—will reunite most of Amounderness. A clever plan. Your sister's future husband holds the rest of the adjoining lands, I understand."

"You've done your work, sir. Your lord will be pleased. Who is he—some land-hungry Scottish baron? Or have you forgotten that King Stephen gave Amounderness to the Scots as a trade for their support in his war with Matilda? I certainly hope your lord is not a Norman. He would be so disappointed to learn he has no legal rights here. Now, if you will excuse me?"

"I know that Amounderness is Scottish by law," the man said, stopping her short. "Would you be so sorry to see it returned to Norman hands?"

Bronwen sighed bitterly. "Neither Stephen nor David of Scotland has deigned to set foot in Amounderness. We are merely a pawn in their game. As far as I am concerned, it matters not who believes himself to own our country, just as long as he does not bring troops here or build fortresses. Tell your lord that we Britons do not intend to forfeit our holding."

Bronwen turned and began walking back along the beach toward Rossall Hall. She felt better for her run, and somehow her father's plan did not seem so far-fetched anymore. Distant lights twinkled through the fog that was rolling in from the west, and she suddenly realized what a long way she had come.

"My lady," the stranger's voice called out behind her.

Bronwen kept walking, unwilling to face again the one who had seen her in her humiliation. She did not care what he reported to his master.

"My lady, you have a bit of a walk ahead of you." The traveler strode forward to join her. "Perhaps I should accompany you to your destination."

"You leave me no choice, I see."

"I am not one to compromise myself, dear lady. I follow the path God has set before me and none other."

"And just who are you?"

"I am called Jacques."

"French. A Norman, as I had suspected."

The man chuckled. "Not nearly as Norman as you are Briton."

As they approached the fortress, Bronwen could see that the guests had not yet begun to disperse. Perhaps no one had missed her, and she could slip quietly into bed beside Gildan.

She turned to go, but he took her arm and studied her face in the moonlight. Then, gently, he drew her into the folds of his hooded cloak. "Perhaps the bride would like the memory of a younger man's embrace to warm her," he whispered.

Astonished, Bronwen attempted to remove his arms from around her waist. But she could not escape his lips as they found her own. The kiss was soft and warm, melting away her resistance like the sun upon the snow. Before she had time to react, he was striding back down the beach.

Bronwen stood stunned for a moment, clutching his woolen mantle about her. Suddenly she cried out, "Wait, Jacques! Your mantle!"

The dark one turned to her. "Keep it for now," he shouted into the wind. "I shall ask for it when we meet again."

DISCUSSION QUESTIONS

1. How had Kitt tried to resolve her feelings toward Michael after he left her? Was she successful? Why or why not?

2. What personality traits, interests and other things do Michael and Kitt have in common?

3. How did Michael choose to deal with the baby's death and the end of his marriage? Why did he make the choices he did?

4. How did Kitt feel toward God after her baby's death? How did Michael feel toward Him? Why does God allow painful things to happen to people who love and worship Him?

5. Trace the path Kitt and Michael each took in their relationship with God—before they married, through their brief marriage, immediately after their divorce, when they meet each other again and at the end of the book.

6. What futures did Kitt and Michael each have planned? How have their plans changed by the end of the book? What does this reveal about God's will? Do you think God changes His plans for us—or do we change by submitting to Him?

7. Toward the beginning of the book, Kitt says, "The past and the future always clash." What did she mean at the time? How does this statement play out in the book?

8. "Forgive and forget" is a common statement. Can people forget? Can they forgive? How?

9. What was Hod's role in the story? Did he affect the relationship between Kitt and Michael? What does Hod mean to them regarding the death of their baby?

10. During her marriage, how did Kitt respond to the death of her baby? What did she choose to do later with her life? Do you think these events are connected in any way?

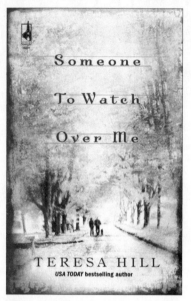

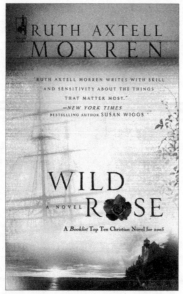

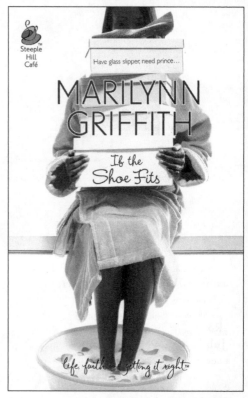

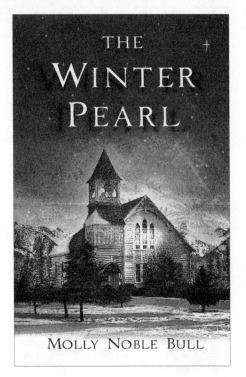